KILLING TIME

BY

M W TAYLOR

SAVANT PRESS

Please support by leaving a review on
www.Amazon.co.uk

M W TAYLOR

www.savantpress.net

First edition March 2017

Chapter 1 – Time to kill

February 2065 – A hotel room in Shoreditch, London.

Knock knock… knock knock knock!

The signal from the whore at the door. Her signal as rough and ready as she is, this buxom trollop, this dirty puzzle, selling her wares to any man with a penny in his pocket. This will be her last moment on this foul earth, of that Jack is certain. What a sense of power to know her destiny before she does, to hold her life in his hands and snuff it out like a church candle.

As soon as he opens the door, the woman's eyes narrow when she sees her client, booked just an hour ago. She is a little surprised by his appearance, but not fazed; she has seen almost everything in her short career.

"Oooh, I wasn't expecting that love… no problem, but it will cost you extra, is that okay?"

Jack isn't feeling talkative, so just grunts his acknowledgement. He is impatient for his kill. This is a very dangerous moment. The allure of this whore sent by her Haymarket Henry, may just make him want to use her for sex first, and that would never do. It is against his strong principles, but he is just human after all. It would devastate him though, to dirty himself upon her saggy body and delay the whole process.

"What is your name?" Speech seems to be a huge effort, so he expels the words from his mouth as quickly as possible.

Her eyes drift up, conveying body language that screams her conceit in trying to remember the name she is using tonight. "You can call me Jade darlin', just like my eyes," and gives a cheap laugh that holds no honesty in it. Her eyes are blue. Eyes that see the gloves Jack is wearing. Eyes that see something is wrong.

"Don't worry, Jade, I just have an aversion to touching skin, which is why I find myself using your... unique services. It's just easier that way, I'm sure you understand."

Now it's his turn to let out a false laugh, and said with a little added estuary inflection to match hers. It reassures her, and mocks her at the same time. He's beginning to enjoy himself in this game; the power and the divine right spurring him on.

The hotel room is the usual American layout but with typically small British dimensions. Bathroom immediately to the left as you walk in past the door, wardrobe on the right, thus providing a tight channel that leads to the bed and a small desk. He quickly maneuvers himself between Jade and the door, confidently cutting out her exit through the pretention of getting cash out of his jacket, which is hanging in the wardrobe. Money will distract her away from any doubts. In an age of credits, cash, though rarely seen these days, still holds the most attention and works its magic on her. It also leaves no evidence trail if you are careful.

Warming up to the event, Jack loosens up and flashes the cash. "Come in, make yourself at home, and really, money is not a problem. I believe in living for the moment Jade, even if it costs a little extra, don't you?" She nods and begins to settle into her own little routine.

"I certainly do darling, mind if I get a drink from the minibar then?"

"Help yourself, and pour me a whiskey please." *You stupid bitch, you jezebel!* The bad thoughts are getting louder in his head now, but the soft side of his nature, his alter ego is fighting against him.

As she bends down to the minibar, it accentuates her hips, and forces her short skirt higher to display the tops of her stockings, taunting him, inviting him in to plunder her goods. This must not happen. In an instant, an explosion of rage tears through his mind as he realises he must kill her now, before her filth infects him.

Using his whole body weight, he slams her face down as hard as possible to the desk, breaking her nose in three places, instantly... which knocks her semi unconscious. As adrenaline courses through her system, fight or flight become her only options offered by a muddled brain, but she is not in control, she cannot think clearly. Instinctively she opens her mouth to let out a scream. Instantly, expertly, the scream is muffled by a hand towel. From Jade's senses, all she can see and feel is fear.

Blood floods her nostrils as the towel gags her mouth, leaving her unable to scream or swallow. Then she feels an arm across her neck, as it slowly squeezes her miserable life out of existence. The pain of her lungs bursting to breaking point is excruciating, until darkness engulfs her, a welcome end to this sudden nightmare. Finally she is only conscious of a ringing in her ears, softly permeated by the dying pulse of her heart, her last moments as predicted by this cruel stranger.

Technically she is now dead. The neural pathways in her brain being starved of oxygen, force it to shut down. She has only minutes to be revived, her brain's only option for survival, but that will never happen. Now it is time for her soul to escape until it can find another body to inhabit; to be reborn. Maybe then her memories can be revived, and one day she will point out her murderer in this new age of Awakening.

Jack is angry with himself. This was very sloppy and he still has to cut her up and lay her in position. It will take time to clear the evidence and he will have to burn his clothes as soon as possible. From now on it will be clean kills, better disguises and possibly drugs to subdue his victims. More discreet venues and simpler meeting methods also need to be employed, but then, he has only just returned, his first murder of a prostitute in a very long time. He is understandably a little rusty and things have changed so much since he was last here.

Now he needs the soft voice in his head to take over, to clear up this mess. It is time for their expertise to complete this partnership against the filth of London...

A filth that seems to have infected the whole world.

Chapter 2 – The Dog and Duck

May - 2065

Wow, at last, an attractive one. How many photos had he seen online, only to be disappointed when arriving at the pub or bar or restaurant? Jason was sure that on the last date the girl's mother had turned up instead... she looked that much older! And yet he should be an expert at this. Not at dating, though of course he'd been forced into more than his fair share by now, but in analysing the data presented on the person's profile page.

Jason then made a quick mental note to himself that thinking words like analysing data, in terms of dating, were probably not a good start. But, as he kept telling himself, as one of the most respected past life investigators in the world, he should excel in routing out dodgy images and funky profiles on these sites. Maybe he was human after all.

A smile crept across his face at this thought, the blessing and the curse of being a mentalist, (a word he has always hated) a person who has an uncanny natural ability to read even the subtlest signs of body language, to the point where it appears like a mind reading trick or some dark magic. He'd furthered these skills through extensive study and utilisation of a mixture of memory techniques: hypnosis, NLP, body language and subliminal ideomotor suggestion. Jason could not only 'virtually' read a person's mind, but manipulate a mental or physical response through his actions and reactions.

In other words, he was good at reading people and persuading them to do what he wanted. Unfortunately, whilst that's great for an investigator, it can be really crap for a steady relationship. It might seem to be a gift from heaven to be able to read a woman's mind and know what she really wants, but it never really seemed to play out that way. With every tiny disappointment screamed at him from her dispassionate face when things are not going well, and the constant temptation to try and sway her to his will, just leaving him hollow inside. A relationship has to be as free as possible to survive; it needs to breathe and grow as organically as possible, from both sides, not just the dominant one.

Time to say hello. "Hi, I'm guessing you are Samantha?" He knows that of course, her left hand defensively clasping her right forearm displaying her nervousness, her clothes attractive enough, but nothing too showy, she wouldn't want to be attracting someone she is not attracted to, or worse, a nutter.

Stop thinking Jason, just turn your bloody sensors off, he told himself.

She seems pleasantly surprised too, a smile forming on her near perfect lips adding warmth to a pretty face.

"And you must be Jason," followed by the awkward moment of not knowing whether to hug, shake hands, or kiss the cheeks. A hug won the day, another one of Jason's little tests to see if she would let him into her personal space.

After the usual pleasantries, Jason went to buy drinks at the bar whilst Samantha found a cosy table with a window overlooking the duck pond outside. It is drizzling, making beautiful ripples spread across the pond, interspersed with ducks flapping their wings as if frolicking in the rain.

"So, Jason, you never really said what you do for a living in your messages?" she asked on his return.

Already the date was turning into the inevitable interview. It always happens. Genuine conversation needs genuine facts about each other, their likes and dislikes, an understanding of their humour. In the end, small talk barges its way in, and that usually involves questions. Questions that Jason didn't really want to answer right now.

It was always awkward explaining his job without making the other person feel uneasy. He'd rather say he was an accountant or store manager for a little normality, or a dolphin trainer if in a devilish mood, but he was just too honest. Silly really, he was able to lie with utter conviction for work, but in a social environment, he felt guilt mounting down on him. At least his father had done one thing right.

"I'm a past life investigator," he mumbled. The usual look of incredulity quickly appeared on her face.

"A what?"

"I'm what most people call a G-eye."

"G-eye?"

"Yes, As in Generations private eye."

"Oh, blimey, that sounds tough, you must hear some horrific details when exploring an Awakening that ends in murder?

Jason was ready for that, a standard response to his job. "Well, yes and no. It is a misconception that we see the death of that person and therefore the whole murder. We only see the events that lead up to it, and the more traumatic the death, the bigger the gap usually is leading up to it. Very frustrating in a way, but that is why we investigate it, rather than just 'see' who it is. I take it that you underwent the usual Awakening foundation?"

Samantha blushed, this conversation was already getting quite personal and her turn to not to want to give an honest answer.

"Only the basics." She stopped to think, amazed by the fact that she was opening up to this person already. People could be quite dismissive of you, if they knew you were ignorant of at least your most recent past lives. Not knowing your past makes you an incomplete person in this modern world.

Samantha had been born just after the huge economic crash of 2027, and somehow her parents had managed to escape the worst of it. Her mother had once told her about Martin Kale's new Awakening technique for past life regression, and how she hadn't taken it seriously at the time. A lot of people thought it was just a cult he had started, and somehow his assassination just confirmed their feelings - until Kale returned in a new body twelve years later. He was just a ten year old boy, but fully aware of all his memories from his life before, and the only person to self-Awaken.

From that point on, Awakening took the world by storm, his death and resurrection the proof that people needed. His murderer had propelled his vision, not killed it off, and now Kale has a new protégé by his side in the form of Adam Capello, the first person to have some scant 'memories' of the future. Awakening is still very new and there is still so much to learn.

"Oh, basics, no problem," Jason reassured her quickly, "I just wondered if you'd had an Awakening in which you saw close to your own death. Believe me, most people say they have seen more past lives than they have, so there really is no need to be embarrassed."

This just made Samantha blush again. She looked across at this man who was catching her attention. He had an athletic build, was about six foot tall, and quite attractive, without looking like a clothes model, and a full head of light brown hair with a trim beard that was well kept.

His manner was relaxed and polite. She appreciated his reassurance and enjoyed his smile, but she couldn't make up her mind if she was intrigued or repelled by his job. After all, he specialises in sifting through people's lives to... well, mostly to catch them murdering someone. She had seen enough TV programmes to know that they were very good at body language and basic psychology, it would be like dating your shrink! Well at least he had a job, better than the last loser she'd spent too much time on, and it probably paid very well too.

"No I haven't," she lied.

No surprise to Jason, but it was just to make a point to her anyway. "Ah, well you are lucky, some can be quite disturbing, even though we never see the actual death; part of the mind's wonderful defence mechanism jumping in and saving us go through the experience again. Of course, if we really could see into that part of our lives, we would probably learn a lot more about the in-between stage, when our souls, spirits, life force or whatever you'd like to call it, departs our bodies."

"Oh, so what do we know about that part?" Her curiosity lighting like a small flame.

Jason laughed. "Ha, nothing at all, still a complete mystery I'm afraid. Maybe Kale or Capello know, but for now it is all quiet. Yes, as part of my work I look as closely into that period as much as I can, but really my investigations deal with the life and character of that person, not the death. Without any record of them to research, I'd have very little to start on."

"So what I see on television isn't true? You can't just see what happened through their eyes? You'll be telling me you don't use magic next," she added coyly.

"If I could perform real magic I'd conjure billions of pounds and be retired by now." His time for a small lie. He loves his job and couldn't think of doing anything else, but he is somehow embarrassed by that fact.

Samantha took another sip of her Gin and tonic. "Hmm, so what is the worst case you have ever dealt with?

"Ah, now that would be confidential I'm afraid. I could tell you..."

"But you'd have to kill me... And then I'd come back, be re-Awakened and have to hand you into the authorities," she laughed. "Seems like a waste of a lot of time."

Jason laughed too, but his alarm bells were ringing about something.

Stop thinking Man!

Jason's constant battle to not over think things was usually at its worst on dates. No wonder he's been single for so long. On the last promising date, he'd lasted almost ninety minutes before realising she was married to an alcoholic judge, and was only going to use him for a 'get back fling.' He might even have gone along with it for a while; after all, it had been a long time since any sex had occurred in his life, and he was really missing it, but her self-loathing became very apparent, and any interest quickly fizzled.

Damn it Jason, if only you could have lost a little self respect long enough to get laid.

Samantha seems fun though, and his alarm bells were always ringing to be honest, like tinnitus. No one is normal any more, everyone has personal shit that they want to keep secret.

Time to counter her question. "And so what do you do?"

"I'm a dolphin trainer."

Jason almost spat his drink out, incredulous, unbelieving, amused. It was so good to be surprised once in a while.

"Get outta town?"

"Okay you got me, didn't think I could lie to you anyway. I run my own little business selling T-shirts with personalised messages. I could do a great one for you."

She grabbed a paper napkin and started writing a special message.

I-spy
a
G-eye

"Ha, don't quit your day job," he mocked.

"That is my day job you cheeky bugger! I think you owe me another drink."

Two hours passed, and for some reason she was still talking to him. Luckily Jason's car had been able to park nearby, so he could relax with a few drinks to calm his nerves and shut off his brain before it drove him home.

This could actually work. I might even get to a second date.

A huge smile crept across his face as the thought of being in a good relationship began to look like a possibility for the first time in over seven months. *Baby steps Jason... baby steps.*

Samantha saw his smile. It was big and beautiful, unforced and sweet. Time to leave before she does anything stupid, like invite him back to her place. Unlikely she knew, but she was definitely attracted to this man.

"Well I better set off, things to do in the morning." Even she didn't believe her own words, but like a gentleman, he walked her to her car anyway.

Crunch time for Jason. He knew he wanted to see her again, but his inherent shyness with women when dating was in full force. His own attraction was masking any certainty over whether she liked him too, so the expert in mind reading couldn't even pick up the subtlest of clues. The irony of the situation never failed to stab Jason in the eyes, and this one was a blinder.

As they reached the car, Jason went to give her a peck on the cheek. Samantha touched his face, beckoning him for something more. As their eyes met, Jason finally got the message that a proper kiss was needed, but he was already committed to the peck on the cheek, and was unable to stop himself. To make matters worse, the kiss was dry, with no moisture on his lips. It was like kissing air.

Acutely embarrassed, he tried to compensate by acting as if that was the plan all along.

"Goodnight, Samantha, was lovely meeting you," and with that, he turned and walked away, wincing as soon as his face was hidden.

Samantha was a little in shock. She thought she'd read all the signs right, she thought he liked her! Embarrassed, she got into the car without saying anything, and tried to work out where it had gone wrong. That's it, she told herself, no more inter-dating.

She must be bloody mad!

Chapter 3 – Preparation

Mad...
  Bloody...

Disgusting women of the night. Three months have passed since his return, and he has been held back from any more kills. Held back by the voices in his head, screaming him down, but the soft one knows better. She is on his side, she has calmed him, told him to prepare for their crusade and is teaching him to be forensically aware, to plan his kills with all the right equipment. She sounds like his mother, even though she was not a soft woman by any measure.

It isn't like the old days, they'd been much simpler, and he'd had fewer voices to contend with. The police had been bumbling idiots then, but now... now they have all sorts of tricks to try and trip him up. How can they be so clever and so stupid at the same time? Scotland Yard, the so called envy of the world as a police force, is respected everywhere, but it is all a sham.

They might have technology and history on their side, but they are handcuffed by their own political bureaucracy and stupidly tight budgets. All that potential fucked up by the government and fear of media and public opinion. So now is a good time to come back, a good time to strike amongst the ruins of London. Now everything is in place to start killing again. Ah, so many to kill, so little time.

Jack laughed out loud at the irony of everything and how it all helps his quest, but then had to quickly stifle it. People are looking at him as if he is mad. He will be quiet for now, even though he wants to butcher everyone in this room for their blindness. They all claim that they want to clean up the filth in this world, but really, they are more interested in their personal projects.

They are just worried about their fancy motorised carriages or electronic toys or relationships or pathetic families. Their dedication lacks conviction... their own purity very much in doubt.

One day... one day they will see the light, and it will burn them.

Chapter 4 – Interrogation

The clock is ticking.

"Describe the room you are in... big, small, well kept or falling apart?"

"I don't know, it is so dark, so cold and clammy. I'm scared, Jason, really scared, I don't think I can carry on."

"I understand that, and not surprised. What you are seeing would scare anyone, but this time there is a difference. This time you are seeing it from the safety of your life as Elizabeth. Remember, no matter how real it looks and feels, you are no longer Thelma, you are Elizabeth, and as Elizabeth, you are in control of what happens to you.

"Everything you see is in the past; your past, your history. If you can face your fears now, then we can find the man that did this to your body; your life as Thelma. I'm here for you, and ready to pull you out as soon as you give me the safe word. Repeat the safe word for me please, Elizabeth."

"Resolution."

"Exactly, resolution is your way out of here. Something you didn't have the last time you were in 1952."

"Oh my God, someone's coming, I can hear them. I think I'm in a cellar and they are opening the door."

"You are doing really well, but you have to describe as

much to me as possible before we lose our place in this Awakening. Everything you describe is a clue to catching your killer. Try to freeze the moment, slow down your thoughts, and that will slow down your personal time."

"Erm, okay. There is a workbench to the left of me. I can't move round because I am chained... oh fuck, I'm chained."

"But your mind is free, Elizabeth. Concentrate on detail. Are there any windows?"

"Yes, a tiny one right up by the ceiling, but it has been blanked out with something. Old carton boxes I think. The hum of the freezer drives me mad at night. The throbbing sound gets inside my head, gives me a headache."

"What's the make?"

"General electric, it has a big GE badge on it, pile of shit. Things are still moving, Jason, slowly, but I can't stop it all, the door is opening, get me the fuck out of here!"

"Breathe deeply, Elizabeth, you are doing brilliantly. Just slow your breath, clench your fists, that always helps me take control a little more. I need photos or names."

"No photos, but there are some old sports trophies. Wrestling I think. Big ugly brute... oh, I remember a bit about him. Hairy, ugly man. Seems huge. I can't remember his face because it frightens me, just his stinking boozy breath when he's raped me. Arghh, bastard, fucking bastard has kept me chained here and raped me so many times. "I want to die, but I want him dead even more. Big fucking ugly bastard... you fucking raped and killed me!"

"We will get him, but I need you to focus right now, Elizabeth. Can you see the names on the trophies? Try really hard to read them. Are you close enough to read them?"

"So dark, Jason, but the light is coming in through the door now, I can see his feet coming down the steps. Can you stop him?"

"I can't, but you can. You have the mental strength. You are in control of your mind. You have still got more time to look around than you think, believe me. I've been in this situation many times. I know you will be okay."

"Hickerson! I can see the name Hickerson on a couple of the trophies."

"Brilliant, that's a name to work with, keep looking. Any first names?"

"Don't have time, I'm fading out. Fuck, this is it. I think this is when I die."

"Hold on, describe him as much as possible before you leave."

"Going blurry now, can just see his legs. He's wearing shorts, and one of his legs is wooden or fake or something. I think he's a war vet. I think it was blasted off in the second world war. He doesn't usually say much, just attacks me, forces himself on me... fuck... resolution! Resolution!"

"Okay, Elizabeth, I'm shining a light on your eyes, follow it."

"I can't see it, where is the light? You said I'd be out... Shit, everything is rushing now, he's in front of me, his face, oh Jesus fucking Christ, his face, help me!"

"Stop looking at him, Elizabeth, it's keeping you locked in. Close your eyes from the cellar and open them to return here in London, in 2065. You are here now, follow the light."

"He's holding the knife that killed me. He's going to cut me up, humiliate and torture me to death. Get me out Jason, get me out right now!"

Pain...........................
    Silence...................
        Light................
            Resolution...

The resolution to live and find her killer over a hundred years later.

Chapter 5 – Chic Geek

Samantha was still a little annoyed to be honest, but couldn't get Jason out of her head. Yes, he'd sent a message the next day to say how much he'd enjoyed the evening, but maybe he was just being polite.

She'd not bothered to reply just yet, partly because she was unsure of what to say back, and partly to teach him a lesson. A night out with her best friend was planned that night, so for now she would just push him out of her mind.

The Bar was a new one to them both, tucked in a narrow lane called Gilbert Place, just a stone's throw from the British Museum in Bloomsbury. It has a chic geek style, with maps of the world stuck next to beautifully faded, expertly worn books, and fake Egyptian artefacts, as if pilfered from the great halls. Lush fabrics covered the seats and sofas, but the girls decided to sit at the bar as they sipped their cocktails.

"So how did your date go, Sammy?" Libby's first question of the evening.

"Nightmare! It was all going so well for most of the evening. He's good looking, funny, intelligent and has a good job, so what more could you want? Well, I say good job, it probably pays well, but he's one of those past life investigators."

Libby screwed up her face. "Oh, he must see some sights."

"That's what I said."

"So he's like one of those guys on the telly? I love a bit of murder and mayhem in the evening."

They both laughed at this, filling the near empty bar with a little atmosphere as it waited for the Thursday night crowd to rush in.

"What's his name?"

"Jason Ives."

Libby looked at her incredulously. "Jason Ives?"

"Er, yeah, do you know him?"

"I wish. Jesus, Sammy, don't you ever keep up with current affairs? He's famous, sort of, been on the news and everything." Her eyes lit up. "Quite dishy too."

"Yeah, well he might be, but he's a lousy kisser."

Libby touched Samantha's arm, delighting in any scandal involving her mate. "You kissed him?"

"Puh! Chance would have been a fine thing. It was going great. We were laughing, the drink was flowing and the conversation was good. I was flirting my arse off."

"What? Not the whole Sammy treatment? Tits out, lips puckered, playing with your hair and sticking your finger in your mouth like a bitch in heat?"

The barman walked in to the conversation midway to ask them if they wanted another drink, turned around, and walked away again. Maybe he'd give them another five minutes.

Samantha blushed. "Shut up, Libby," she said laughing, "you'll get us both thrown out."

"Hmm, well you can play little Miss Innocent with your other friends, but I've seen you in full force and it's scary."

"Yeah, well not on this occasion, I was all sweetness and light."

"So what happened?"

"Nothing, he just gave me a quick peck on the cheek and ran off as soon as possible, he couldn't get away fast enough. I think I've lost my sex appeal, Libby."

"Don't be so silly, Sammy... you never had it in the first place."

"Oh ha ha."

"Sammy, you are beautiful, you know that. He might just be a bit shy."

"Yeah right, you should have seen him. All confident and smiling that daft big grin of his. He's probably a player, picks up girls all the time and I just didn't make the grade."

"And you believe what you are saying do you?"

"Oh I don't know, he was lovely and he ran off."

"And so are you, but you didn't make the first move either. Well, apart from opening all the buttons on your shirt."

Samantha rolled her eyes. "It's as if you were there," she replied sarcastically.

"Well message him, Sammy, even if it's just so I can meet him. He's seriously important in the G-eye world thingy. A few years back he caught Pol Pot from the 1970's Khmer Rouge in Cambodia."

"Pol Pot who?"

"I give up. Seriously, Sammy, read a Kindle sometime," Libby said scornfully, but with a glint in her eye, goading her friend on. "He also got in a bit of trouble for catching a guy who'd been a war Nazi but didn't even know it. Tricked him into having Awakening sessions and then had him arrested when he remembered his Nazi life. Don't you remember, it was a whole new form of entrapment and Kale had to get involved? Oh my God, Sammy, he's worked with Martin Kale!"

"He never mentioned that."

"Well, maybe he's shy **and** modest."

"Oh Bugger."

"Well not on a first date, but maybe you've added that to your flirting repertoire too."

Chapter 6 – Killing Time

Brick Lane, on the corner of Chicksand Street, and it's a miserably cold evening, sodden by the relentless rain that belies the fact that summer should just be around the corner. It works for Jack in a way though, gives him the chance to pull his hood over his head and disappear amongst the detritus of human society that lives in this 'desirable' area.

He thought he'd plan his next murder here for old time's sake, close to his old stomping ground, but doesn't recognise any of it. The only thing that hasn't changed is that it's still a shit hole, but now it's a different kind of shit hole, with different shops and different people from all over the world. He can't decide whether it's better or worse, just that he might as well be in any part of London now, but at least he can hide here, or can he?

Security cameras are almost everywhere in London now. Council ones on poles, shop fronts, clubs, pubs and people wearing cameras on almost every piece of clothing they can think of. 'Mother' was right; disguise and keeping in the shadows are a bare minimum now in this age of the electric camera. Thank the heavens she had found a contraption for messing with their signals.

His mother's voice still in his head after all these years, the voice that he hates - but loves much more. One of only two women he has ever loved, but in those last few days she never gave him any peace. Never forgave him for sleeping with prostitutes and catching syphilis. It had killed him in the end, before the police could find his disfigured form riddled with the disease.

He's so lost in thought, that a bus full of sad looking people narrowly misses him on the street. The driver mouths obscenities at him, but can't be heard through the vast glass windscreen, separating him from the world, as if in a fishbowl. He was almost killed. Jack smiles as he feels the adrenaline surge through his new body. How ironic that you have to be so close to death to feel so alive, or cause the death of someone else.

Murder had not been his mission originally, just outrage as he discovered his body was being ravaged by the pox he'd caught from one of the trollops in Whitechapel he'd screwed, his Russian roulette with syphilis.

He went to confront the woman, he was so incensed. Just to talk like, but she'd been so gobby and told him to fuck off! After a few punches to her face, he didn't see her any more, the red mist just hid everything as he lashed his anger out on her broken body. That is when the voices started, and Jack was born.

Amazing to think that had been almost two hundred years ago. Who would have thought that he'd be alive again after all this time - and Pox free too. His voices have been right all along, it makes his mission more important, as if his resurrection is proof that he is on the right path. A cruel choice of body, that is for sure, and probably his mother had some hand in the abomination he now inhabits, but it only makes things easier for his destiny, and probably his punishment for shagging a whore in the first place.

Yes, the pox had killed him in the end, painfully, and without grace from the madness in his head. He must have been found in his bed chamber, covered in the warts and puss-filled boils that raped his skin, with only the sound of the sea to keep him company.

Instantly he tries to blot the thoughts out. *Push those memories away, they only bring back the pain.*

At least they never discovered his dark secret, and in some way, his death had ensured that he was never caught. It has made him famous, or infamous, he can't really work out which. His murders immortalised him in London folklore, and his death had sealed the mystery. Now he is known all over the world as 'Jack the Ripper.'

Jack... that's not even my real name.

Memories flick through his head of his student days. Painful memories of a love lost, that almost surpass his last few months of painful death, lead to tears running down his cheeks as violent emotions flood his body. No, he hadn't really gotten away with the murders, God had seen to that. The urge to scream becomes so much that he has to bite his arm as if it is a piece of wood, drawing blood and bruising the surrounding skin.

I need to kill now!

Oh, if only he could find the bitch that gave him the pox and kill her once more. The thought is so delicious that it halts him mid stride. His whole mind suddenly transported to the flea pit where he slaughtered her the first time. He would fuck her up again; good and proper, just like he did the other blowsy girls, ripping the whores open and cutting out their 'innards.' But this time he would keep her alive as long as possible, to chat about old times as he flays her skin. Two souls transported to this futuristic London; brought together through pain and suffering, over and over again.

What a wonderful idea, that must happen, it will happen.

Fashion Street, his destination finally reached. Jack looks at the narrow thoroughfare. It reminds him of a quote from Charles Dickens describing nearby Spitalfields as, 'Squalid streets, lying like narrow black trenches... where sallow, unshaven weavers... prowl languidly about, or lean against posts, or sit brooding on doorsteps'.

It had been full of Jewish tailors in his time. They'd bastardised the name from Fossan Street to suit their commercial purpose, but even he has to admire their tenacity and entrepreneurial spirit. It had been one of the worst slums in London at the time. Where most men saw despair, they had seen hope and opportunity, and even though it still looks like a sow's arse, it is a million times better than it had been.

He isn't here to reminisce though. He has an appointment with Zandra, another disease-ridden tart, his next victim, his next step to salvation. Gloves on, hood up, disguise of moustache firmly placed on his upper lip, and sunglasses hiding his eyes. It's killing time.

Knock knock... knock knock knock.

Jack has stolen Jade's secret signal. Now he is calling upon Zandra's 'knocking shop'.

"You're late," her first words before she's even opened the door completely, and Jack's blood starts to boil already. How dare this harlot speak to him as if she is his superior! But he needs to calm down, do this properly, not rushed and bodged as with Jade.

"Traffic," is all he can muster. Projecting his voice is always difficult at first. He hardly uses it with anyone apart from his mother.

Zandra looks at him as he takes his sunglasses off. His deep blue eyes seem intense, but quite attractive.

"Well, I've got another appointment in an hour and we don't want you both meeting in the hallway do we." She softens up on this, knowing that she should be nice to the 'Johns' if she wants them to come back. Just because she's had a shitty day doesn't mean she should take it out on everyone else. "No problem hun, let's take a few clothes off and see what we both have," she says as she gives a little laugh.

Jack pulls his hood down, hoping his disguise will hide his shame. It doesn't.

"Oh for fuck's sake, why doesn't anyone tell me anything?" she exclaims, but then gives a warm smile to break the tension. Is that pity in her eyes?

"It's okay, I'll pay you double, but I get to keep my gloves on as well." He's learnt fast from his time with Jade.

"Whatever you say my lover, my... big strong man. Now get your kit off so you can give me a right old rodgering."

Jack knows she is patronising him, all part of the act, but he likes it. She is making him feel strong again, like he used to in his old body, not this weak and feeble shell. He feels a stirring in his loins, an old passion. He wants to fuck this thrupenny bit's sauce-box, but he knows he can't right now. It is as if his cock has withered and died; dropped off, redundant, still obliterated by the pox.

Tears start forming in his eyes again. He doesn't want any of this. He just wants to be normal. He knows he is consumed by hate and driven by demons, but he is powerless to stop it. His damnation is almost certain, even though he is on a righteous path. Good and bad voices scream in his head, as if this woman before him is on trial. He has to kill her, he has no choice; she is part of the vermin that is corrupting the world.

Slipping his hand down to his back pocket, he grabs a steel asp; a telescopic baton that expands with an expert flick of the wrist. Just time to see the horror in her eyes before he smashes it into her skull, extinguishing her scream before it can properly escape from her lungs.

He catches her as she collapses to the ground to avoid the thud, and holds his breath to listen intently to the outside world; waiting to see if anyone heard anything and is on their way. Nothing, but her flesh peddling pimp won't be far away. Time is of the essence.

With speed he dons disposable white paper overalls from the small rucksack he is carrying, then pulls out a bowie knife, freshly sharpened that morning, and slices it across her throat as if it is a ripe blood orange. He uses such force that it cuts through the windpipe and carries on through the spinal cortex, thus partially severing her head from her body.

The mess is incredible as the blood pumps out of her throat, her heart's last few moments of trying to keep her alive, only add to her death by emptying her body of this vital fluid. Jack can feel her die in his hands and he feels energised by it. He is in control. He is the dominant one at this moment. He is in charge and he has the almighty power to snuff out people's lives.

Now it is time to cut out her ridiculously shaved purse and rearrange those vile organs to make her pure again.

Time to dice and splice and all things nice; end her vice... that will suffice.

Chapter 7 – Writing up the Report

What a crap day.

7pm and Jason is still dictating the case notes from Elizabeth's last investigative Awakening. She is majorly pissed off with him, but not as much as she is scared. Still angry that he couldn't pull her out of it any sooner...

"Get me out, Jason, get me out right now!"

Well, that's what he'd told her, but that last minute in the session had brought up the greatest detail, so the little white lie that he couldn't pull her out earlier had to be worth it. Hmm, maybe she wouldn't agree with that right now, and she definitely wouldn't see it as a little white lie, but Jason felt justified in what he had done. Those last few memories could save countless further sessions and thus save her the agony of re-living those moments again and again.

"Big fucking ugly bastard... you fucking raped and killed me!"

"Don't have time, I'm fading out. Fuck, this is it. I think this is when I die."

"...Oh Jesus fucking Christ, his face, help me!"

Elizabeth's words still haunting him, but now she can identify her killer from a photo. Up until then, he'd been masked in earlier attacks, as if he was going to toss her out like the trash after he'd finished with her, but then decided he'd have to kill her instead.

So, what other details did Jason have to work with? The layout of the cellar with the small window so close to the roof is not really a UK architectural style. The refrigerator with the big GE logo does indeed indicate General Electric, which is American, and being 1952, much less likely it was an import.

That and the wrestling trophy (less likely it was Canadian then) was also written in English, making Jason 99% sure that his killer was American. In this game, you have to be very sure before going down a path of inquiry, otherwise a lot of time and effort is wasted on false leads.

The name Hickerson is also typically American, which is good and bad. Good because it further validates his hunches, bad because it is a bigger pool of names to sift through. The last few images of him walking down the stairs were also invaluable. A World War II vet who'd been left with a wooden leg? Gold dust when married with the name and records, which would have to exist for someone like that.

He'd have had psychological reports made, as well as medical records for his recovery, so identifying him now should be a lot easier. The difficult part as usual, is to follow the investigation through and find the body that he is inhabiting now, if indeed he is even alive right now.

And of course, even if he is alive, and findable, is he even aware of his past life? Although he'd made quite a name for himself with the Mueller Nazi trial, it hadn't exactly painted him in a good light, and Martin Kale had warned him against entrapping anyone ever again. It is a difficult tightrope to cross. Can you truly justify protecting the rights of a murderer in this lifetime just because he does not remember being a murderer in another lifetime?

It reminds Jason of the Jewish school girl who 'remembered' she'd been Adolph Hitler. If she hadn't been Awakened in the first place, she'd never have known. She was put on trial and originally condemned to losing ten lifetimes to act as a deterrent to any would be despot, tyrant, genocidal maniac or serial killer. The message was clear, just because you have changed the body you are in, doesn't mean you can escape your past crimes and start a new life completely free of any penalty. People want justice.

Jason was hugely grateful that he hadn't been involved in that case, as it had been incredibly complex and controversial, and he still wasn't quite sure what the answer should have been. Since her death, trials of this nature now have to include new factors, such as their history of nurture and social environment at the time of the crimes being committed. It helps to try and find the true character of the soul / personality that is the core of everyone's being. Maybe one day his skills would make him the perfect judge in such trials. The thought makes the hairs on the back of his neck stand on end.

One day I'll get a job like that though, and the moral consequences could tear me apart.

It scares the hell out of him. For someone as outwardly confident and collected as he is, Jason knows he is in fact a sensitive and slightly insecure person, but has learnt to hide these elements behind an air of professionalism.

Interviews like the one he'd had with Elizabeth really take it out of him. Not only does he have to coax the subject into remembering incredibly traumatic events through their Awakenings, but he also has to build up a mental relationship with the killer. In effect, Jason has to get to know the murderer and their victims intimately. He is the man in the middle, and has to try and see not only

34

why a person might commit a murder, but, sadly, in some small way, why sometimes the victim is a victim. That is the level of detail needed to hunt your murderer through time.

Jason shakes his head to drag himself out of this ugly thought process that he has been down a thousand times. It feels like he is disappearing down a rabbit hole, chasing some elusive logic whilst running out of time.

Back to work Jason. Whatever happens, I'm going to find you Hickerson, he promised quietly to himself.

Thirty minutes later, he was Vid-linking New York.

"Hey, Cody, how's it going?" Jason suddenly developed an American twang the moment the call went through. He can't help himself, part of his innate ability to mirror people, but more a result of him always trying to fit in, than a professional trick to build rapport and thus get better results.

"Hey, is that, Jason? It's been so long I thought you'd died."

"Ha, what are you talking about, it has only been a few months? How's the wife and kids?" *Damn, I knew I should have called him ages ago, and now he's playing hardball*, thought Jason.

Cody raised an eyebrow. "Try a year."

"A year? Are you sure? Wow, time flies when you're having fun."

"Yep, last time we spoke you needed some info on the Burgundy case."

"Oh I remember, you were invaluable, Cody, we couldn't have solved that one without you."

"So I'm guessing you need some more of that invaluable help? Boy, does that piss me off. What am I, just a cop on a leash that you take out for a walk every now and then?" He genuinely looked upset.

"Jeez, you got me, although I must add in my defence that I've been meaning to catch up with you for quite a while."

"Yeah, yeah... save it for the judge." A slight delay on the second yeah and the softness of the H indicated compliance and warmth, maybe he was going to help after all.

"You are just messing with me aren't you?"

A big grin suddenly appeared on Cody's face. "Yep, just busting your balls, Mr Ives, ha-ha, got ya!"

Jason gave a wry smile. "You sure did. Look, I'm sorry to just call you out of the blue and then instantly ask for help again, but I'm working on a particularly nasty case of abduction, rape and murder from 1952. I could veeeerrrrry slowwwwly get some info through my systems, but you are so much better at it, and your computers are much bigger and shinier than mine. Not to mention that you have direct access to your historical records. You'll get results in no time at all."

"Wow, you must be desperate; you're being polite and everything."

"Well, let's just say our last session kinda spooked her, and I kept her in longer than I should have. So the sooner I can get some results, the sooner I can calm her down and keep my investigation going."

"Ha, you never were good at keeping the ladies happy."

"Yeah, well, nothing much has changed there, I can assure you. Look, can I send you over what few details I have, and you work your magic for me?"

"Sure thing, Jason."

"Thanks, Cody, I really appreciate it."

"Oh and, Jason..., (in his worst English accent) the wife and kids are just spiffy, thank you so much for asking. Let

36

me know when you finally get hitched, and we'll be there on the big day."

"Yeah right, now you're just being mean."

As soon as the call was finished, the room was filled with an eerie silence. Not even the sound of traffic, and it just highlighted how alone he was. Cody was a good friend, and they'd been almost inseparable twelve years ago when working for the NYPD, and yet now he couldn't even spare ten minutes to keep in touch. Sure, Cody could have called as well, but he has a young family and stupid hours to work. If Jason wasn't working now, all he'd be doing was eating a TV dinner and wishing he had a dog.

Does everyone know about my bloody personal life?

He thinks he is a nice guy, and some may say quite a catch, but his 'extraordinary' ability to read people had always played havoc with his relationships.

Jasmine was lovely... well, most of the time, but he could see she was a nest builder, just craving for a family because she had been an only child from two parents too busy to give her the love and attention she naturally desired. She was more in love with the idea of marriage than love itself, and he just wasn't ready for that, or sure she actually loved him.

Beth was adventurous, but very private. She hated talking about herself, as if every piece of information she gave would be used against her. It was a disaster. Whilst the passion was great, she soon learnt that he could read her like a book and quickly started to resent him and his abilities.

And then there is Nicole. Truth be told, he was still a little in love with her, so any memories hurt like hell. Their moments together were always hiding behind his eyes, thrown up at the worst times as if he was being punished for allowing himself to fall in love.

If only I was more... normal, we might still be together and happy. What is it she had said? "*It is like every move I make is being studied by you Jason, nothing at all is left to chance or forgotten or diagnosed. I just can't live that way anymore.*" *Women... relationships... it's just simpler being single. Give up the dating Jason, focus on your work and see you friends more often.*

Ping!

A message flashed up on his wall screen with a map:

'Hi Jason, it's Samantha. Sorry, I'm crap at getting back and replying to your last message. What would you say to going on a second date? I know this great bar in Bloomsbury'.

Chapter 8 – The Way of the Warrior

Jason stared into the eyes of the Samurai warrior screaming at him in Japanese. Although only about 5 and a half feet in height, the soldier still projected an air of cold, calculated menace as he stood firm in his elaborate, but very effective armour.

Most disturbing of all is his 'Mempo', a protective mask that is also designed to look like the Daemons of their folklore, and it sent a shiver down Jason's neck as distant memories flickered through his mind. Echoes of screams, crying, pain and fire that Awakening had returned to him, and now he was trying to suppress.

Just the shadowy eyes could be seen through the mask, his whole body otherwise completely covered, ready for battle, and now he was issuing Jason a war cry! Jason wasn't sure if it was the style of armour that frightened him the most, or the fact that there was no face to read on him. He was effectively hidden in his war suit.

Jeez, Jason, it's only a dummy, you dummy! He reminded himself.

Both with busy schedules, it had been easier to meet Samantha during the day than a night time drink at a bar, and she had suggested the Victoria and Albert Museum in South Kensington, as it is an excellent place to stroll, chat and admire the exhibits... or each other. And whilst she likes the elegant museum for many reasons, it appears Samantha loves the cream teas in the opulent Morris, Gamble and Poynter rooms even more.

The Ancient Japan gallery had taken Jason by surprise with its interactive models though. They were so lifelike.

"Aw, did the little soldier scare you," mocked

Samantha, "you've gone as white as a sheet?"

Jason laughed it off, but inside his mind, a part of him died again.

"He might be little, but he has a big sword," he whined, playing to the coward line.

"Hmm, reminds me of an ex," she replied, a glint in her eye.

"Ha, I have no response to that right now, but give me five minutes for a funny answer and I promise it'll be worth it."

"Five minutes? By that time I'd hope to have delivered ten jokes and three more insults. You gotta lot of catching up to do, G-eye man."

Jason was enjoying the playful conversation, but was already feeling the 'museum fatigue' that he always felt in these places. "Well let's sit over there by the other masks to give my brain a fighting chance then."

They went and sat on one of the museum benches. Smart, firm and functional, but not so comfortable that you'd want to spend the whole day sitting on it, as if designed with the words 'temporary stop' as its primary task. In walking over, the conversation dried up a little, causing the humorous moment to dissipate a little, and leaving Jason to ponder more on the warrior who'd intruded his thoughts.

"Have you had any past lives in Japan, Sam?"

Samantha stiffened up a little. Anyone could see that Awakening was a touchy subject with her, no expert required, but Jason felt he needed to know a little more about his latest date, and pressing certain emotional buttons could bring out the most information in the shortest time.

"No, not that I know of, although as I'd somehow found myself telling you, I didn't really finish my

Awakening foundation," Samantha exclaimed. "Actually, I was going to ask you, how do you do that, Jason?"

"Do what?"

"Get people to open up about their most personal feelings. I mean, I haven't really told any of my friends that embarrassing fact, and yet I spilled the beans on our first date as if we have known each other for years."

"Ah, I'm sorry, I really wasn't doing it consciously, it's just that..," he let out a big sigh and let himself open up to her, the tables turned towards him for a while. "I was always very good at reading people's body language, and now use it so intensively at work that it's almost impossible to turn off. As a by-product, I unconsciously mirror people's actions and reactions, and give back a positive nudge that builds up rapport and trust. Then, as you say, they spill the beans. It sounds like a gift, and it is in some respects, but I wish more than anyone that I could discard it when I wanted."

Samantha saw his eyes dull as he spoke, unable to look at her directly for the first time that day, and instantly felt a sense of wonder at this amazing skill, and sorry for him at the same time. Then it occurred to her that he could be playing her along with any idea he wished, and she'd stand little chance at knowing she was been played like a fool. This was going to take some getting used to.

"Oh, that's okay, I probably need to open up a bit more anyway" she offered. "So, were you a Samurai warrior once?"

"Twice actually, I must have been a sucker for punishment in my spiritual form. The first time I found myself in the Heiji Rebellion in 1160AD, fighting under Taira No Kiyomori, an imperial advisor. We won, but it was a horrific battle, and for what? Only twenty years of peace till the next big war, and... well, to cut a long story short, that was the end of that body. I had become a strategic casualty for Kiyomori."

"Wow, you must be royally pissed off with him."

Nah, it was a long time ago, no bad feelings, I just hope he's a dung beetle now, or worse, a traffic cop."

Samantha laughed. Maybe the date was going okay after all. "Well I have no memories of Japan, but I did spend some time in Rome around that time, but nothing as dramatic as your experience, thankfully. Quite fond memories actually, especially when compared to other lives. That's why I quit Awakening as soon as possible, too many bad memories and I was getting sick of them. Of course, reclaiming the ability to talk in Latin and French and other mildly useful languages was, and is, useful at times, but I don't really think it is worth the price."

Jason nodded. "To be honest, Sammy, most people find it a difficult line between the excitement of seeing into the past and regaining useful skills, against the pain of remembering loves lost or pain inflicted. And then you have to wait till you die before the gift of forgetting them again. What was it Shakespeare said in Hamlet about dying?"

"Er, something about 'To be or not to be'?"

"Yes, that, but he also spoke about death releasing the pain of life." His eyes looked up, trying to remember the lines from his English studies. "To die, to sleep no more, and by a sleep to say, we end the heartache and the thousand natural shocks that flesh is heir to - 'tis a consummation devoutly to be wished!"

"I'm impressed, although some might say you are trying too hard to impress on a second date," Samantha said, winking at him. It felt good to be with someone intelligent again, and felt like an eon since that had happened; the baggage of her last two relationships niggling at her mind and making her overly cautious at getting 'involved'. In retaliation to these thoughts, she stood up and took Jason's hand to press on. A smile spread across his face.

"Shall we move on to the room with all the giant casts in them?" she suggested.

∞-∞-∞-∞-∞-∞

The night before, and only a few miles from the V&A. Jack had been prowling the streets of London again, looking for his third victim in only four months, with only caution slowing down his blood lust.

God... It feels so good to be alive again! Even the rain on my face feels so fresh, as if this modern world uses mountain water to sprinkle the earth, rather than the grimy, smoked-filled smog that pissed out rain in my day. Hmm, this world is more sterile and cleaner on the surface, but it is hiding its shameful moral decline, and putrid inequity to the righteous and God-loving community that is fast becoming extinct.

A gurgling emanated by his feet, shaking him out of his reverie.

She's still alive.

Even though he'd cut deep enough into her throat to cause blood to foam around the wound, her breast was slowly expanding and contracting as her heart was engaged in a desperate battle to pump what little blood was left around her system. It was time to add to his repertoire as Jack, and safeguard him being discovered by their magic-like technology.

Placing her head back over his paper suited knee, he pulled out a razor blade he'd prepared earlier, being extremely careful not to cut himself in the process.

We don't want to be leaving our blood signature at this scene, do we Jacky.

"Look at me!" He growled into her ear, but she was past any action.

Pulling back her eyelid, the pupil was wide with shock as she stared into the face of her executioner. Then, he deftly sliced across the eyeball as precisely as a surgeon, splitting the ball until it oozed the pus like vitreous humor towards her tear duct. He squeezed what was left of the eye, curious to see if it held any secrets within, then repeated the whole process to the other.

The young girl writhed a little from the extreme pain, her last actions leading to her last breath. Within minutes her spirit was ejected from her body. Alone and cold but for a second, then transported to a better place.

Even with Awakening opening up so many paths to our past and our future, this is the point that human knowledge stops. This is the borderline between life and death, being a body, or being a soul. The unknown, but for how long? Maybe when mankind finally sheds light on this mystery, the clock will be set back and we'll start again. All saints and sinners balanced against the books, ready for a brave new world.

∞-∞-∞-∞-∞-∞

The Weston cast courts were opened in 1873, with the galleries conceived as a definitive collection of great works from Europe. Full-size fragments of exotic cathedrals and palaces, duplicated in London for all to see, and complimented by giant statues and columns. It was an aristocratic grand tour for the curious Victorian with a sense of adventure, but without the time or means to travel.

"This room is amazing," commented Jason, "I can't

believe I've never been here before."

"I know, it's practically a secret for most Londoners. They usually go to the Science or Natural History Museum, leaving this overlooked sibling to quietly preserve history. The Ceiling is 24 metres high, and yet that huge portal from the San Petronio basilica, only just fits inside."

"And these are just copies of the originals? They look so real."

"Yep, and even though they are old exhibits now, they have never been more relevant. The Victorians looked at them for clues to history. Now we look at them to jog our memories and see history through our own eyes. I'm surprised you have never used this place for your work."

Jason laughed. "Ha, it's not quite as simple as that. Most of the Awakenings I run would freak out the tourists and school kids. They'd end up screaming through the galleries."

He ran his hand over the smooth intricate figures originally carved out on Trajan's Column and seemingly, as if by magic, replicated in plaster by the industrious Victorians. In this new age, people travel all over the world to see this copy to confirm or even just reminisce about their time in Rome, when it stood as a focal point in the Emperor's forum to inspire or impose authority.

He'd lived in ancient Greece at one point, but never had the amazing experience of seeing the capital of Athens or nearby Rome at that time. A pang of jealousy went out to Samantha, but it was short lived. Almost everyone he knew had had at least one life in an important time point or city in the world.

"Enough history for now Buster. I'm going to treat you to the best cream tea this side of the Cromwell Road." said Samantha.

Jason laughed out loud. "Did you just call me, Buster?"

"Might have."

"Is that an ex, or just a really bad expression of speech?"

"That is for me to know, and you to find out... Buster."

There's definitely a good rapport between us, thought Jason, *and that is distracting me away from my over-thinking. Okay, so just thinking this is over-thinking, so stop thinking!*

This felt good and he didn't want to spoil anything with his analytical side, so he shoved it out the way and took her hand as she had taken his earlier. Samantha responded by clasping his hand back, and smiled, inside and out.

They walked to the cafe area along the slightly circuitous route, via a little bit of Korea, then strolled the whole length of Medieval and Renaissance Europe to get to the grand entrance. Walking hand in hand, they both went quiet as the exhibits took them back through their own personal time lines. People everywhere were doing the same, with only the children in their pre-Awakened innocence, using their imagination rather than their memories.

Then, walking through the shop and past a few statues, they crossed the delightful courtyard known as the inner quadrangle near the rear of the building that leads to the Refreshment Rooms at the end.

The Morris, Gamble and Poynter rooms were the original Refreshment Rooms, with the most lavishly decorated, and original restaurant being The Gamble Room. It was built to impress, and provide yet another way to entertain the Victorian people, where you could breakfast, dine or enjoy high tea whilst immersed in world culture.

Jason found himself impressed yet again by the central

Gamble Room. Decorated in stunning ceramic tiles and lit by three impressive sphere-shaped chandeliers hanging from its high ceiling, he felt special just by the fact that he was allowed to walk in there, even if he was wearing scruffy jeans.

His mobile then decided to pierce the gentle chatter of people enjoying their meals, with the sound of The Beatles screaming 'Help!' Samantha threw a glare at Jason that instantly wiped out any good impression he'd made earlier.

"Sorry," he said sheepishly, then ran out of the room cursing his mobile whilst being watched by the whole room. It was Cody.

"Hey, big guy, is this a convenient moment?"

Jason sighed, and then let out a little laugh. "No, just on a date with a beautiful girl who now hates me because I've left her alone in a museum restaurant filled with a gazillion disgusted diners, but that's okay."

Wow, really?"

"What, you don't believe I can get a date with an attractive woman these days?"

"No not at all, the internet is full of losers. I just can't believe your uncultured ass is in a museum."

"Maybe, but not for long at this rate."

"Well, look at the bright side, now you can blame me for it going sour."

"What bright side, it is your fault!"

Cody gave a mischievous laugh. "Okay, I'll help you out and take the rap for another failed date, but it's worth it. I've got those details you wanted re the Hickerson case. Turns out he is already serving time for carrying out the same kinda crime from 1954. Hickerson is now a Canadian, so suffering in the cold already I guess, and now called Tony Balcarey. He's residing at a penitentiary called Toronto South Detention Centre.

"Yeah I know it, quite a popular resort for past life crims. Thanks, Cody, I really owe you. Could you send me the files?"

"Already on your system my friend, complete with holographic profiles of him and his 1954 scene for you to wander round."

Jason was embarrassed by his friend's helpfulness. "Thank you so much, Cody, I owe you big time. I would chat but I better get back to Sam."

"Ooh, you dating men now."

Jason slapped his head in realising the ammunition he'd given his friend. "No goddamit, Samantha. Her name is Samantha."

"Yeah, I believe you, thousands wouldn't."

"Look, thanks again, I really appreciate this. I'll give you a call soon. I'm finally catching up with my workload."

Cody went back into Dick Van Dyke mode. "Take care me old China, and gimme a call on the dog and bone soon."

Jason flinched. "Shocking, Cody, really shocking. Somehow you are getting even worse at that accent."

But he was gone, leaving before he could hear his critique, even though it was all part of their comedy routine, probably guessing that Jason should get back to Samantha as soon as possible.

Jason found her already tucking into half a scone topped with clotted cream and raspberry preserve, whilst washing it down with a pot of Earl Grey. She looked up at him, a little peeved, but understanding that he obviously has the type of job that invades into his private life too.

More to get used to, she thought.

"Sorry about that," he offered, "Duty calls, and usually when you least want it too. Great news about a case I'm working on though."

Samantha's eyes lit up, maybe a little juicy gossip was going to come her way. "Oh that's okay, but I had to start, otherwise I'd look a little stupid sitting alone with no tea. What's happening in the world of Jason Ives then?"

"Ah, I can't really tell you much."

"Jason!"

His hands flew up, palms facing her in submission and an embarrassed smile on his face. "Ahem, apart from it's a nasty case from 1952, and I now have the name of the current identity of the killer!" He blurted out. "Can I have half your scone?"

"No, get your own you cheeky git." She then winked and produced another scone with a cup and saucer that she'd hidden on the seat next to them. "I hope you like Earl Grey."

Within five minutes they were chatting away again as if nothing had happened. Jason explained that he had to be available on the phone to a few people, such was the nature of his work, but that he always tried as hard as possible to not let it interfere with his life.

"Okay, I'll let you off this time, but you're on probation," quipped Samantha. "So have you got time to go and look at the 2020's fashion exhibition with me, I'll let you hold my hand a little more?" Her eyes lit up a little as she smiled, and went a little bashful.

"There was a fashion in the 2020's?"

"Apparently so."

Jason thought he'd rather bite his thumb off than look at fashion, but he was eager to make a good impression. "Sure, I've got all the time in the world."

Samantha looked past his left shoulder. "Oh, so why are those police officers coming towards us Jason? Oh god, I hope I'm not going to be embarrassed again in this tea room. I'll never be able to set foot in here again."

Two uniformed officers flanked the sides of a tall, thickly set man in a cheap suit. His goatee beard tried to distract from his greasy hair and large nose, but was losing the battle. The social chatter stopped for the second time that day as all the diners looked on in fascination at the new entertainment on show.

"Mr Jason Ives, I wonder if we could have a word with you down at the station?"

Chapter 9 – Police station

Jason wasn't impressed. He knew his work was important, and thus it makes certain demands on his personal life, but this was ridiculous. Samantha had positively seethed when she saw the police officers approach him in the museum tea rooms, but it had been made a thousand times worse by the fact that they could not tell them what the matter was about. And although it was all official business, it made him look guiltier of something more than just 'helping officers with their enquiries'.

Samantha followed Jason back to the Grand Entrance on Cromwell Road, only to witness him being driven off in a squad car with the blue light flashing and two tones blaring, as if purposefully trying to draw even more attention to them both. She knew it wasn't his fault of course, but she'd already had her doubts about being involved with someone 'like him' who held a job 'like that'. It was bloody frustrating, because she knew she was attracted to him and was already beginning to have feelings for him forming... but she couldn't even be sure about those new feelings, thanks to skills 'like his'. Of course, she also knew that if she wasn't so jaded by the relationships of her past, she might not be so suspicious of him, or afraid to be in a relationship again, but life isn't that simple.

Jason sat in the back of the car, mouthing the words, "I'll get in touch" through the rear window as they sped off. A Japanese tourist started filming the drama on the street, his retro style camera covering his face, looking for all the world like a steel Mempo mask from the museum. Jason shook his head in disbelief. It really was not his day.

The police car sped northeast along the Brompton Road until it was soon passing Harrods in Knightsbridge. Jason looked on at the people milling about, some shopping for luxury items, the rest just wishing they could afford them, but happy to gawp.

From there, the young officer driving the vehicle on manual pursuit mode, took them around Wellington Arch, until they reached the small entrance to Constitution Hill. It felt like an express tour of London, with the highlights blurring past, but it was the most direct route to their destination at Charing Cross. In respect to the King, the driver turned the siren off and slowed down to a more respectable speed as they passed Buckingham Palace. Even in this day and age, a degree of decorum is still expected.

Pressing on along The Mall adjacent to St. James's Park, they soon reached Nelson's column at the heart of the West End. The siren returned, with buses and auto-cabs sluggishly pulling over to let this noisy irritant get past to reach William IV Street, home of Charing Cross police station. If he wasn't so pissed off, Jason felt he would have enjoyed his exclusive tour.

"Would you like a tea or coffee sir?" A uniformed officer with pimples asked as soon as they arrived.

Detective Sergeant Pascal stroked his goatee beard with his thumb and forefinger, possibly with the intent of making himself look more authoritative, but failing miserably. He hadn't said much in the car, except that he was extremely thankful to Ives for agreeing to come back to the station, and that it was a matter of some sensitivity and urgency.

"Coffee please, milk and one sugar," answered Jason with a smile to the police constable. Then, he sat down, crossed his right leg over his knee, leant back and gave Pascal a steady gaze; a signal to indicate that he was comfortable and in control, ready to argue any point if needed. "Can you now tell me what this is all about Sergeant?"

"Of course, sorry about all the cloak and dagger stuff, but we are trying to contain a situation before the press work out what's happening and create mayhem with their sensationalist reports."

Ives raised an eyebrow, signalling the sergeant to apologise further. "And how did you know where I was?"

Pascal looked at the floor. "Ah, sorry, but as this is a bit of an emergency, we had to trace you through your medi-chip."

"You did what?"

"Chief Super's orders."

Luckily for Pascal, Ives was more intrigued than he was annoyed. "So what is so important that you need my immediate help with?" he said with a little anger in his voice. A warning shot to stand his ground.

"In February of this year, a prostitute was found murdered in a hotel in Shoreditch. It was particularly gruesome, as the killer decided not only to end her life, but make sure she'd be found cut open with her entrails hanging out. I have some photos if you'd like to see them?"

Ives put his hand up to the officer and shook his head. "I'll pass on those for the time being. I have enough blood and death in my own line of work without looking for more of it. So how can I help? I only deal with past life murders."

We think it was the first of three murders, all linked with the same modus operandi. That of murdering a prostitute, and then mutilating their bodies before leaving them lying on the floor with their legs open, as if ready for sex. Trouble is, there's no forensic evidence left at the scene, and he's getting more sophisticated in his methods, and he's picking up speed. Last night we found the body of a young girl in Soho."

"Christ, that's a very public area." Ives interjected.

"Yes, it is, but with lots of alleyways. The killer obviously knows his way around London, but the first two were in Shoreditch, the hunting area for the infamous Jack the Ripper, which is where you come in."

Ives was blown away. Could that be possible? "Sergeant, that is very unlikely. Not only would someone have to find out that they had been Jack the Ripper through Awakening, they also would have had to do it in some form of secrecy, as all sessions are recorded. Their observer, the person putting the client through the Awakening, would also know they had been Jack the Ripper and thus reported it."

"Still possible though, Mr Ives?"

"Yes, I guess so, but even then, these are our old personalities from our past lives. Our current identity is our core identity, and thus in total control. Just because you remember being a murderer doesn't make you want to do it again. And even if you did, your skills would still be compromised by your current identity."

DS Pascal nodded in agreement. "I guessed you might say something like that sir. I was once a pirate in the South Seas, but I don't feel the urge to hoist the mast and shiver my timbers."

They both laughed. Even in a society fully aware of past lives, talk of such tales in such an abstract fashion still sounded odd.

"But," the sergeant added, "the MO in terms of victim choice and mutilation style is very clear, so it is either the Ripper or someone copying him. The only deviations from that MO are the last victim being out of Shoreditch and that he's added an extra mutilation."

"Really, what is he doing now?"

"He cut out the eyes."

The words kicked Jason in the stomach. To him, maybe more than most people, eyes are that window to the soul that everyone talks about. They are the basis of a lot of his body language skills. By looking at a person's eyes you can tell if they are remembering something, or just making it up. You can tell if someone is attracted to you or angry. In his mind, this was the final straw.

"Okay, you got me. How can I help you with your enquiries?

"Our superintendant, Mr Hopkins, hopes that you can use your skills to delve into the Ripper's past to find out who he is today."

"What, it's been almost two hundred years since Jack the Ripper was last seen, and his identity back then is still a mystery. I've got nothing to go on to set a profile for today."

Pascal sympathised. "That's what my governor DCI Bjorkman said. She's certain that it would be wasting your time, but the Chief Super hopes you could find and interview some of the original Ripper's victims to find some vital clue that could lead to his arrest in the here and now. There's no time to waste. He has killed three victims in just four months, so it's only a matter of time before he strikes again."

Ives let out a big sigh. He wanted to help, but he didn't know how. "I'm already wrapped up in a case. I can't just drop it." What about you own past life investigators?"

Pascal shrugged his large shoulders. "To be perfectly frank with you sir, they are just not up to it. The team is small and inexperienced in major cases, because the Met won't fund past life crime anywhere near as much as current crime. We can hardly keep up with things happening in 2065, never mind all the crap from the past. But now the past has thrown this huge challenge at us, we need the best, and according to the media, that's you."

"You're just buttering me up to get me to help, aren't you?" said Ives with a smirk.

"Might be, it's desperate measures for desperate times," Pascal joked. Then he gave Ives a steady gaze. "Don't worry, we will get our team to assist with your existing case that I'm guessing is more time tolerant. It will free you up for this more urgent matter and hopefully we can save lives rather than just pick up the pieces after the event."

Well that's the personal life out the window for another year at least, thought Jason; *I'll never get time to sort things out with Samantha now.*

Somewhere between Ancient Japan and the Pillars of Rome, he'd quite fallen for her. Yes she had baggage, that was abundantly clear to anyone, but then who hasn't? He loved her sense of humour and her passion for art and history, in spite of her own troubled Awakenings, and was now intrigued. He wanted to know more about Samantha, which is probably why fate seems to have stepped in to quash any hope of happiness for him.

But lives are at stake and he has a chance of catching this lunatic.

How could he say no?

Chapter 10 – DCI Bjorkman

Some days you just know what you will be doing in your day at work. Meetings, time reading messages, chats in the hallway about how much you hate your boss. That never happens with Jason Ives, in fact, it is so rare, he actually longs for a normal day. It is a special occasion.

True to form, today had started off on his first promising date in an eon, only to be dashed within a few hours, and any kind of personal life put on indefinite hold. Jason also knew this would probably be his toughest ever assignment. Was he really capable of finding and catching the most mysterious serial killer in history? Part of him relished the challenge, but the rest just wondered if his day could get any worse.

Detective chief inspector Sabina Bjorkman walked into the room. Five foot eight, shoulder length golden blonde hair, lapis blue eyes and extremely attractive, in a Scandinavian way that seems so casual. She took Jason completely by surprise and all the effort he could muster to not leave his mouth gaping. For a short while at least, Samantha became but a distant memory.

His attraction was palpable, instant, magnetic... no, stronger; gravitational. Jason could feel it, as if it was an energy buzzing in the room and he knew it would be trouble.

Unfortunately for him, Bjorkman looked at Ives as if he was a piece of dirt... no, worse, as if he was a miserable piece of dog turd stuck to her shoe.

DS Pascal practically stood to attention. "Afternoon guv, this is Jason Ives. I have just been telling him about Operation Talisman, and he's very kindly agreed to assist us with our investigation."

A smile appeared on her face, but it was completely disconnected from her eyes. A political smile forced through need rather than want. You don't have to be a Jason Ives to see that she didn't like Jason Ives.

A small prick of resentment stabbed at Jason. "Nice to feel wanted," he blurted out sarcastically, surprising himself with his honesty.

The eyes finally caught up with the mouth. Now she was enjoying his discomfort. "And hello to you, Mr Ives. At least I don't have to expend time explaining how I feel about bringing you into the investigation. I'm sorry that we have wasted your time and interrupted your date," she gave a little wink at Pascal who'd obviously brought her up to speed on the day's events, "but my superintendent has been reading the headlines and watching YouTube for five minutes and now thinks you're the bee's knees. I'll be blunt, I don't."

Brave face Jason, he thought to himself.

"I admire your candour chief inspector, and to be honest, I'd rather not get involved anyway, but your sergeant says three women have been butchered and more lives are at risk, so it looks like neither of us has much choice. Of course, I could talk to your superior officers if you like and maybe we can find a solution?"

Bjorkman instantly bit at the word 'superior' as Jason knew she would; a little touch of resistance just to show he wasn't a pushover. Her eyes narrowed for a fraction of a second, tainted by an anger lurking within, before quickly returning to her professional facade.

"Oh, my *Superiors* want your help, Mr Ives, that is without doubt. This trio of murders is going to hit the media at any moment and they are desperate for any new path. But remember, they are also *my superiors* because they know how to play the game."

Ives looked at her disdainfully. "Cat and mouse or Cluedo?"

"Politics and media, Mr Ives. When the shit hits the fan, and it will, and the public start braying for results, who do you think *my superiors* will blame?" She paused for a moment for dramatic effect, pointing at Ives. "The civilian of course. The world famous G-Eye known for entrapping otherwise innocent people who find out they were once a Nazi, or that they murdered someone hundreds of years ago. Not everyone believes in next life justice, Mr Ives."

"Ah, so you are a clean slate kind of person then; new life, new beginning?"

Bjorkman tilted her head and nodded gently. "Yes I am."

Jason's eyes lowered, this was a sensitive issue that he fought with almost every day from like minded people, and he could completely see their point. Once again he thought of the case that haunted him the most; the Jewish girl finding out she had been Hitler and the anti next life justice marches it had caused. The press had gone wild, inflaming passions from both side of the argument.

That is one of the problems with Awakening. It is still very new, and yet had such a huge impact on the perceptions and consciousness of society. It has formed a new consciousness, leading to changes that are being made all the time. Only last year, Martin Kale finally persuaded the American courts to review her sentence once more, and change it to a custodial sentence starting from her next life. They also reduced it to four life times with new reviews every ten years. Better to watch and study the life force that had once been Hitler, than to possibly turn it into something worse.

When that news came out, the press made another loud

noise about paying dues with your bodies, and the other half of the general public became very vocal in wanting the original sentence kept. This is a very emotive subject, and is always going to divide opinion. Jason knew there would never be a satisfactory solution.

"I understand that chief inspector, but unfortunately a lot of people want closure, and they want that through their idea of justice. Ultimately, it is a tally of karma."

"Karma can be played out over many lifetimes, Ives," said Bjorkman, dropping the Mr as if dropping that last modicum of respect for him.

"Yes, maybe, but five years ago I was called in to find Pol Pot, who'd led the Khmer Rouge in Cambodia and was personally responsible for the genocide of at least two million people. Relatives of those that had died were still very distressed. Not because they could not reconcile themselves with the death, but that he had died peacefully in his sleep. He had escaped judgement or karma or whatever you want to call it, and it seemed too unfair to bear. So where is the point in which people should be able to escape, Ms Bjorkman? Should we be able to murder people and then run away to death as if it is the Mexican border?

Bjorkman looked rattled, this was obviously very close to her heart, and she was genuinely upset by the matter. "And should a law-abiding family man be suddenly thrown into prison just because he was unfortunate enough to have committed a crime in a past life? Is that fair to his wife and kids?" She countered.

Jason put his hands up in submission. "Okay, I get it, I'm sorry. Plenty of people feel just the way you do and I respect that, I honestly do. There is no simple argument, but ultimately our aim right now is the same, and I'd like to help if I can, and I'd like to do it working with you and your team's blessing."

"That's not going to happen, Mr Ives, but we can offer you a cubical to work from until the Super gets bored with you," she said with a sneer.

Ives had had enough. His time working for the Met, and the NYPD in the past, had quickly taught him how their particular style of politics could fuck up most multi-agency investigations. This was too big a case to throw away, and he certainly didn't want to see anyone else get hurt. He got up to leave.

"Then I'll just have to investigate this as a private matter to cut through the bullshit. Whether I get paid by the Met or by selling my story, it doesn't matter to me as long as I get results," he bluffed.

Bjorkman looked Ives up and down as if she was scanning him in a way that felt very familiar. *He was being read* just as he would read a suspect. Yes, in an amateurish, obvious, clunky style, but she definitely had some basic body language skills and was using them now to look for clues to his personality. Looking for whether he was telling the truth in wanting to help or just trying to add another high profile assignment for his résumé. He blanked any thoughts or signs instantly.

Something clicked in her logical brain. A decision had been made and the sun came out. A warm, genuine looking smile that filled the room and disarmed Jason completely as she held out her hand. Her whole demeanour completed a u-turn to reveal someone who was truly apologetic. Pascal just remained quiet, caught up in the event.

"I'm sorry, you are right of course. It's been a rough few months for the team. The stress must be getting to me. I won't lie though, I obviously have my doubts about you, and most certainly about G-Eyes in general, but I also appreciate you offering your services. Pascal will assist you with anything you need, but keep me in the loop at all times."

Jason cautiously took her hand to shake it. Her Nordic features affording her a strong beauty which was still in danger of overwhelming his senses. Soft light skin that felt warm and sensual to touch, passing that energy he'd felt earlier, right through his body.

Step back Jason. You've been here before, remember?

"So," added the chief inspector trying to lighten the mood, "has DS Pascal told you about Isambard Smythe?"

Chapter 11 – Isambard Smythe

Jason couldn't help focusing on Smythe's nose. It matched his name exactly, in a Dickensian sort of way, and his odd choice of clothing didn't help. Isambard Buckton Smythe was in his early forties but looked older, with grey hair that was balding in the middle. An old fashioned look, as most people choose to keep their hair with med shampoo or shave it all off to enjoy the freedom of a bald head. His suit was lined with velvet and completed with a silver pocket watch hanging from his left pocket. Smythe was the living embodiment of a modern Victorian gentleman, reminding Jason of a steampunk style, a character out of time and place.

Right now that *place* was Horseferry Road Coroner's mortuary in Westminster, and everyone was waiting for the pathologist to arrive. Inspector Bjorkman had insisted Ives tag along if he wanted to be part of the case, but Jason felt it was just one of her tests to see what he was made of. Now she was outside fielding calls in the warm sunlight of the early afternoon, whilst DS Pascal was chatting to the mortuary technicians about their weekend, as if they were down at the pub.

Isambard noted Ives signing the registration book and introduced himself with a sweaty hand. It gave Jason a chance to examine him methodically; there was just so much 'wrong' about this guy. Isambard's hunched, almost apologetic demeanour made it pretty obvious that he had grown up unhappy in his current identity, but he had moved from trying to fit in, to purposefully sticking out.

His aim now was to emphasise his differences, it makes him 'special,' and Jason could appreciate that. Either he had chosen to become 'Victorian' in adulthood as a fashion statement, or he had lived and preferred his life in Victorian England after Awakening, and wished to emulate it. Not an unusual move by any means, but it was to this extent.

His name... of course, he's probably changed it by deed poll. He is hiding behind this elaborate identity, thought Ives, *and possibly explains his profession as a Ripperologist!*

Usually giving lectures, writing books or taking tourists round on tours, Ripperologists have been in existence almost as long as Jack the Ripper himself. All of them want to solve the mystery of who the man really was, and why he committed the atrocious murders. Suspects range from royalty to pub owners to cotton merchants to surgeons to artists and impoverished Europeans.

There are so many 'clues' to the identity of the Ripper that it is almost impossible to be able to know what is real and what is fake. DNA and fingerprint samples have been taken, as well as psychological profiles from witnesses and x-rays of paintings by suspects to see if there are any clues in what lies beneath the canvas, but nothing has stood the real test, leaving the Ripper to languish in the shadows, even in modern times.

Jason finally took his eyes of Isambard's nose and shook his sweaty palm. "Hi, Jason Ives, another civilian specialist brought in to crack the crime," he joked.

Isambard took it at face value. "Oh yes, I'm very much looking forward to working with you, Mr Ives, watched much of your work I have, on many mediums."

Jeez, even his speech is skewed.

"Please, call me Jason."

"Oh, thank you kindly for your generous offer, boss, but I actually feel more comfortable adhering to formalities; they are what keep us above beast and our burdens. You may of course feel free to call me by any name that puts you at ease." He spoke as if he was in a high brow play and said the word 'boss' with a slight femininity that completely changed the feel of the word. Ives could not guess what, or why he'd used it. Had he been bullied so badly at school that he was in subservience to most people?

"Just Jason or Ives is cool, thank you, Isambard. I'm going to need your help every step of the way on this case as I'm a little rusty on my Ripper knowledge. I'll need to know as much as you can tell me on ideas to his identity, and what his habits were. I'll also need to know his victims and where he liked to hang out; pubs, brothels anywhere that the experts agree on."

Isambard looked a little uncomfortable. "Sadly, with this regard, none of the 'experts' agree on much. Jacky boy is still a slippery character. Surmount to say, many of us enjoy the riddle more than the answer. To find him would remove his mystique."

Jason felt himself getting a little irritated by this weasel of a man. "You know that's the idea, Smythe... we have to catch him, and catch him fast?"

"Don't worry boss, we'll catch him."

"And don't call me boss, it creeps me out!" snapped Ives with a shiver going down his spine. He knew it wasn't Isambard's fault, all part of his social conditioning than any ill intent, matched by an unfortunate physical appearance that emphasised his quirky nature.

Isambard looked at him from his beady, bird like eyes, taking two blinks to digest the information. "Oh, but of course, Mr Ives, forgive my vernacular, it rubs a lot of people the wrong way, but it is part of my very nature. I mean nothing by it."

Jason felt guilty all of a sudden, as if he'd spoken like the school bully in Smythe's past. "Sorry, it's no problem, Isambard, I just don't like being called boss. It's my hang up really."

Doctor Bartholomew eventually turned up, having rushed from the edge of London to the centre, fresh from giving evidence in court that morning. It was only a distance of seven miles, but in the thick London traffic it can take hours.

"There were reporters at the gate when I came in," remarked the pathologist, "looks like they have finally put together all three murders and now know a serial killer is on the loose."

Bjorkman groaned. "Motherfuckers, looks like it's going to be another late night boys."

"It's all overtime to me, guv," said Pascal, trying to put a silver lining on the matter."

You'll be lucky, Pascal, it'll probably be time off in lieu by the time the Super sanctions anything."

"Bloomin nora, any more time off in Lieu and I'll have to retire early."

A cough filled the room. "Shall we get started?" offered the pathologist.

Ives could smell the examination room a mile off. It stank. A mixture of chemicals and death that conspired together to try and induce vomiting from the beginning, as if it were a challenge. This was not Ives' first dead body, that event had passed years ago, but it was his first 'special'.

A special post mortem is a complete post mortem carried out by a forensic pathologist for any death considered 'suspicious', and any non-suspicious sudden death has a standard PM, just in case something suspicious turns up later. If that happens, they then call the homicide team in, and a forensic pathologist.

A body was already lying on a slab at the end of the room. A standard post mortem from earlier, just waiting for the busy technicians to sew his face back on and stitch the length of his body and arms in a way that allows the family of the deceased to view their loved ones in as dignified a way as possible. Right now, with a name tag on his foot and lying stark bollock naked, it was as far from dignity as you could imagine.

Ives was already feeling 'peaky' and they hadn't even started yet.

Dr Bartholomew looked at Ives and Smythe. "Not a good one to lose your PM virginity to gentlemen, but at least she hasn't shat herself. I hate it when they do that."

Jason gave a feeble smile as Smythe jutted his latex covered thumb into the air with a big grin. *He's enjoying this*, thought Jason. Many people do of course; they find the whole experience of seeing the body opened up as fascinating, especially when the brain is pulled out of its skull. Jason wasn't one of those people.

The mortuary technician called Steve pushed a trolley holding a white body bag into the examination room. He then scanned the ID tag and let the Soco take photos of the bag as they opened it up to discover what was left of her body.

"Looks like someone's beaten you to it this time doc," said Steve in jest. "She's already been cut up just the way you like them."

The pathologist looked at Steve with mock contempt. "And it will take you twice as long to sew her up in that state, so you better shut your trap so we can get on with it."

Whatever Jason was expecting, this was worse. As the bag was unzipped and removed, the absolute carnage became clear. Her whole body had been ripped apart... the MO of the killer known as Jack the Ripper. In other ways though, it was easier, as the victim didn't look human anymore. Even a butcher would have had more respect for his meat.

Her sallow skin was cut from inside the vagina, right up to her sternum by an incredibly sharp knife, but then that could be from most kitchen blocks these days. Her entrails had also been left scattered at the scene, right next to her seemingly empty body, leaving the forensic team to scoop what they could into plastic bags and lay them beside her frail frame. A body that had been so full of life, left hollow and silent.

Isambard moved closer to look at the neck, cut so deep it severed the voice box and continued into the spine till the knife finally met resistance on the final vertebrae. A little more force would have severed the head completely. Isambard's main focus of attention was the eyes though, or at least, the lack of them. Jason could hardly look.

"What the hell must have been going through the killer's warped head?" remarked DS Pascal. He was taking exhibits, but had to pause to take in the horror of the scene.

Bjorkman joined Isambard by the head, equally fascinated by the sliced open eyes and eager to listen to her team's guesses as to why the killer had introduced this new mutilation to his routine. "What do you think doctor?"

Doctor Bartholomew shrugged his shoulders. "It wasn't to kill her, that's for sure. Unfortunately, I can't tell you if her eyes were cut out post or anti mortem, but if she had been still alive, she'd have been struggling with all her strength, and would therefore have made it very difficult for the killer to perform this mutilation." Then he pulled an eyelid over his forefinger, spreading the tissue to inspect it. "No cuts, no damage, I can only imagine that they'd been held back whilst he was gouging the eyes."

Isambard suddenly turned to Jason, interested to hear his suggestion before declaring his own. Jason stared back from as far as he felt was reasonable without looking like a complete wimp. "What say you, Mr Ives?"

Ives shook his head. "No idea... maybe he wanted to blind her first, just in case she is interviewed in her next body and would thus know the killer." The idea gripped him, pushing him to expand on his theory. "Yes, the killer was maybe masked, then subdued her, then cut out her eyes so that she couldn't see what a sadistic bastard he was." He looked at his hands that were quietly shaking.

Isambard was almost euphoric. "Excellent hypothesis sir, and almost correct, but borne from the summation of the assumed facts than the facts themselves, and thus just wide of the proverbial mark. History of the Ripper holds the answer I fear."

Bjorkman was getting impatient. "Today, Isambard, before someone else dies."

Isambard nervously swept his hair back and licked his lips. "As I was implying before your interjection, Ma'am, when the original victims of Jack the Ripper were photographed, explicit instructions were given to take extreme close ups of the eyes, using specialist lenses and bellows to exact a macro image."

"Skip the photography lesson," exhaled the pathologist, eager to move on.

"Well, they took close ups of the eyes in the vain hope that the technology of the future would catch up with the dreams and aspirations of Victorian pride. They believed that one day they would have the capability of seeing the killer through the eyes of the victim, using special photographic techniques as yet undiscovered."

"You're shitting me?" was all the technician could add

to the conversation.

"I poop you not fine sir." Isambard was on a roll now, his place at this post mortem validated.

Jason was curious. "So even now, almost two hundred years later, we still have nothing that could do anything like that. And yet this killer is still afraid of something as absurd but curiously plausible in a Victorian way, that he would take the trouble to cut their eyes out. I'm sorry Isambard, but only you would have come up with that. I'm impressed."

Isambard put his hands up to humbly play down any praise. "On the contrary, any Ripperologist worth his salt would know that nugget of information. I'm surprised it has never come up in your line of work."

"No, Isambard, it hasn't funny enough, but it has now."

DCI Bjorkman grew restless. She looked at the corpse quietly waiting on the table for any secrets to be extracted, and then looked to her personal Ripperologist. "So, tell me, do you think this is the work of a copycat or the man himself?"

All eyes were on Isambard... his moment had come. At last he could revel in the grimy limelight of this case. Pausing for thought and suspense, he straightened his bow tie and swept back his grey hair.

"Yes dear boss, I think this is Jack's grand work, and he won't stop till he gets buckled good and proper."

Chapter 12 – Angela

Now that the lights are out at the mortuary, there is something in the air. Something intangible... but it is definitely there. The pathologist left hours ago, followed by the officers, the civilians and the technicians. Even the press have left, safe in the knowledge that this story will feed their families for months to come with their frenzied reporting of a new Ripper on the loose. A new Ripper, how close to the truth they really are.

Total peace now, save for the fan whirring in the freezer, but it is not disturbing Angela, it is too late for that as she lies on a metal tray, her organs reunited with her, but in no usable way, just stuffed into a black plastic bag and pushed into her empty carcass.

The freezer is the only thing keeping her body from putrefying. As it went from life, to death, to rigor mortis in a matter of hours; her cells breaking down, the next step in the cycle of life as it begins to rot from the inside out; gasses forming and released through her mouth or anus or one of the many new holes in her body, roughly sewn together by the mortician.

Her body's life has ended, but it will provide nutrients to the insects that swarm her grave. Her life providing for their life, a life snuffed out before it even began, a life full of mistakes, even though she was only nineteen years old when the killer crossed her path.

Nineteen and walking the streets to pay for her drug habit, another mistake that started from hanging out with the wrong crowd, and now she is dead. It will be years before she can even contemplate taking a new form after this awful trauma. Pain and fear has a habit of doing that, sometimes for decades, but that's okay, time is different out here.

And yet she was killed by someone who shouldn't even be walking around, someone evil who has been given another bite of the cherry by overpowering their new body. How unfair is that? Their suffering is also very bad though, some might think it is even worse, in a dragged out, lifetime sort of way. Karma is a bitch, and still no one truly understands it.

Worst of all, she now knows her killer's secret...

...but can't tell anyone, no matter how hard she screams.

Chapter 13 – A Swift Half

Samantha checked her messages, and yet still nothing from Jason. She's had seventeen emails this week from eager men (mostly) on lovematch.com. Seventeen messages saying they want to know more about her and maybe even have a relationship. One of those men might be Mr Right, with a good job and good teeth, who is strong and charming and funny. Someone who knows his own mind, but can have it changed on her whim because he loves her so much. Someone cool and handsome, but extremely loyal. Someone who isn't clingy, but wants to settle down and have kids in the next couple of years.

Samantha then realised she was letting her mind run away with her dreams, and that virtually no one has all those qualities she is looking for. Her thirtieth birthday is looming (28th on lovematch.com) and yet she still has to trawl through bloody dating websites. Her biological clock is screaming at her, and yet, she isn't really interested in looking through the latest lot of human rejects that want to talk about their work or football or how big their cock is!

She let out a big sigh. Oh hell, why did she have to like the bloody awkward one? Jason, the guy with the lovely smile, good manners and confident air, (when not being shy) but who has a job that will completely dominate his life and anyone he is in a relationship with.

Patrick had had a job like that. If she'd have married him... and thank fuck she hadn't because he is a complete loser, she would have ended up with four kids running around the house whilst he was always out working, or seeing his mistress. Bastard! Why is life so bloody difficult?

What she needs is to meet up with Libby again. Talk it through with her sensibly over a few drinks, and who knows, Mr Right might even be there at the pub. It would be about bloody time. Honestly, where the hell is he hiding?

∞-∞-∞-∞-∞-∞

Jack was lying low in the corner of the Ten Bells pub in Spitalfields trying to not get noticed, but he was still attracting some attention for some reason, probably his damn body sticking out like a sore thumb, but he hadn't had time for a disguise. Anyway, he was having a day off from killing today, and just fancied going to his local from the good old days.

Ah, the Ten Bells, den of inequity and watering hole to most of his victims. Long Liz used to stand outside the doorway selling her wares as if she was selling flowers. Brazen hussy; she'd had no shame till he'd taught her the error of her ways. Annie hadn't fared much better.

He couldn't believe how many original features he recognised. Yes it was cleaner, everywhere is bloody cleaner now, but the narrow Roman pillars at the entrance were still there, and the beautiful blue and white floral tiles on the walls, he'd always liked those.

A noisy couple were kissing and cuddling by the huge mural, making it difficult for Jack to read the title at the bottom, but he knew it off by heart. He'd read it thousands of times before.

'SPITALFIELDS in ye OLDEN TIME -
Visiting a Weaver's shop'.

Christ, the mural had been old even in his day, now it

was positively ancient amongst the 21st century technology; magic by any other name.

He closed his eyes to block out the modern day and imagined himself back in 1888. They had been hard times, enough to drive him to the brink, but he still finds himself reminiscing with a golden glow. No mobile devices, no computers, no electronic cameras, no wall screens with 'structured reality' crap on all day and night. No celebrity gossip... well, maybe a little, but it was with people he knew, real stars of the stage, not some talentless dandy.

Jack closed off his mind and concentrated really hard, even managing to silent the voices in his head for a short while. Long enough to hear the horse and trap outside delivering the beer, or the Hackney carriages ferrying patrons to the theatre district. The squalor came rushing back in as if it was yesterday. There were people so poor that it was not unknown to see dead bodies lying in the gutter amongst the rotting vegetables and manure.

The sweep used to pop in with his sweet little lad in tow. Little Tommy had been pushed into the business to help pay for his father's alcoholism, and was already coughing up a pile. Ironic that when his father dried out for a while, they'd have to come in and clean the pub chimneys and wash away the soot with ale.

Then a pang of guilt suddenly hit Jack as he remembered 'Old Scotty' sitting outside. She had been married to a wealthy man who spent all his money before dying and leaving her penniless as one of London's crawlers. Maybe he should toss her a coin when he sees her next.

He had asked her once if she was okay begging on the street, and she had answered quite pragmatically. She had grown accustomed to it. What, however, she could not endure, was the awful, lazy, idle life she was forced to lead. To her, it was a thousand times worse than the hardest labour, and would much rather her hands were cut, blistered, and sore with toil, than just swollen and smarting from the exposure to the sun, the rain, and the cold whilst doing nothing. She would also borrow babies for begging, as it always raised more pennies, and then split the proceeds with the mothers.

Jack slowly opened his eyes and returned to present day as soon as the light hit his retinas. Real poverty was extinct in London now, but replaced by a proliferation of sin. Sex has always been the devil's lure, but now it is openly accompanied by pride, envy, wrath, gluttony, sloth and greed. The seven deadly sins have never been so visible. Billboards and commercials advertising a non-stop stream of this filth, to tempt even the most righteous, are on the streets and busses, and in our homes, with scantily clad women selling provocative make-up or underwear to find a man... or woman in these days of moral turpitude.

∞-∞-∞-∞-∞-∞

Samantha stuffed her boobs firmly into her Wonderbra. She'd finally made contact with Libby, who was only too ready for a night out on the town, and if she didn't hear back from Jason soon, she was going to ignore her feelings for him and just snag another man into her life.

"We should go to Spitalfields for a change," Libby had suggested, "it's getting quite trendy now."

Chapter 14 – Scarface

Jason was shattered. What had meant to be a rare day off had turned into one of the biggest challenges of his life. He was used to chasing people through history, but he usually had their names to start with. And with high profile suspects / victims he'd also have a stack of biographies of the killer he was looking for. True, there are probably thousands of books on Jack the Ripper, but they are mostly written with the author's private views, often with a suspect in mind, and then the whole investigation engineered to make the face fit.

All this information to sift through, and yet it was only the starting point. To find the possible name to begin with, and then build the investigation into the Ripper's life, on what would probably be very little written information to put together a profile. Jason could only hope that the Ripper's identity would turn out to be someone well known, or arrested for some other murder, and therefore traceable through the usual classified Awakening legal records - preferably in Britain.

He looked out of the window of his Putney apartment, craning his neck around the small balcony that the sales blurb had promised was a view of the river Thames. It certainly delivered in its promise, as long as you were on tiptoes and risking life and limb to peer over the side. The full river view Apartments demanded at least 40% more money and were 10% smaller. 'Welcome to London living' it had said.

London living, from crack dens in Hackney to billionaire mansions in Holland Park, London had it all, and now it even had its most infamous serial killer on the loose again. Jason couldn't decide if that would push the value of his apartment up or down, such is the madness of the market these days.

After the post mortem, He'd gone straight to the office to cancel appointments and transfer his current investigations to the Met's past crimes unit. He felt bad about Elizabeth's case, but fortunately the info Cody had found regarding the already documented link between Hickerson and his current identity provided an excellent short cut to closing the case. Hopefully Hickerson would confess to further crimes to save jail time and find a way to make an apology to his victims. Funny how an act of genuine contrition can help heal so many wounds.

The case reminded Jason that neither of them had known her killer's identity at the start of the investigation, so he should just apply the same process to finding Jack and they could move on from there. This time however, he would be hampered by having to work with a DCI who was busting his balls about everything he did, and a Ripperologist who acted like the main suspect would act in a cheap novel. Isambard was harmless enough, but his obsession with Victoriana and the Ripper himself makes him a very difficult character to read.

Bjorkman's character was also hidden from him. It had become quite clear to Jason that she too held a natural ability to read people's body language. Her's was a raw skill, honed through whatever kind of life she'd had growing up, than in classrooms and through books. And, as Jason had seen in her presence, she was blocking her own outgoing signals to stop being read herself. It takes a very private nature to be able to keep the barrier up all the time though, to the point that it is done automatically through her subconscious.

The irony hit him. Here was this incredibly attractive woman who he could not read, and thus have some semblance of a normal relationship with. Someone who is also an investigator and understands the demands of the job. She is perfect for him... if only she wasn't such a bitch.

That's the Ives magic, he thought to himself, and then smacked his hand against his head as he remembered something important. *Oh God... I better call Samantha!*

The enormity of the day and the unpleasantness of the post mortem had pushed everything else to the back of his mind.

But what should he say? He definitely liked her, physically, and on a personal level, where he felt they shared the same type of humour and interests. It was also quite clear that she was intelligent and liked a little culture, museums, movies, music etc. Now if only she liked Rugby Union, it would push her even higher into the dating league.

But what to say? Jason knew from experience that a major case like this would become all consuming. It wouldn't be fair to her, or even him to start anything new right now. Sure, if they were in an established long term relationship it might just weather the storms, but in its infancy? It was just too difficult an ask.

∞-∞-∞-∞-∞-∞

"Two pints of lager and a packet of crisps please."

"What?"

"Two pints of lager and a packet of crisps... please!" Samantha screamed at the barman in a noisy Brick lane pub.

Libby quickly pushed in. "You're bloody joking, I'm

not drinking lager. I'll have a whisky and Coke."

"Good idea. With the mood I'm in, it will get us drunk quicker. The daft bugger can't hear us anyway though, or doesn't speak English."

Samantha looked back up to the barman to try and order again, but he had already moved on to serving someone else, and they seemed to be ordering a round for a football team.

Libby was livid. "Oi mate, what the fuck?"

The barman suddenly possessed perfect hearing and replied in sign language using his middle finger.

Samantha burst out laughing. The first time that evening, and was quite relieved in a way. "Come on, Libby, let's go somewhere quieter."

∞-∞-∞-∞-∞-∞

Jason was still sitting on his tiny balcony, his city version of a back yard, only it was about 75ft up in the air rather than surrounded by grass and flowers. He knew he had to make a decision about seeing Samantha again. He wanted to see her, so why not just arrange another date, or at least to have a chat over coffee sometime. Play it by ear, see what happens, take a chance on it working out okay.

He somehow felt it was the coward's way out though, and that he should be upfront and say his life was just too complicated to get into a relationship right now. That would be the sensible thing. Stop it now with a clear message that she is lovely, but that the timing was just wrong.

He picked up his mobile ready to call her…

∞-∞-∞-∞-∞-∞

Samantha and Libby walked past the slim Roman style posts at the front door of the pub and revelled in its old London style décor. With no music piped through, it presented itself more as a gastro pub for diners and drinkers to chat about their day, than a young person's party bar.

"Ah, perfect, just what the doctor ordered," remarked Samantha with a glint in her eye.

"Oh, okay I'll have what he's having then." Libby quipped.

"Who?"

"The doctor... nope, scrub that, I'll still have the whisky and coke... your round," winked Libby, "and make it a double, I have a feeling that you need to talk about your new fella again."

Samantha shook her head in disbelief. "He's not *my* fella," she shouted back on the way to the bar. The gentleman sitting there looked up and smiled as she approached.

"Problems with men?" he offered as a question.

Samantha took a deep breath. "Well I have now," she said with a smile to be polite, but also to show she wasn't really interested.

Poor guy, she thought, *he's almost good looking, but that scar across his face is really quite scary.* Then felt a little guilty for being so flippant with him.

It didn't seem to bother the guy though, as if he was used to women reacting to his scar and would just try harder to make conversation. "Difficult to find a good man in a wicked city like this," he joked.

Samantha rolled her eyes. "You can say that again."

The man gently laughed. "Look, I'm quite new to London and don't know anyone yet. Would you mind if I bought you and your friend a drink and joined you?"

∞-∞-∞-∞-∞-∞

Jason's mobile rang the moment he picked it up, almost causing him to drop it with surprise.

"Hello," was all he could muster.

"Evening, Jason, DS Pascal here. Sorry to call you this time of the evening. Just to let you know we are having a team meeting at 9am tomorrow morning and the boss wants you there."

"Really?"

"Well... no, but it's probably best you turn up anyway."

∞-∞-∞-∞-∞-∞

Libby had just excused herself to pop to the toilets, leaving Samantha alone with their new 'friend'. He seems harmless enough, and is happy to keep buying drinks. She was beginning to feel quite tipsy.

He leant over and smiled. The smile crisscrossed his scar, with the unfortunate effect of making it zigzagged, as if a bolt of lightning had struck his face for some atrocious act against God.

"Now that your friend's popped off, it gives us the chance to be alone." He said it so close to her ear that she could feel his breath, then put a hand on her knee to seal the deal.

Samantha felt lost, she didn't know what to do. She suddenly felt so vulnerable, as if he was showing his real personality for a moment. "Libby will be back soon," she countered weakly.

"Then we better leave now," he winked as he said this, "and then we can have a little fun."

Samantha grabbed his hand to pull it off, but he was

going nowhere. "Get off me."

∞-∞-∞-∞-∞-∞

With his mind made up, Jason dialled Samantha's number. God he hated situations like this. No one likes being rejected, but he knew he had no choice; he was just going to be too involved in the case to start anything serious right now. He would have to let her go.

∞-∞-∞-∞-∞-∞

"Aw, come on my sweet, let's not start playing games now, I've bought your drinks and you have been coming onto me for the past hour and a half. I know a little quick bang hotel only a couple of minutes away. Perfect for a little hanky panky, no strings attached."

Samantha was shocked by his boldness, and by the way he was holding her wrist so tightly. She was too afraid to move lest he have a knife or punch her in the face. His eyes had fire in them; reason had departed his mind.

"Let me go or I'll scream the pub down." She was punching the words out through tears.

He instantly let go, as if reminded that they were in a public place. "Ah you got me on that one sweet cheeks. I'll just go and wait outside for you, that way your friend can join in too. I've got plenty to go round." He pushed out his tongue in a grotesque licking motion, then got up and left just as Libby was returning from the Ladies.

∞-∞-∞-∞-∞-∞

The phone rang three times. Jason was hoping that she wouldn't reply so that he could put off making the call, but then she answered, sounding very upset.

"Jason?" He could hear panic in her voice, the broken notes in just that one word saying everything and nothing.

"Hi, Samantha, what's wrong?"

She couldn't get the words out straight, the adrenaline and fear muddling her brain, but eventually she managed to get across the fact that a guy had scared her just a few moments ago.

"Where are you, Sammy?"

"I'm with my friend Libby in Spitalfields."

What? Of all the places.

Jason went into full protective mode. This was probably the most dangerous place in London right now and she had just been threatened. "You better get out of there, Sammy. Get a cab or take the Tube home with Libby."

"I can't do that, I think he's waiting outside."

"Okay, call the police and stay where you are. I'm coming over now to take you both home. In the meantime, sit at the bar, have a coffee and just keep talking to the barman. What is the name of the pub?"

"The Ten Bells."

Chapter 15 – Team Meeting

Jason was late, and the events of the night before had denied him most of the sleep that he needed to function properly. Bjorkman growled at him as he walked through the door. It might have even seemed sexy at any other time, but right now she was just kicking him while he was down.

"Ah, Mr Ives, so kind of you to join us. Late night was it? Too much partying with some of your celebrity friends?" With every punch line she looked over to DS Pascal playing the wingman, laughing with his boss. Jason could see that he was doing it reluctantly, which at least softened the blows. Isambard sniggered, but immediately stopped when he saw the look on Jason's face.

"I was working." A little white lie that was kind of true. After all, was the man with the scar a suspect? Could Samantha actually have stumbled across his target without even trying? Surely it was too much of a coincidence - but then the universe has a way of throwing such scenarios into the mix. Just her being in that exact pub; Jack the Ripper's most infamous drinking spot, on exactly the same day that Jason and this... reluctant 'team' agreed that they are probably looking for the original Ripper, not a copycat.

Of course, he couldn't tell Samantha any of this. The public would fly into an absolute panic if they heard the original serial killer was on the loose again. Once he had got her home, Jason had called the police (Sammy hadn't wanted too, she just thought it was wasting their time) to alert them to a sexually aggressive man with a large scar on his face, hanging around the area. He was hoping they'd come back with some info soon, but he definitely didn't want to bring it up at the meeting. The link seemed too tenuous, and with Bjorkman berating him so hard, it was too personal.

Bjorkman pulled a mock face of surprise. "Oh, and what progress have you made?"

Maybe more than you can ever imagine, he thought to himself.

Jason quickly gathered his thoughts together. "The most logical start would be for Isambard and me to go over the victims identified as most likely to have been murdered by the Ripper, then check the past life crimes unit to see if we have any of them on file. Personally, I'm doubting we do, as it would have probably made the news, or at least I'd have heard about it before now."

Isambard shifted on his seat, a bundle of nervous energy with a thousand thoughts running through his mind. "Ah, that would be the 'Canonical five' victims: Mary Anne Nichols, Annie Chapman, Elizabeth Stride, Catherine Eddowes and Mary Jane Kelly, although there is huge bone of contention even with that brief list."

"So are there more or less names?" asked Pascal, still stroking his goatee and looking confused.

"Well," started Isambard with a big sigh, "to ask me is to ask for my own humble opinion, which is based on the works of other Ripperologists with their own interpretations of the events surrounding the period 1888-1889, or earlier, or later."

Pascal looked at Isambard with an air of annoyance. "Can't you just give a straight answer?"

"He is giving you an answer, Pascal," Bjorkman said defensively, "and he's saying that there are so many theories that it's difficult to find the truth."

Isambard was more surprised than anyone by Bjorkman

jumping in to defend his point of view. It spurred him on to add more to his summary of action. "Exactly, dear boss, there were some very strange and brutal attacks earlier in the year of our lord 1888, especially against the fairer sex, at a time when that was quite rare. It may have been arduous in those destitute times, but local law was governed and dictated by the Peelers and the local gangs. It was very effective, as was the threat of hanging by the rope in those days."

Isambard suddenly sprang out of his chair and rushed over to the nearby office doorway, eager to act out a scene from history that was so strong in his mind. "On March 28th, 1888, Ada Wilson was attacked on the doorstep of her own domicile by a man fitting the Ripper's later descriptions. He stabbed her several times in the throat as he demanded money, a key element that throws this tale into a negative light regarding the Ripper's MO, as he normally had no motives at all. Miraculously she survived, but nobody made a link at the time."

No one interrupted this performance, so, still holding the floor, Isambard continued. "Annie Milwood was stabbed by a complete stranger in February 1888, with numerous stab wounds to her arms, legs and groin. She survived for a few months, before expiring via natural causes, which seems odd given the circumstances. But, her attack was very much like that of Martha Tabram in August 1888, who also sustained stab wounds to the breast, belly and groin, but died as a result. Many people regard her as the sixth Canonical victim."

Jason started taking notes. "Really? How many possible victims are there estimated to be?"

"Almost twenty women could have been a victim of this daemon of the night. The events are sporadically documented, but hypothesised by some truly talented investigators. I have many a personal note that we can scrutinise in our mission, Mr Ives, and therein draw up a list of modern day witnesses for you to interview. I look very much forward to witnessing your prowess in this magical skill you possess."

Jason didn't want Isambard anywhere near his interview sessions. One look at him would have them closing like a clam. He'd get nothing out of them. "Hmm, we can certainly review my sessions when needed, Isambard, but I'll also need a list of names of the officers who were working on the cases at the time. Maybe we can marry up their memories with some of our more modern forensic evidence. It might trigger something new that they have missed before. The trail is not completely cold."

Bjorkman looked slightly impressed, although as usual, it was all hidden behind that wall of ice she used as a defence.

Maybe she fancies you Jason and is just too embarrassed to admit it, he pondered.

"Don't forget, Ives that we are here to catch today's killer. No going off on a personal hunt for curiosity. Just keep to the absolute bare minimum of witnesses, get them processed as fast as possible and get me a name pronto!"

Or maybe not.

"And what do we know from the latest murder scenes so far?" added Ives.

DCI Bjorkman then looked a little uncomfortable and passed the responsibility to her sergeant. "Pascal?"

Pascal was caught short sipping his hot coffee. "Oh, er, not a lot I'm afraid. It's a corny line, but it's as if he is a ghost. Absolutely no forensic evidence left at any of the scenes apart from a partial shoe mark."

Ives noted it down. "Well that's something."

"Not really, it's a Nike trainer – Soco code 412.

Millions of them made, so pretty generic in a way, and because it's a partial, it makes it difficult to work out the foot size.

"Our biggest break is a small piece of cctv footage from the second murder in the series, taken in Fashion Street on the corner of Brick Lane, at about the time of the murder. It is a poor quality, three quarter view of him, but better than nothing, as he seems to be using some type of video signal disrupter for cctv cameras, that screw-up any image that he's close to.

Ives sat bolt upright. "What? But you still got an image, so why didn't you mention that before? That's fantastic news."

Bjorkman waded in. "We didn't mention it before because it is our part of the investigation, Ives. You know, good old fashioned 'modern' detective work."

Pascal continued before his guv got carried away. "To be honest, Jason, we have only just identified the cctv footage, and had this still image analysed by the image mapping team. From the surrounding street furniture in the image, they estimate the man to be about 1.78 metres in height and medium build."

As he was talking, Pascal reached into his satchel and pulled out an A4 photo. The image was blurred and pixelated, making identification much trickier. Looking through the pixels gave the impression of looking through time itself.

"Unfortunately the subject was across the road about twenty metres away and the cctv was set on wide angle to see the whole street, so this is a selected enlargement from a small area of the video grab. He was in a dark corner of the street too, which doesn't help. So far he's had luck on his side, but we'll get something better soon."

Everyone nodded in agreement, but also knew that it

would need another attack for another chance to catch him in this way.

Pascal continued. "As we can see, he's wearing a hoody fully over his head, but we can also see he has long hair and a straight bushy moustache. His eyes are obviously hidden by the sunglasses, which would seem odd in most places at night, but in London... well, anything goes. I'd hazard a guess that the hair and moustache could be a disguise too."

Isambard put his hand up in the air as if he was at school.

Pascal tried to suppress a groan, but failed. "Yes Isambard?"

"If I may interject, many of the descriptions of the Ripper described a man of about this height, and having a moustache. It wouldn't be incomprehensible to think that he might be resuming some of his previous physical features."

"Fine, it could be a real moustache, but unfortunately that still narrows us down to maybe a million people in London," Pascal exaggerated, "but it is better than nothing I suppose, which is exactly what we had last week."

Jason looked again at the image. *Hmm, I can't see an obvious scar, so unless it was on the other side of his face, that takes him out of the frame.* He'd ask Samantha later, relieved that it took the pressure off him to mention what was now beginning to feel like a foolish notion from his worry over her, and decided to discard the whole matter unless he heard differently through the police officers dealing with Samantha directly.

The room went silent for a few seconds, everyone digesting the few facts they had, and trying to formulate a way ahead. Isambard suddenly sneezed, but in a way that he was trying to suppress, with his hand over his nose, as if he was trying to swallow the involuntary action, rather than let something out. Yet another one of his odd little habits.

Jason broke the moment, which was in danger of taking over the meeting. "Which leads us back to seeking his past until we get a lucky break with some forensic evidence or a witness comes forward. Isambard, who would be the best officer to interview first?"

Isambard finished wiping his nose with a silk handkerchief that he had stowed away in a secret pocket of his jacket. "The most famous officer dealing with the case at the time was Frederick George Abberline. He was a Detective Inspector 'first class' for the London Metropolitan Police, and put in charge of the case after the Polly Nichols murder. He lived and breathed the hunt for the Ripper, and was ridiculed for never catching him."

Bjorkman looked at her watch. "Well gentlemen, let's get a plan of action. Isambard, do we know if he has been Awakened?"

"Indeed we do, boss. He is very well known on the Ripper circuit as a G-historian, but there is inevitably a complication I fear."

"And what would that be?" prompted Bjorkman.

Isambard shuffled his feet, looking suddenly embarrassed.

"Because, DI Frederick Abberline is also a suspect."

Chapter 16 – God's Will

The voices have been even louder lately. Maybe they are rallying together to fight his new found faith in God, but that only makes Seb smile. It shows that they are afraid of something. Could they be fearing his salvation?

There is a new presence in his mind now though. A stranger with a hate and madness that far outstrips his own. A fear and hate of women derived from pain and loss. Someone out of time.

But why? Why in his mind? Why now when he is making such good progress with his new friends? Hopefully this is just a desperate last pitched effort from the demons that have plagued his mind since childhood.

Or maybe, it is a test from God himself?

Chapter 17 – The Ripper's Diary

Jason passed the salt. A lot was on his mind. The case, the press wanting a comment from him, and that kiss. That damned kiss. He had rung Samantha to tell her that any idea of a relationship was going to be impossible, and instead found himself running to her rescue, taking her home and the evening ending in a kiss. A good kiss. A bloody good kiss! Life could be really shit to him sometimes.

Now he wanted more. Now she was a greater distraction when he could least afford it. He smiled at his dumb luck. It felt good to be wanted by someone attractive again, no matter the situation, and now he didn't want it to stop. They would just have to find a way to manage a relationship somehow, if she still wanted one.

He then passed the vinegar. Isambard was tucking into fish and chips at the local pub as a working lunch, and it was giving Jason a few minutes respite from his chatter. His own lunch of a salt beef sandwich was waiting forlornly for him to start, but instead he played with the potato chips decorating the side of the plate. His appetite had deserted him, the nerves of what was about to start, personally and professionally, overriding his thoughts.

Against his better judgement he restarted the conversation. "So, tell me about DI Frank Abberline, is he seriously a suspect? I mean, how? How does the officer in charge become a suspect?"

Isambard politely placed his knife and fork down to speak. "Oh, most students of Ripper history agree with your doubts, Mr Ives, but there are several reasons for placing him in the ever increasing list of suspects. At the turn of the 21st century, a French writer and handwriting expert compared the handwriting of Abberline with the handwriting of the equally dubious, but undeniably compelling Ripper Diaries, and said it was in his hand."

Jason was caught by surprise at this sudden revelation. "Hold on, they found a diary by Jack the Ripper?"

"It might be... a phrase you will hear a lot when it comes to details surrounding everything Ripper. The spurious diaries surfaced in 1992. They have been tested and retested countless times, and yet, they remain as mysterious as every other detail in this sordid affair. In fact, Mr Ives, so much about Jack the Ripper is contradictory and supernatural in its ability to stupefy and discombobulate, that it borders on the realms of black magic."

Jason let out a welcome laugh. "In English, Isambard, and my name is Jason, please feel free to use it sometime," he said with a smile on his face.

Isambard blinked, looked down at his plate and popped a chip into his mouth whilst he thought of what to say next. "In short, Mr... ahem," he couldn't bring himself to say Jason. "In short, sir, many, many details have been lost in history. Police officers on the original case took souvenirs, as have researchers over time, to our great shame. The Yard were also very haphazard in their storage methods in that period, and would nonchalantly throw away records and exhibits to make way for new cases when they ran out of space. The Second World War also destroyed a lot of records through fire and outright destruction. In fact, it is only when some of those original items and records find their way back to the police or the public domain, that new facts come to light."

"So what do you think about this diary?"

"It is said to be the diary of James Maybrick, a cotton

merchant from Liverpool, and although it only ever gives the name of Jack the Ripper as the author rather than Maybrick's, many of the details reflect Maybrick's life.

"So it is Maybrick's diary?"

Isambard lifted his index finger to make a point. "Only possibly. The Liverpudlian scrap metal merchant Michael Barrett, who discovered and published the diaries, then later went on record saying his wife wrote the diaries under his dictation. It is very mysterious, because he then refuted his refuted statement, and went on to reclaim the 'fraud' all over again. Some students feel he may have buckled under pressure of the press coverage, and wanted to claim they were fake just to make them go away. Some think that a much darker pressure was applied to him to make the diaries look fake. Chemical analysis of ink and paper point to them being of the right period, but other tests deny this fact."

"What a bloody mess."

"An astute summation, Mr Ives, and why our search for the truth still continues to this very day."

"So what has Abberline got to do with these diaries apart from some French expert claiming it is the writing of Abberline?"

Isambard let out another long sigh and opened his palms to the air. "That, I'm afraid, is also very complicated. In short, there are many merry theories apart from the handwriting. There is speculative information that Abberline was helping to cover the real Ripper's tracks, due to royal connections, or that it was part of some Masonic cover up. Even failing that, Abberline's own dubious diary has been passed from pillar to post, and is rumoured to now be held in the Vatican libraries. I'm sorry, Mr Ives, but this line of inquiry will only drive you to Bedlam." And with that, he gave an odd little laugh, as if to confirm it had done precisely that.

"So where do we start? I'm beginning to feel Bjorkman is right in that I'm a waste of time in this investigation. I only hunt out known criminals from the past, not investigate those who might have been. Even if we found the answer to this 'ghost', building up any kind of clue to who he is *now* seems highly unlikely."

"You do yourself a disservice sir. Remember, if we find a name that is already known and is on record somewhere, we can catch him. For the time being at least, his past identity is our only 'fingerprint' of him in this day and age."

Jason was touched by his support, but still felt overwhelmed by the amount of information to analyse. "Thank you, Isambard, but can we catch him before he kills again?"

"Yes boss, don't forget, I have the knowledge and support of thousands of Ripperologists all over the world to assist. Right now they are talking about this new Ripper. They are primed and ready for a new chapter in this disturbing, but compelling story. With their help we can sift through all the silt to find the golden nuggets of information that seem most logical. Our databases online hold many facts and theories that have been debated for almost two hundred years. I suggest you read them, Mr Ives, and become a Ripperologist yourself, or at least, a temporary one." He sniggered again, shrugged his shoulders and returned to his meal.

Jason went through a quick rundown of everything they knew so far. It was pretty evident that a lot of the facts from the case had been lost or covered up. Yes, countless hours of research had been done by keen amateur investigators, ever since the crimes had first started, and many of their findings were documented. The problem was going to be finding the relevant and true details that they could work with.

Abberline as the main OIC had to be interviewed, but maybe this Maybrick character, if easily found, could add or dispel this diary, or hold information to any Royal or Masonic connection. And, most importantly, the victims would be invaluable. As usual though, the fact that the act of death is so traumatic that almost no one can remember their last hour or so before they die, was still as frustrating as hell, but you can't blame people for not confronting their deaths.

Well, almost no one. Some people remember right up to the last few minutes, but it was rare, and bloody difficult to work through. As soon as he got back to the office, Jason was going to have to look into finding the canonical five and then interview them as soon as possible.

Jason stopped to think for a moment. Over the years he'd had to push some of his clients to the brink, and whilst it had always bothered him, he knew it was for their greater good. Now this was a little different. Now he was going to have to ask them to help save other women's lives. Was it still enough to warrant putting the original victims of the Ripper through the experience of their murders again?

"Isambard, which victim do I ask first?" Jason asked with a grave voice.

"I have just been pondering that exact same question, Mr Ives, and whilst there are many different elements to consider in the canonical five victims, I'd say that the last victim, Mary Jane Kelly would be an excellent start."

"Based on what?"

"Well, she has always of been particular interest to me in that she was a little different. She was a class above the other working women of the night, and had been known to sell her services to rich gentlemen. She'd been known to frequently ride in a carriage through London, and once accompanied a gentleman to Paris. This is interesting, because on the night of her murder, she was seen with an affluent gentleman wearing very white cuffs and a thick gold chain on his waistcoat."

"How does that fit in with the Ripper?"

"Not a great match, but still possible. The interesting facts are twofold. Firstly, she was the only canonical victim killed in her own home, and secondly, not only was she the most mutilated, but the Ripper also completely destroyed her face."

Jason instantly knew what this could mean. It was a basic psychological profile element of a murderer. "So you are saying that he savaged her face because he knew her, and therefore she knew him?"

Isambard picked up a napkin from the table to wipe his face, blocking his expression at this precise moment from Jason's gaze.

"Precisely boss. It is my humble opinion that Mary Jane Kelly not only knew the Ripper, but that she was the only victim that he had a true motive to kill."

Then he rubbed his hands together and looked Jason directly in the eye.

"There was a history between those two. By my heavens, I truly believe that."

Chapter 18 – In Jack's Mind

Three a.m. Jack's mind has pushed through his restless, resistant host, the pain wanting to break out and inflict itself on the easiest of targets – the painted ladies of the night, on every street of Whitechapel. Their disease-riddled bodies acting as killer traps for desperate men to fall into, just as he had. Mother had known the symptoms when she saw the ugly blisters on his arms. It was how she'd lost her husband eight years earlier, and the bitterness had infected her too.

Maybe she would have even guessed he was the Ripper from his character changing, if he hadn't told her anyway. A woman's intuition is a powerful thing, especially when so raw. And although she hated prostitutes too, she'd hated his father more for cheating on her and dying, thus leaving her a widow in such a dishonourable way. That is why she'd sent a carriage and two large men to take him back to Bournemouth to spend his last few months; telling everyone that consumption was claiming her son. That convenient disease was claiming one in four people at the time, and could cover a multitude of sins.

A painful death in that seaside abode. A prisoner of his male nurses, and eventually a prisoner in his own rotting body, lacking the strength to carry on. At one point he wondered if he was being poisoned by his watchers... and later praying that he was.

His mother's voice? Was that the one in his head so often? It is so hard to tell amongst all the other voices scrambling for position. Her voice is soft and sharp at the same time. Strong, but weakened by her position in his head. Trying to stop him murdering more women, but also protecting him, and protecting his dirty secret once more.

He hadn't given a damn if he was caught on the streets of Whitechapel all those years ago. He knew he was dying anyway, and maybe the rope would have been a kinder death. How ironic that the lack of fear had given him the ability to kill so easily.

He then remembered his little routine. It had been so much easier in those days. "Just stand there my dear and lift your skirts so I can see your quim before I stuff it," he'd say to them, and the stupid tarts would do just that. With their hands busy holding their skirts, all he had to do was grab their throat and squeeze the fucking life out of them. It kept them from screaming out, and gave him the joy of watching their life ebb away, their eyes bulging, tongue flaying in their ugly mouths till they'd pass out.

Then, ever so softly, lower them to the ground... out of sight, out of mind. Jack would then kneel by their side, as if praying for forgiveness, but it was anything but that. He was kneeling on their right side, and using his left hand... yes, his damned affliction even then, when to be left handed was seen as evil or deviant. Even the word sinister is derived from the Latin term for being left handed. A fact that his Latin teacher would never let him forget, and had repeatedly whacked his left hand whenever he tried to use it, whilst delivering quotes from the Bible. Jacky could even hear him now.

"Listen boy! Even Jesus himself said that on Judgment Day the blessed should sit at the right hand of God, while the accursed and damned should be cast away by the left. So what does that make you?"

Painful memories from so long ago, but still so fresh, as if it was just yesterday. This strange rebirth in this strange time is also an abomination. Maybe he is sinister after all.

So Jack would kneel down on the right side of his prey,

and then use his veterinary knife to cut her throat from left to right, thus draining the meat of its blood. If she was still alive, her heart would pump and spray the blood in almost every direction but his own, allowing him to stay clean to find another victim, another day.

Once drained, it was time to try and hack off her head, but it had always proved too hard; the upper vertebrae refusing to let go of its precious cargo. And then the source of his anger, her vile vagina, offering his larger knife a handy hole to start from, cutting right up to her sternum. They were the basics, the rest was made up as he pleased, as he always liked to experiment. He couldn't use the skirt trick now of course, things were just too different, so he'd had to adapt, and listen to the voices in his head offering advice. As if they had been here all along, waiting for him to return.

Although his mind would be raging when he butchered these women, he would also feel very calm, almost invincible, as if he really was carrying out God's work to clean the streets of London from this proliferation of vice. Vice and alcohol and drugs and gangs and crime and debauchery. On every street in those days. Now, is this sterile world it is positively glamourised, but Jack can still see the filth.

And all this killing had been with his final victim in mind. The first girls were just his pox suspects, and Catherine Eddowes; she'd stupidly been snooping about asking too many questions about him from Mary, and telling people she knew who the Ripper was.

The final straw came when the bitch started using Mary's name to try and drum up some extra business of her own. What luck it had been to bump into Catherine after having to run from the body of Long Liz in Dutfield's Yard. He'd almost been discovered by that idiot with his pony that night, but instead he bumped into Catherine... and then *bumped* her off. Two deaths within an hour. It had completely drained him of all his strength that eventful night, but it had also made him an international monster.

Five weeks then passed, with studies and duties in Bournemouth to attend to. A semblance of normality, but he knew all that time that he was going to have to deal with Mary. He could not put it off any longer.

Jack suddenly screamed out in his host's quiet home, gasping for breath, fighting tears as he remembered what he had had to do on that bitterly cold morning in November 1888. Time to find Mary. Time to Kill. Time to take her heart.

Revenge on his beloved.

The whore to adore.

His mate, that fate made him hate.

Chapter 19 – Samantha

Knock knock... The sound at the door.

Samantha was still in bed trying to wake up, and thanking her lucky stars it was a Saturday morning with a chance to have a lie in after the late night before in Spitalfields.

Who the hell is that?

She stood still in her own home, feeling like a little girl playing hide and seek because she didn't want to rush down the stairs and answer the door. She could even hear her own breathing offset by the tick-tock of the clock. Hopefully it was a parcel. Hopefully they would leave it at the door or with a neighbour. Or maybe it was the Jehovah's Witness group that occasionally stop by.

Knock knock... knock knock knock.

Louder this time, it made her jump in spite of herself, her heart now beating rapidly.

Sod it. Samantha threw her dressing gown on over her thin nightie and walked down the stairs. The outline of a man wearing some kind of hat, rippled through the glass door. For a minute she hoped it was Jason, coming back for another kiss and a whole lot more. She'd had a few fantasies that night dreaming of Jason's kiss, his hair, his body, his...

Knock knock!

"Okay, I'm coming, hold your horses," she shouted down the stairs.

Just as she went to open the door, a sudden feeling of foreboding embraced her, reminding her to attach the safety chain... just in case. Now she was fumbling with the lock, her sleep addled brain finding even the simplest of tasks difficult before that all important first coffee of the day.

She feels like death without it.

∞-∞-∞-∞-∞-∞

Back from Hell: Has Jack the Ripper been Awakened?

The headlines were everywhere, with the media on a feeding frenzy looking for more details.

Triple murder count Victims gutted alive!

The press had finally put together the details from the three murders that year, even though the Metropolitan police had been suppressing most of the details. And now, with statements from several historians and 'experts' of psychology, they were declaring that this was no series of copycat killings. Even Martin Kale, the founder of Awakening, was being questioned on whether it was possible for a past identity to completely overwhelm their present identity.

DCI Sabina Bjorkman pushed herself to read through all the articles with a sense of real dread. She was in danger of losing this case to a higher department, and although it felt like she was holding onto a tiger's tail, she knew she couldn't afford to let go.

∞-∞-∞-∞-∞-∞

A police officer in uniform stood on the other side, looking a little irritated by having to wait at the doorway for so long.

Ooh, a man in uniform... now you've got men literally queuing at your door, she thought to herself in amusement.

"Oops, sorry officer, I was getting dressed."

The young officer suddenly went a little red, embarrassed that he'd caught her with so few clothes on. Samantha was amused by this fact, and realised that she had finally reached that age where police officers looked too young to do their job.

"Sorry madam."

She groaned at the word madam too.

"I've been asked to come and take a statement regarding an incident you were involved in last night."

Samantha smiled to herself. *Oh well, a little company will be fun for an hour or so.*

"Come in officer, I'll put the kettle on."

∞-∞-∞-∞-∞-∞

Bjorkman let out a groan as she flicked through all the different news channels on her wall screen.

Fox News, BBC, NBC, ABC, Russia Today... all the major news services were waking up to the opportunities that this new Ripper story had to offer. A goldmine of airtime, if the fevered coverage of the original Victorian papers at the time were anything to go by.

She remembered the Victorian headlines she'd seen posted:

GHASTLY MURDER IN THE EAST-END

DREADFUL MUTILATION OF A WOMAN. CAPTURE: LEATHER APRON!

Another murder of a character even more diabolical than that perpetrated in Buck's Row on Friday week.

WHO IS THE WHITECHAPEL MURDERER?

And after Mary Jane Kelly, the LONDON DAILY POST.

"JACK the RIPPER" CLAIMS 5th VICTIM - WOMAN BRUTALLY HACKED TO DEATH

When the reporters couldn't get details from the cautious police of Great Scotland Yard, they started adding to the legend themselves by sending fake Ripper letters to their agencies, or Detective Abberline or George Lusk, president of the Whitechapel vigilance committee. All these extra letters and parcels adding to the confusion, adding to the death toll by delaying his capture.

WHO WILL BE NEXT?

She didn't think Jason had a chance in working out who the Ripper had been, never mind Ripper Version 2.0, and that was exactly the way she wanted it. There was no way she was going to let that civilian poke his nose into her affairs. God how she hated the whole concept of past life investigation. It had left her without a father. The bastards had ruined her life.

She could see the argument of course, but it still didn't make it okay to ruin people's lives in the here and now, just because they suddenly 'remembered' doing something bad.

Jason did intrigue her though. A man she could not guess, which was so refreshing because all her boyfriends in the past had been so damn predictable. He was the yin and the yang of her affections. If only he was an accountant or hotel manager, anything normal that she wouldn't despise. Sabina knew she was good at reading people of course, it is what makes her such a good detective. Not only was she able to get valuable information from suspects, but, more importantly, she was able to read her managers perfectly to make the necessary moves needed in the Met police. It was how she had overcome her dreadful past to rise so high and so quickly in this dog-eat-dog world, and be promoted just last year to DCI.

Being a Detective Chief Inspector had always felt the right fit for her. Still active at scenes, but with the power to send your team to do all your dirty work.

∞-∞-∞-∞-∞-∞

"Sugar?"

"No thank you," replied the officer. He took the small coffee cup and placed it onto the glass table in front of him. "Right," he started, "I've read the crime report, and we have looked into this character with the scar, but we don't have much information on him. Even the local neighbour team don't seem to know someone like that."

"Oh, that's right, sorry, I forgot to mention last night. He said that he was from out of town, but I didn't get where from."

"What kind of accent did he have?"

"It sounded a bit like a Liverpudlian accent, but then maybe a little Irish in it too. Sorry, I'm not very good with accents."

The young PC made some notes as he thought of some more questions. "Did he say what he does for a living?"

"He was quite vague about that. When I asked he just laughed and said that he was a Jack of all trades, and often travelled into London on business. It gave me the creeps when he said that to be honest."

The officer could see he wasn't going to get a good description this morning. "Okay Madam..."

"Miss."

"Miss?"

"Yep, not married yet... but don't get any ideas." She winked at him and laughed, but he acted as if nothing had happened, causing Samantha to blush from her own joke.

The officer ploughed on regardless. "We have the description you gave from last night, and of course, a report on how he behaved, so we should get something very soon. Do you still think he could be a risk to anyone?"

Samantha shrugged her shoulders. "I've no idea, but he did seem to get pretty nasty. I don't scare easy, but he had an evil look in his eye and seemed very determined."

He mouthed the word 'determined' as he wrote down the details. "Was he well dressed or casual?"

"Oh well dressed, he obviously has plenty of money, probably from selling drugs or running a vice ring." Still no laugh, not even a smile. Honestly, was this police constable even human?

∞-∞-∞-∞-∞-∞

Of course, most of her colleagues just thought of her as a robot, or the Snow Queen. DCI Sabina Bjorkman, as cold as the icy mountain blood in her Swedish veins. She knew she wasn't though, she felt pain and love and hurt just as much as any other woman, but had learnt to hide it all after her father's death. It was all part of her survival mode, and these days she needed it more than ever.

She'd had to push hard to get this Ripper case, and even take the chance on suggesting it was a Ripper copycat to grab her Superintendant's attention. Working for Scotland Yard carries a lot of kudos around the world, but in reality it is falling apart at the seams from budget cuts and political scandal. Now you have to really fight hard for the cases you want. Isambard had sealed the deal though, pressing the Super with photos and files on the Ripper murders, saying how close the mutilations resembled Jack's work.

He even pointed out how and why the original MO had changed due to modern circumstances, but that the basic elements bore a strong resemblance, almost an homage to the Ripper. Details such as the areas in London (till the third victim), laying them on the ground and cutting the jugular to avoid being covered in their blood. Using two different types of knife and the cruel mutilations, including extracting their wombs before posing them on the ground with their legs open, ready for sex.

It was Isambard that had suggested to the Superintendant to use Jason Ives to build a new profile, and the Super had jumped at the chance. He was lining himself up for his next promotion and didn't want a serial killer running around London getting in his way. But everything about the Ripper was getting out of hand.

Sabina's head was now on the block and she didn't know how it was going to end.

∞-∞-∞-∞-∞-∞

The young officer had finally left after a barrage of questions. She was quite surprised by his attention to detail, but impressed that the police were taking it so seriously. Whatever Jason had told them last night, it had definitely made them sit up and listen.

Personally, she thought it was just all a storm in a teacup, yet another lecherous man overstepping the mark after a few drinks too many. She felt quite guilty causing the police to put all this work into her crime report. A thought suddenly occurred to her. Maybe they knew more about this man than they were letting on? Seriously though, how bad could he be?

As Samantha jumped into the shower, she turned the radio on to keep her company. By the time she started washing her hair, the news came on with details of this new Jack the Ripper roaming the streets of London, especially in his old stomping ground of Whitechapel.

Samantha let out a scream. Both from the realisation of what may have happened... and because she had shampoo in her eyes.

Chapter 20 – Abberline Witness

"Come in, come in," welcomed Abberline with his melodic Parisian tones, "please make yourselves comfortable."

It had been a busy weekend. Jason and Isambard had drawn up a list of witnesses to interview via Awakening, and because Inspector Abberline was already fairly well known on the Ripperology circuit, he was the easiest to find and start with. Abberline was known to be a colourful character, who played on his dubious reputation of being both in charge of the investigation for 'The Whitechapel Murderer' (as he preferred to call him) and a minor suspect.

He was a showman in many ways, carefully balancing the information he gives to perpetuate his popularity as an after dinner speaker and expert on the matter without ever giving too much away. It is an act to neither confirm nor deny his absolute position. This keeps interest in him high enough to make a comfortable living as a G-historian; someone with the advanced experience and fortunate timing to have been somewhere important in history, and able to pass that knowledge on to interested parties - for a fee.

Isambard admitted to Jason that this showmanship frustrates most of his colleagues, who just want the truth in plain English. No vagaries or messing around with the facts to tell a good story, just the whole truth and nothing but the truth. Hopefully, his being questioned by representatives of Scotland Yard would push him to be as straight talking as possible.

One advantage of Abberline working as a G-historian

on the Ripper, was that he lived in London for his work. Born in this lifetime in Paris, and christened Guy Rochelle, he was now a sixty-two year old man aging very gracefully, with silver streaks enhancing his roguish good looks, which he bolstered by retaining just enough of his French accent to charm his way through life.

He'd agreed to meet Jason, Isambard and DCI Bjorkman in his home, nestled down a side street of Wimbledon Village, SW19. Although the tennis tournament was still a few weeks away, the 'village' shops were decorated with racquets, bunting, posters of strawberries with cream, and photos of past champions from as far back as its inception in 1877, eleven years before Jack the Ripper had even started striking terror into the hearts of Whitechapel.

On arrival, Jason noticed that Guy Rochelle's front door was Met police blue, causing him to wonder if it was pure chance, a subconscious choice, or if he was a man who liked to plan and control everything. Abberline had been a stickler for attention to detail in his time, and considered by many to look and act more like a bank manager than a proper copper, but he had been highly respected for his work and skills as a police officer.

On seeing DCI Bjorkman, Rochelle carefully swept his hair back to smarten himself up for the attractive woman in charge. "Bonjour Mademoiselle, it eez a pleasure to 'ave you as my guest."

Against her better judgement, Sabina Bjorkman warmed to this charismatic man giving her his undivided attention. "Thank you for agreeing to see us at such short notice, Monsieur Rochelle, we won't take up too much of your time."

"S'il vous plait, it is no trouble at all for ze Met's finest."

Jason looked at Isambard, his eyes rising in exasperation as if to say 'get me out of here', but Isambard was too enthralled by meeting one of his heroes to see Jason pulling faces. Frederick Abberline, Inspector 'first class' at the time of the Whitechapel murders, newly promoted and raring to go. His intimate knowledge of the area had seen him quickly seconded back from Scotland Yard after the death of Polly Nicholls in Bucks Row, on the 31st of August that same year.

Ives waded in. "Monsieur Rochelle, as you are probably quite aware, there is either a copycat killer on the loose, or Jack the Ripper has been Awakened and somehow is either dominating their current body's persona, or that person actually likes the idea of being a killer, and is using his past knowledge and skills to start his butchering again."

"Yez, I 'ave seen such things said on ze news, it ez awful, but I must stress that I cannot really add any more than ez already documented by myself, and thousands of others interested in ze Whitechapel murderer."

"We thought you might say that," said Ives, "but we are hoping to jog your memory with some current information."

"I will do what I can do to 'elp. Pleaze, just give me a minute to bring Mr Abberline back to ze front of my memory. I find it makes things a lot clearer, and use 'eez characteristics a lot for my work."

With that, Rochelle closed his eyes and started muttering little key words to himself. Softly calling in his past memories. On opening them again, his whole body language and tone changed. He wasn't being taken over by another personality, just letting others see another side to his nature, but with Rochelle in full control.

"Ah, thank you. I've had so many Awakening sessions

as Abberline that I'm able to utilise my memories of him quite easily. Fantastic little party trick after a speech," said Rochelle with an old fashioned Dorset accent. Bjorkman was taken aback by it, spooked even, but to Jason and Isambard, they had both seen many examples of this wonderful ability in their line of work: to recapture and reuse old skills.

He was still a flirt though. "So nice to have women in important roles for the Yard nowadays, DCI Bjorkman," he said with a smile, "although you would have been quite a distraction for my young lads."

Bjorkman didn't know whether to take that as a compliment, or be slightly annoyed that he was bringing her femininity into the conversation. She decided to push ahead with her professional smile. "My officers are too afraid of having a sexual harassment charge made against them to bother me," she said with a wink, then stopped short. "Sorry, do I call you Monsieur Rochelle or Mr Abberline when you are like this? I've never questioned anyone looking back before."

"Don't you worry, I've been doing this long enough to not care about what I get called as long as it's polite, but it might help you to focus your questions if you just call me Fred, or DI Abberline if you want to keep it professional."

"Thank you, Fred, you can call me Sabina then." She was working her charm on him, getting as much cooperation as possible, as softly as possible. "So tell me, in your own words, who you think Jack the Ripper was and why?"

He shrugged his shoulders. "That young lady, is the billion pound question. Honestly, I have no idea."

Isambard quickly jumped into the conversation. "Forgive me, Mr Abberline, but in 1903 you seemed quite certain it was George Chapman."

"That is true, but that was over 150 years ago. I've changed my mind somewhat. Back then I was pretty desperate to finally put a name to the killer, and George Chapman seemed to fit the bill for me at the time. He was a wife killer several times over by 1903, but had been living in the Whitechapel area in 1888 under his original name, Severin Antoniovich Klosowski. He had a penchant for winning the favours of as many young women as possible and didn't care how he got rid of the previous women holding him back."

"So what changed your mind?" asked Ives.

"Poison. Yes, he'd been an evil man, but his murders at the turn of the century against his wives had all been by poison. With the benefit of seeing everything from today's perspective, I can see that a leopard does not change its spots. Meaning, he does not go from being a brutal, sadistic murderer of strangers through mutilation, to being a man of potions and poisons against women he knows."

Isambard nodded in agreement. It was a fact that had already been discussed to the point that there were very few people who thought it could be the Polish wife murderer any more, even though his profile fitted that of a multi-killer. Very strange though, because serial killers are rare, and yet here he was living in the middle of Whitechapel whilst another serial killer was rampaging the same streets. Maybe seeing someone like the Ripper do what he liked and never getting caught was an influence on him, making life seem cheap in comparison. The Ripper's legacy of murder rippling into the swarm of deprived Londoners affected by poverty and booze.

Bjorkman touched Abberline's knee and leant in, coyly using her feminine charm before swooping in for the kill. "I have just read that there were many conspiracies regarding your involvement, Fred. How could that be for such a respected officer? Tales of royal or Masonic connections, and even that your handwriting matches that of the so called Maybrick - Ripper diary.

I think you have some serious explaining to do!"

Chapter 21 – Flashbacks

Flashes in Seb's mind of squalid streets kept interrupting his sleep last week, but that is nothing new. What really disturbs him is the 'feel' of everything he now sees. The damp coldness that seeps into his bones and remains for a few minutes after waking, or the screams of women ringing in his ears like vixens in the night. Blood curdling screams that remind him of his own past.

But last night Seb saw a new image. It was a young man in a dark cloak and hat, sobbing. He is trying to tell Seb that he is Jack the Ripper, and pleading for his soul because he knows he will burn in Hell. This new Ripper in the news is really affecting him, and he doesn't yet know why.

Better not tell anyone though. He doesn't want to go back *there* again. Not now that he's doing so well in the outside world.

Chapter 22 – Abberline Suspect

Abberline reeled back from the sudden attack, but was experienced enough to know when the tables had been turned. With one quick action, he had gone from being a witness to a suspect. Whether it was for extra time to find his feet, or just to play with this female detective chief inspector's patience and show he wasn't flustered, he changed the subject.

"Oh I'm sorry, I'm a terrible host. I've neglected to offer anyone a drink. Would anyone like a cup of tea?"

Bjorkman wasn't going to be put off the scent that easily. "We are fine, thank you, DI Abberline, just answer the question please."

Isambard looked a little disappointed at not getting a cup of Darjeeling.

Abberline gave a little sarcastic laugh. "Desperation young lady. A lot of people want to solve this riddle, and believe me, I was the first person to know how that feels. I've read and heard all the rumours and conspiracy theories, and to be honest, they are comical. Okay, I was a Mason, but not until a year after the murders, and truth be told, the Masons are just an empty mystery. The group just oils the cogs and gears of promotion, so a lot of officers were Masons, they still are. Why would they realistically want to protect a madman?"

He continued to laugh it off and took a sip of water from his glass before continuing. "And as for protecting royalty... that's a load of hokum too. Any royal would have been locked up for his own good before a second or third victim was made. Can you imagine the catastrophic

118

disaster if a relative of Queen Victoria had been found leaning over the body of a victim? Even just being corralled into a group to be questioned at a scene would have led to the secret getting out. Utter nonsense!"

"What about the diaries acclaimed to be written by your own fair hand, DI Abberline? You have always remained quite vague as to their authenticity when questioned by my most esteemed colleagues," asked Isambard politely.

Abberline shifted his weight to the other side of the chair, leant back and crossed his arms in a protective manner. "Also utter poppycock my fine man, but I have to retain an air of mystery in my strange profession as a Ripper G-historian, so I'd appreciate it if you kept this to yourself."

Isambard didn't seem so sure. "But you must have kept some diaries at the time, and what about the rumour that they are kept at the Vatican?"

Abberline suddenly looked very tired. "Rumours are much easier to start than they are to finish, you must know that. I did of course keep a diary at the time, but it was pretty dull stuff about people in my life and ideas towards my profession. I find it hard to believe that my boring record of my life has been stowed away in the Vatican libraries, even if written at a very sensitive time. Could be my diary of course, but no one has offered to show it to me and I've never bothered to ask."

Jason was curious about the last canonical victim. "What can you tell us about Mary Jane Kelly's death and your investigation at the scene?"

Abberline turned to look straight into Jason's eyes. "Bloody frustrating in all honesty. When we got there, I'd been given strict instructions to not disturb the scene. We had to wait for the police dogs to come over, pick up a scent, and then hopefully lead us on a trail. As it turned out, the dog owner hadn't been paid and was almost two hundred miles away. He refused to come. Over two hours we waited outside! Two hours for the Ripper to get away even further. It still raises my hackles."

"But what do you think about a link between Mary and Jack?"

Abberline's eyes dipped down to break eye contact as he put a hand to his mouth. "I don't know what you are talking about, Mr Ives, what link?"

Jason could see Abberline knew something but was keeping quiet. He was covering something up. "I'm sorry, Inspector Abberline, but I think you do."

All eyes were on the two of them. Abberline capitulated a little. "Only a few little ideas lad, but nothing concrete. Nothing worth your while, and I'm putting them all together for a new presentation myself. All bollocks of course, but the Ripper fans love it, and as I've said before, it is how I make my living."

Jason pulled out some photos of the last victim in Soho. "Would you like to give that reason to this girl's parents Inspector? Her name was Angela. She was only nineteen. A runaway from home who got lost in the city lights and was surrounded by bad people giving her the wrong choices. Imagine if she was your daughter, Inspector Abberline, how would you feel if there was even the slightest piece of information that could lead to the killer's name?"

Abberline went pale. He looked left to right and turned red, ashamed that he had even contemplated keeping his little titbits of information to himself.

"I... I don't know. It's stupid really, and only something I've thought since coming back as Rochelle. Being able to read all the information online has given me a better overview of the investigation, but I still don't know who he

120

is. It is embarrassing, and still driving me mad."

He wrung his hands as if covered in the blood of Mary Kelly. "It was just a bit strange that day when we went in. The fireplace was smouldering from the fire of the night before, but it had some of her clothing on it. I thought at the time that the killer had just been trying to keep warm, and see what he was doing from the light of the fire, but now... now I think he might have been burning a hanky that one of our witnesses had seen, or a present that he had given her. Something that indicated a connection between those two."

Ives kept the pressure up. "Is that it, a few items on the fire?"

"No, not just that son, more the overall feeling of the place. Her face was so disfigured, but of course I didn't know at the time that it might indicate that he knew her. None of us knew anything like that in our day. I might even have put two and two together at the post mortem if I had today's knowledge of criminal psychology. You know he took her heart away don't you, it was missing at the scene?"

Jason nodded his head. "Yes, I read that in one of the many books I've been reading on the matter."

"Well, I thought it was very personal at the time, a natural token of love in a sick way, but then he'd taken every other organ from his victims before, so I shook off that idea. You have to remember that we thought we were chasing a lunatic who had no motives at the time, so why would we think he suddenly picked on someone he knew?"

Bjorkman also nodded her head in agreement. "To be honest Fred, we still don't know if he had a motive for anyone... or all of them, which is unfortunately why we will have to keep coming back to you with fresh questions. Your case has been reopened sir, and it is now as urgent again as the days when you were in charge."

Isambard wanted to push a little harder with an idea of his own. "Was it not you that interviewed her live-in lover Joseph Barnett as a suspect? Many hold suspicions that he was your man and had only killed the other girls to take the suspicion off him as a prime suspect. Some even believe he invented the whole Jack the Ripper identity to fool the police when he would finally murder his partner, or that he just murdered the other girls to frighten Mary away from prostitution because he loved her so much. They hypothesise that it didn't work, and in a lover's rage, he murdered her just as he had the others. Then the cycle was complete, or that he'd been scared off by the police questioning him, or that he had no hunger for murder anymore?"

"Yes, that has obviously occurred to me since coming back, Mr Smythe, especially as Catherine Eddowes had mentioned knowing the suspect. She had come back from the countryside to collect the reward offered, just before being cut down as the fourth victim. She had mentioned the name Joe on several occasions apparently. Even said to one of my officers on that fateful night just before her death, while she was drying out from her drinking, that Mary's Joe was dangerous."

Isambard grew excited. "So it was Joseph Barnett then?"

"No sir, I honestly don't think it was because the term 'my Joe' was rarely used in the context of Barnett. Things just didn't feel right at the time. It is something you cannot explain; an investigator's gut instinct if you like. I don't think her Joe was Joseph Barnett at all. I think it was someone else, and Cathy knew her secret. There was a rivalry between those two ladies, and maybe Cathy knew more than we think.

"I think her Joe was someone from Mary's past, maybe a client, someone from her better days, or an old sweetheart. He had money. Enough money to make her desperate enough to let him back into her life, even though she didn't trust his nature, and her desperation eventually led to her death."

DCI Bjorkman went pale at the implication. Jason guessed that she must know from a woman's perspective how desperate and vulnerable Mary Kelly must have felt, and it was temporarily breaking her wall down.

For a short moment he could see darkness behind those steely blue eyes, some kind of tragedy that was bringing on this reaction, and it was ringing his alarm bells.

Chapter 23 – The Drive Back

Jason was manually driving the car back to Charing Cross police station to clear his mind, but it was DCI Bjorkman who was driving him up the wall. After their meeting with Abberline, she had gone silent for a little while before launching into a series of excuses why Abberline was lying in an attempt to put them off the scent.

"Why would he act to protect this killer after all these years, Sabina? It just doesn't make sense."

Bjorkman was sitting in the front next to him, rebuilding the wall around herself once more and determined to take control. "Because he could very well be the Ripper himself. We know some experts have good reason to believe he was involved. And what about his diary that has mysteriously and conveniently disappeared. Then there are the possible links to the Masons that could have given him cause, no matter what he says. Don't forget, Ives, he knew Whitechapel better than most. He knew many of the girls, and was an ambitious man rapidly climbing the ranks of Scotland Yard."

"It still doesn't make sense. Where is the real motive? He never caught the Ripper, so it hardly helped his career, did it? What do you think, Isambard?

Isambard was hunched in the back seat, trying to remain anonymous in this verbal scuffle. "There are reasons for and against many of these contiguous accusations, and historic examination has still not revealed any definable yea or nay for any of the suspects Mr Ives. I am still of the opinion that Mary Kelly knew something, and the fact that Abberline feels the same only strengthens my humble resolve on the matter."

124

Bjorkman snapped back at him before he could draw another breath. "Mary Kelly is an easy guess for anyone to make. He's probably giving some slight truth to draw us in. If anything, I think his game of giving us false leads only makes him more interesting. Let me be clear, I don't want us wasting time looking for Kelly when we have Abberline as a strong suspect right on our doorstep."

Jason had to brake hard to let an Uber push past. "So what would your plan be?"

"As I've said before, I really don't think looking to past lives is the answer. I'm going to be keeping tabs on Abberline for the moment, and see if we can trace his footsteps on the nights of the murders. If you want, we could also try and trace that diary of his. Surely that is a good start?"

Ives was not so sure. "Fine, but you have a big enough team to search on many levels. I must admit that diary could prove crucial to uncover the real Ripper, or even to implicate Abberline himself, but I've had to deal with the Vatican myself in the past, and they are notoriously difficult to get any information from. In fact, if they do talk, they usually throw a lot of red herrings into the mix to hide bigger secrets."

"I know how to investigate, Ives. You keep to the past and I'll deal with the more pressing matters in our present."

Jason was furious with her attitude. "Sabina, for God's sake be more open minded. Your clouded judgement, and quite frankly, rude non co-operation is really pissing me off."

"Then leave. We don't need you anyway. I told you that right at the start. Go back to your past life shit stirring and leave my own team to get on with it. To be honest, I've seen nothing special in you anyway. I don't know what the big fuss is about your so-called skill set."

Ives knew when he was being goaded. She was afraid of something, whether it be the fact that his methods were in direct contradiction to hers, or that there was some other darker secret lurking in the background. She was either afraid of this investigation politically damaging her career or she was afraid of him. He hadn't made his mind up yet, and it was infuriating him that she was one of the few people in this world that he could not read. Maybe it was time to press a few psychological buttons to try and crack her defences.

"Maybe Abberline isn't the only one with something to hide, Sabina. I mean, I get the whole past life justice argument, but you are wedging it right in the middle of our investigation when there are lives at stake. Are you just afraid of the competition, or has something happened in your past that we should know about?"

"What? She screamed.

"Is there something we should know from your past? Remember, you are duty bound to disclose anything that might conflict with this investigation."

"Stop the fucking car!" She was almost in tears.

Jason instantly regretted what he had said. He knew he had gone too far, but the frustration had got the better of him. "Ah come on, Sabina, I'm sorry, I just meant..."

"Stop the fucking car now, Jason, or I'll jump out while we are still moving."

Jason pulled over and stopped by the curb, his hazard lights flashing. He felt he needed a few hazard lights himself at the moment. "Sabina, don't be silly."

Bjorkman grabbed her things, jumped out of the car and looked back in. "How dare you talk to me like that. How dare you accuse me of anything that would jeopardise this case. Do you know the pressure I am under from my so called superiors as you put it? You don't know me, nobody knows me, but I'm going to warn you now," Bjorkman paused for a second to try and control her temper, her voice belying her pain by focusing on her aggression. "Do not cross my path, Jason, it is just too dangerous a place to be."

Jason tried all his tricks to try and placate her. He looked down in a subservient way, he opened up his palms to try and show he had nothing to hide, he tried a hundred little tricks to pull her back into the car, but she was impervious to his methods. It made him feel small and useless, and a bit of an unfeeling bastard.

But then you have to be a bastard sometimes to get results, and this bastard had learnt more about her in the last minute than probably anyone else in her life.

Chapter 24 – An Hour in the Day

Sabina was furious for so many reasons. She was angry at Jason for saying all those things about her, but she knew in her heart of hearts that he was right. She should never have gotten involved in this case, but then she didn't really seem to have any choice anyway. Maybe she should have mentioned her past to her managers. Maybe she should have said a lot of things a lot earlier, but it was too late now; her path in this matter has been laid. Her life would be ruined if she tried opening up to her bosses now, and the political backlash was unthinkable.

She was definitely pissed off with Jason, and knew that she had shown him more of her nature than she wanted, but for some reason it only made her more attracted to him. Most men were so weak willed and obvious that she normally grew bored of them, but here was a man who constantly surprised her and was able to dig deep into her psyche. It would be a dangerous game getting involved with someone like him though; someone who could delve into her past if she ever let her guard down.

And for fuck's sake - she hates past life investigators with every fibre in her body!

∞-∞-∞-∞-∞-∞

Jason threw his keys on the table by the front door as he slammed the outside world out of existence. He was shattered, and wasn't quite sure what his next few steps should be. One thing he had been putting off though was messaging Samantha. Not because he didn't want to see

128

her, far from it, but because he just felt he was becoming more and more embroiled in this case and it was hogging all his time and energy.

In fact, time with someone like Sammy was exactly what he needed right now. Time to relax and talk to someone about something other than the Ripper. We all need down time and someone to share the stresses of life with, otherwise we begin to fall apart at the seams. Jason wondered what Isambard did to relax, and imagined him alone in a darkened room with a Ouija board trying to summon up the spirits of all his Victorian friends.

Actually, with the way things were going, it might even be worth a shot.

∞-∞-∞-∞-∞-∞

Isambard propped his bicycle against the wall of his basement flat in Battersea, just a few hundred metres from the royal park with its Buddhist Peace Pagoda, tall trees and gentle paths. It was a clear night, thus providing a slight chill in the air to wash his thoughts on today's interview with Abberline. He could see both Ives' and Bjorkman's point of view, and had some doubts of his own about Abberline's statement. He knew Abberline to be a self serving opportunist, who would keep the juiciest of details for himself if it meant he could make some money out of it. That said, there were quite a few of his colleagues who could be accused of the same thing.

He was so glad to be back home after such a trying day, with his two cats Sherlock and Mycroft welcoming him in with soft purrs and excited tails. Was that the smell of Shepherd's pie? He entered the kitchen to find his wife singing a song to a media centre made to look like an old art deco radio, whilst scraping some carrots.

His home. His small sanctuary that makes him happy as he basks in its warm atmosphere.

∞-∞-∞-∞-∞-∞

Samantha received a message on her wall screen from Jason. He had called her a few days ago and had been kind enough to try and be as honest as possible about his situation. She could see how busy he was every time she turned the news on. But whilst she admired the truth and respected his position, she felt that she needed to prioritise her own feelings and situation too. She still wasn't sure whether it was a good idea to start something with him now.

She felt like she should suggest waiting until this new Ripper was caught. And, if she was still single when that happens (or indeed he was) they could, or should, get together at that point. All very sensible, all boring, and anything but satisfying, but it could save a lot of pain. You always want what you can't have though, so suggesting this action might only make things worse. It was an impossible decision considering her attraction to him.

His message was rambling a bit, as if he too was conflicted. Seems like he's had a bad day, but at least he is suggesting a meet up soon. Dinner somewhere nice, as far away from the claustrophobic feel of Whitechapel as you can manage in London. Suddenly Samantha pushes away her doubts, and thinks of all the positive advantages of having Jason in her life.

Holding hands over a romantic table for two seems like a good start.

∞-∞-∞-∞-∞-∞

DS Pascal was on night watch, and waiting for a fish to bite. He was using some of his 'time off in lieu', the Met's way of making you to take time off rather than receive money for any overtime earned. And even though they'd been incredibly busy this last week, Bjorkman had warned him that he was already way over his limit and would therefore lose a whole chunk of it if not taken soon.

John Pascal is a conscientious police officer and almost ignored the warning, but he also hates being ripped off by his bosses in their high level offices, working a more normal Monday to Friday. He had quite fancied a fishing trip with his brother which was also long overdue. So that is how he found himself in the middle of the night wrapped up in a thick jacket, drinking malt whiskey and chatting with him about his part in the case.

The fish however, were yet to bite.

∞-∞-∞-∞-∞-∞

After his guest had left, Rochelle kept in his Abberline frame of mind for just a little longer to think back to his more personal moments. Using 'Kale's advanced visualisation method,' he was able to dig a little deeper into those memories he had uncovered with his Awakening Observer over the years. Maybe it was time to see him again for a few more sessions to try and remember the details he had left in that mysterious diary of his.

Maybe it was time to push the Vatican again for access to his own words. There was a secret buried there somewhere... he was sure of it.

Chapter 25 – A Date with Fate

Jack is back.

His voices are screaming louder than ever, but this time at each other. Demanding murder, demanding he turn himself in, demanding him to commit suicide. The loudest voice is usually his mother's, warning him that Scotland Yard are getting closer to knowing who he is every day. But tonight she is quiet; she has disappeared into the furthest reaches of his mind. Probably because his blood is boiling from the madness of the world that he has to witness every day.

He feels compelled to murder once again, to taste the blood, to sniff their hair, to gauge their eyes and hear their pleas for mercy through a muffled mouth. Maybe he should strike again whilst she is silent.

Quickly, the disguise goes on, the forensic suit gets packed, the gloves stretched over the hands.

Time to find another painted lady and drag her to a gutter.

Down with all whores!

∞-∞-∞-∞-∞-∞

Date night, and Jason plays nervously with his tie. The investigation hasn't made much progress in the last few days, which only adds to his feeling of guilt by taking the evening off for a little romantic interlude. *Come on Jason, you can't live like a monk all your life. Get out there and have some fun... doctor's orders.*

He caught the train from Putney to Waterloo, then used the Jubilee line on the tube to get to London Bridge. Packed with city types going home from work and tourists eager to explore everything that London has to offer, it made him feel a little trapped with the amount of bodies milling about.

∞-∞-∞-∞-∞-∞

The wonderful London underground. My how it has grown... its tentacles now reaching out to every nook and cranny of London.

Jack is in a good mood as he rides along the noisy tracks of the London underground system, known the world over as 'The Tube'. In his day of course, it had been known as The District Railway. All brand spanking new, clean and shiny, until the steam driven locomotives sooted it all up. Handy too, for getting into Whitechapel from his lodgings. Quicker and more discreet than a handsome carriage, or walking for over an hour in the middle of the night to avoid suspicion; keeping to the shadows if he'd been sloppy and spilt blood on himself.

All these new stops at places he'd never heard of before in Victorian London, but then he wasn't exactly local then either. As soon as he started his Veterinary sciences studies, the other gentlemen had regaled him with their sordid stories of Whitechapel, where thrupenny uprights brazenly advertised their goods to anyone with money to spare. If only he had taken heed of his friend Fredrick's warning, or learnt by his own father's death, but then mother hadn't told him the whole truth until it was too late anyway.

Memories of his father were clouded by the last few years. A vicious man, unafraid to teach him the rules of life with the back of his hand, or his walking cane slapped against his back. His father had finally grown weak though, his whole stature crumbling into itself as he rotted from within. Another victim of the pox. Like father, like son. A chip off the old block some might say, through rotted clenched teeth, and spittle full of hate.

In an instant, Jack's mind was forced forward to the 21st century by the announcement of his stop. Time again to find those girls not on the legalised prostitution register. They are too well protected by their colleagues and cameras. Now, it is time to find the girls who don't quite fit the criteria. The desperate ones willing to take the bigger risks, just like his blowsy girls had still been when walking the streets, even though they feared the Leather Apron.

The internet has found him another victim.

∞-∞-∞-∞-∞-∞

The ultimate inter-date, but things are different this time. Jason isn't leaving anything to chance. A window seat at 'Neo Apollonian', the Greek / Italian fusion restaurant on the thirtieth floor of the Shard, that promises great flavours with finesse, a warm welcome and the best views of London. Or at least, that is what 'Time Out' had posted in their review.

This time his mobile is turned off and he hasn't told anyone from the station what he was up to tonight. No Pascal turning up unannounced, no embarrassing ringtones sending him into a panic and dunking his mobile into the soup to try and mute it.

Suited and booted, shaved and showered, Jason felt

ready to be a human being again and have a proper relationship. Okay, so he has a thousand reports to read, books to skim, websites to absorb in their entirety in his bid to learn as much about his quarry as fast as possible, but for one night at least, he is off duty.

Samantha appeared from the corner of the main entrance to London Bridge railway station, nestled by the base of the Shard. Dressed in a simple but elegant dress, pinched at the waist and coloured in the most attractive Moroccan blue, it shows off her amazing petite figure in a serene and understated way. Jason knew he'd made the right decision, and was glad he'd made the extra effort of wearing a smart suit for this posh venue.

He couldn't help himself as he blew a wolf whistle to welcome her arrival. Smiles all round, and a calmness he had not felt in ages; it was a good start to the evening. Samantha faked a look behind her.

"Ooh, someone nice passing or are you calling a cab?"

Jason chuckled at her self-depreciating humour. "I'm calling you, and you look gorgeous by the way." As they met, they hugged and he could feel her letting him into her personal space without reserve. She was happy to embrace him, with a hand on his back to hold him even closer. *Stop analysing*, he warned himself, and with a great effort, he switched that part of his mind off as well as he could to enjoy the evening and her company.

As soon as they were seated, they drank in the view. Looking north over the Thames, it was possible to see the capital's majestic river snake around the landmarks of one of the most beautiful cities in the world. From east to west, with Greenwich leading to Putney in the foreground, and Heathrow airport in the far distance surrounded by circling planes waiting to land. A metropolis being visited by millions of visitors every year.

Jason was still on his best behaviour. "I hope you like my choice, Sam, it was pretty difficult to think of somewhere that could outdo your choice of the V&A?"

Samantha pulled a face. "I suppose it will have to do... as long as they do chips, I'm happy."

"Ah, you should have said something earlier, we could have just met at Mr Cod, and I wouldn't have had to remortgage my apartment to just book the seat." He said with a wink.

"Hmm, I wasn't going to let you off that easily, Mr Ives. I want posh chips and only the best Mayo."

"Mayo with your chips? You psycho."

∞-∞-∞-∞-∞-∞

Jack looked in the broken hallway mirror to try and find himself in the cracked glass. This accursed body, so strangely attractive, and yet such an abomination to him, seems so alien to his whole sense of being. The piercing eyes staring back at him are those of a stranger, but there's an energy and intelligence that he recognises. Can it really be possible that he is trapped within this feeble frame?

He found the tired looking doorway of his walk-in appointment on the corner of Duncan Street, just as promised on the new website he'd been using; dedicated to swingers and depraved denizens of this filthy land. Somehow he'd known back then that all the failing morals of the lower classes was going to lead to this. He knew that he had been infected morally and intellectually way before his stupid cock had been infected. That was just the natural course of events, and he was paying his dues.

On the side of the door in the dimly lit street, it had said 'Models upstairs'. Models indeed. Everyone knows what that really means; a knocking shop by any other name, and yet the Peelers still can't work it out – or just don't want too. Probably on a back-hander.

And tonight's tasty victim is Nadia... Fresh from the Ukraine.

∞-∞-∞-∞-∞-∞

The menu was exhaustive, promising delicacies ranging from an ancient Greece recipe for Stifado, to an ultra modern version of a kebab, with each separate succulent cube of lamb trimmed to perfection and injected with a different exotic sauce to thrill the palette. In the end they settled on sharing a Meze, a 24 course meal of small plates, offering tastes from different sections of the menu.

Aubergine dip, stuffed vine leaves, dolmades, tahini; each Greek tradition wrapped in phyllo, every conversation accompanied with hummus, and each topic made fresh with tzatziki. The starters before the kleftiko, souvlaki, mousaka, Keftedakia, each dish trying to outdo the other in a celebration of food.

Accompanied by a simple rich red wine, the colour of blood.

∞-∞-∞-∞-∞-∞

Nadia's blood spurted from her jugular, staining the taupe coloured carpet in an instant, as it tries to find a new home to settle into. Her life-giving liquid escaping from her body before her soul could.

This girl had been difficult; she'd put up a hard fight and had almost overcome her attacker. Only by luck had

Jack managed to regain his balance when the bitch had kicked his shin with the back of her foot. A frenzied moment, a battle for control. A moment in which her life could have been saved, and history could have been made. How satisfying it would have been to the general populace, to hear on the morning news that Jack the Ripper had finally been caught... by a common prostitute!

The old communist blood in her veins had given her a strength beyond her size, a mental toughness and a survival instinct much higher than Jack was used to from his drunk Cheapside floozies, but it was of no use to her now, soaked in the carpet. Her strength was almost gone, but her arms were still twitching, still fighting death to the very last drop.

Time to rip her body apart whilst it is still warm. Maybe even eat her kidney.

∞-∞-∞-∞-∞-∞

To be honest, there was too much food. They were little dishes, but lots of them, and they were both trying to be good. No one feels sexy when feeling bloated, but it tasted amazing. Samantha dipped into the plate of kidney beans, covered in a rich, warm tomato sauce, seasoned with herbs a shepherd might find in his field whilst tending to his flock.

"Wow, this is amazing," she managed through mouthfuls.

"I know, but I can't decide on whether to chew first or take another look at the view."

∞-∞-∞-∞-∞-∞

Jack spread her legs, but not to fuck her... that would be vile with this creature. He grabbed from his rucksack the biggest knife in his collection. The French chef's knife, a heftier blade that works well for splitting, stripping and cutting meat, but still shaped like a blunt instrument as he rammed it into her filthy hole with all his strength. This is the point at which he needs to reposition himself, to grip the blade and pull back, cutting through her Venus mound, slicing her uterus, her stomach, her vital organs, right up to her chest.

Nadia's last few moments on Earth... for a while at least.

∞-∞-∞-∞-∞-∞

The sun was setting over the landscape on what had been a beautiful summer's day. A day of respite from the typically inclement British weather, and a promise of warmer days to come. From the thirtieth floor of the Shard, it looked as if the sun was melting into the sea of buildings on the far reaches of London. The crimson glow warming the eyes of Jason and Samantha as they held hands over the table.

It was made all the more beautiful by the momentary silence between them. Soaking up the atmosphere of the setting, and full of awe by the show displayed by Mother Nature. No wonder it had been almost impossible to book this table at sunset; it was a cabaret, the show to end all shows, a celebration of light.

The waiter cleared their final plates, congratulating them on their attempt to eat almost everything. "Would you both like an Ouzo to finish the meal? On the house, of course." The wine was already working its wonders, but neither of them could refuse the offer of a free drink. It would be rude not to after all. With a coffee bean in each glass, the waiter lit them both with a practiced flourish. The flames whispering on the surface, cooking the beans to infuse its flavour through the aniseed liquor, until Jason snuffed the flames out with his hand, a trick he had been shown by his father.

∞-∞-∞-∞-∞-∞

Jack snuffed the last particle of life from her battling body by stabbing her directly in the heart. The fight was over at last, and Jack made a mental note to himself to avoid such women in the future. No old guard, no stocky women or ones that 'go to the gym'. It was not right, everything is unbalanced. Here he was, stuck in this new, but weaker body, at a time when women have never been stronger! The prostitutes are a lot more sober, and the world has electric cameras protecting them on every corner. The challenge is greater than ever.

Time to dice and slice and all things nice, Jack's sick motto running through his head again as he begins to strip the flesh from her naked body. He has already popped her eyes out, and stamped on them until they became a gelatinous mush... no images will ever be recovered from those visual portals. So now it is time to remove her insides.

His father had taught him how to gut his first animal, a rabbit caught on his first hunting expedition, aged six. He remembered the warmth of the poor creature as he fumbled like an idiot trying to cut off its furry jacket, without cutting himself first, and crying because he hadn't wanted too. His father had been strict though, told him that it would make him into a man.

From rabbits to pheasants to pigs to deer. These poor creatures grew bigger as he did. Maybe that is why he had chosen to become a vet, to quietly protest against his father's sporting bloodlust or simply to try and make amends for all his forced misdeeds. Funny how he felt guilty for those poor creatures and not his victims. Animals are innocent in his eyes, they don't make the choices that humans do, they don't stray from the path because they don't know what they are doing.

Lust is such a human element. It makes us all weak, and those trollops just exploit that weakness to pay for their next drink.

∞-∞-∞-∞-∞-∞

One Ouzo had turned into two to accompany their coffee, their final course in this fine restaurant, and both were thinking the same thing as they looked into each other's eyes. Both wanted to feel the touch of each other's bodies, to rip each other's clothes off and feel the softness of flesh. To take and be taken, to force and to yield, to love and to lust.

It is the point in which our civilised modern intelligence battles against our primitive instincts. To have what we want, but to obey the rules of engagement in respect of each other. Logic and passion at loggerheads.

As they left, Jason passed the waiter. "My compliments to the chef."

Chapter 26 – The Morning After

On the dawn of a new day, Jason found himself entangled in Samantha's arms as the light seeped through her blinds. His head seemed slightly muggy, but he was generally feeling really good. The sex had been good too, a relief to the system and a reminder of how important physical contact is. Sure, nothing beats the raw feeling of rolling around naked and satisfying that primitive urge to copulate, but when it all comes down to basics, it is ultimately the intimacy that he loves the most.

To be able to see and touch and taste each other in a way that you just cannot do in your local supermarket, well, not for most people at least. To Jason it supersedes sex and is an example of feelings and emotions that are so human. The embrace after the orgasmic spasms that relaxes your body like nothing else. The whispers of sweet nothings that tease your mind, the caresses and soft kisses, especially when you are still getting to know each other. He felt recharged and ready to face the world.

But not quite yet. His mobile was still turned off and Samantha was still asleep, so he just lay there listening to the traffic and thinking about nothing at all, until his other call of nature forced him to get up and find the toilet. That strange first journey alone through someone else's property as they sleep, making him feel awkward, even though he had just seen her naked.

On his return she was lying face down in an attempt to grab a bit more sleep before starting her day. It showed off her perfect peach of a bum, which quite frankly was just asking for trouble. He felt himself stiffening. Perhaps there was time for another round before letting the world back into his life.

Later, a sumptuous brunch made from leftovers and titbits matched the weekend feel. Now all they needed was a brisk walk in the woods with their nonexistent dog to blow the cobwebs away.

Samantha could see Jason looking at this mobile with a slight jittery look on his face.

"Have you still not turned it on?"

He picked it up. "I know, I better call in to at least see how the land lies. Silly really, it's probably just been a quiet night in the office."

"Hmm, another kiss first before that's allowed," she demanded.

Jason laughed, pulling her close for a long sensual kiss.

Samantha squeezed his arm. "You better call the office quick if you're going to kiss me like that, or you'll be otherwise engaged."

"What, again? Please, I need a rest," he begged.

Samantha gave Jason a playful slap, then went to make some fresh coffee to give him the space to check-in.

As soon as turned his mobile on it went wild. All sorts of messages and missed calls coming in, asking him where the hell he was. The Ripper had struck again, and quite literally under his very nose from the thirtieth floor of the Shard.

He grabbed his keys and walked to the door with a sense of urgency.

"I have to go."

Chapter 27 – Crime Scene

Duncan Street, Angel Islington. Normally a quiet road near the Regent's Canal, but now it is surrounded by a swarm of police vehicles trying to block out the reporters and general public. Their main objective is to keep the scene sterile and avoid any images leaking out to the media or world wide web. A thankless task most of the time, but necessary to get as much forensic information as possible without contaminating the scene.

The golden hour is the sixty minutes deemed the most important in an investigation of a serious crime. To get the scene shut off, the investigators at the door, and the forensic teams mobilised. From that point on, the crime scene manager can devise a plan of action with the senior investigator, the homicide advisory team, the lead forensic scientist and the SOCO acting as photographer and evidence gatherer.

It is vital to get as much information as possible, as quickly as possible in the hope that they can catch the killer out. Jason was late. At least nine hours late from when the body had first been discovered.

Pascal met him at the cordon tape near the door to the location, a smirk on his face because he knew how much trouble Jason was in with Bjorkman. "Good afternoon, Mr Ives, so sorry to have woken you up on such a fine day."

Ives blushed, completely embarrassed to be in this position. He thought about lying, saying that his mobile had died, but just couldn't bring himself to do it. "Sorry, John, I just needed one night off the grid, but of course the Ripper had to choose that night for his next attack. It's as if the bugger knew what I was up to."

Pascal laughed. "I doubt he's planning his moves around your private life, Jason... unless you want to fess up to something?"

"Only to the terrible sense of timing that plagues my life."

Pascal swiped his ID to let Jason pass through the low shock holo-barrier marking the scene's outer boundary, and rested a hand on his shoulder. "Honestly, don't worry about it, Jason. No offence, but your skills, clever as they may be, aren't so urgent at the scene, so it's not vital for you to be here at stupid o'clock like the rest of us. Plus you are in luck, the body is still in position. We had to wait for the pathologist to get here to take a look, and he has been extraordinarily vigilant on this one. He wanted lots of photos, and the blood spatter guys to work around the body. They are really hoping to get something this time."

Ives looked relieved. "Oh thank Christ for that, I thought they would have carted it out by now. Would it be okay to suit up and take a look?"

"Of course, but just try to stay out of the guv's way, she's been in a foul mood since getting here, and for once, I don't think it's your fault."

Jason grabbed the forensic gear that he needed from one of the SOCOs. A paper scene suit with elastic cuffs around the hands and feet, and a hood to completely cover the head, even though he also was given a hairnet to wear. Gloves, a face mask and overshoes to help stop him leaving shoe marks at the scene completed the set. On a warm summer's day like today, he was going to roast in that outfit for the next few hours at least. Pascal led him into the scene.

Past the 'Models upstairs' sign by the dingy entrance. Past the broken mirror in the hall, leading to a bedsit room, with a mattress in the corner and a body lying next to it.

"Oh, how did the fishing trip go with your brother?" Ives was trying to normalise his surroundings by asking 'normal' questions. A common occurrence by most officers in this bizarre occupational setting.

"Fine thanks mate. Would have been better if I'd have caught something though."

"Well today's the day for that big catch I guess." Jason then looked at the scene properly for the first time. "What a mess."

The room was covered in blood and the poor girl's body parts. Pascal stretched from one stepping plate to another to move around the body in an effort to not disturb anything. The metal plates are used to keep the investigators from touching the floor, and thus disturb any marks left underneath.

Pascal then held out a hand to assist Ives across the largest gap as he began to describe the scene. "Yep, claret everywhere. The spatter bods have isolated that large spurt over there, which again correlates with the previous Ripper scenes. He quite literally bleeds the victims as if he's at an abattoir. It makes the whole ripping process a lot cleaner apparently, as there is less blood left in the body to leak out, especially once the heart has stopped beating."

Jason nodded in understanding. He felt suffocated by the surroundings and the mask over his face, but at least it lessened the smell of death a little. The carcass of the young girl was barely recognisable as a human being, and even in worse shape than Angela in the post mortem he'd been to. Flies were already laying their eggs all over her body, so that their maggot larvae could feed on the dead flesh when they hatch. They seemed to be concentrating on the empty eye sockets for some reason, as if it is the tastiest part.

Jason wondered how many years it would take for this

kind of sight to become less horrific. And how many years it would take to get over each and every event like this; these mini traumas thrust into the lives of officers having to deal with murders on a daily basis. Does anyone truly get away without being affected?

He shook his head to clear the gruesome thoughts clouding his mind. "So what have we got so far, Pascal, any clues?"

Pascal just shrugged those huge shoulders of his. "Nothing yet, but the specialist lighting team will be over later to do their magic laser thing."

"Wow, you sound like a pro. I'm surprised you aren't doing it yourself with a torch and some sticky tape. What laser thingy?"

"Careful, Jason, you're beginning to sound like the guv." He pointed to a wall right by the body and continued with his explanation. "They blank out all the windows to cut out the light, as it has to be done in complete darkness. Then they treat the most likely areas that might have finger prints, using some kind of laser or intense light to bring the marks up. I think the chemical glows if it has some kind of bodily fluid on it such as sweat or semen. Then they can photograph finger marks on a different wavelength from the background, even though it had been previously invisible to the eye. It'll take them a few days with this lot though."

Jason was happy to see there was still more to do. "Well thank God for modern technology. Makes you feel quite sorry for Abberline and his colleagues back then, trying to find the most basic of clues. They didn't even have fingerprints in those days. Seems unbelievable now that they ever caught anyone."

"I know, but that was in the days of good old fashioned detective work, just like her Ladyship keeps banging on about. And she has a point in a way. They knew their local area really well, and the public were too afraid to even think about crossing a police officer's path. Their hunches were usually spot on too. That's why I think Abberline might have a point about this 'my Joe' theory."

"Hmm, you might be right, but Joe the Ripper doesn't sound so menacing for some reason, and I can't think of any clear suspects with that name apart from Barnett." Ives started taking a few photos himself as he walked around the room as he talked.

Pascal still seemed pretty convinced. "But worth looking into with Isambard though? Abberline was a bloody good detective, at a time when a hunch could make or break a case."

"Really, you think a simple hunch is worth putting a lot of manpower into?" Ives asked, even though he already agreed with Pascal.

Pascal moved into the small kitchen area to get away from the body. "Aye, I do, especially when we have so little to go on anyway." He opened a cupboard out of curiosity. "Oh look at all this tea. I could murder a cuppa right now."

Ives laughed. "Poor choice of words, my friend."

Pascal look confused for a second, and then twigged. "Oh right, yeah. I've obviously been doing this job too long."

"There seems to have been quite a struggle, or do you think she lives in this mess all the time?"

"Nah, definitely a struggle, look at the kitchen, it's spotless. I also think the girl got a few hits to our murderer before she went down, judging by the amount of things knocked over."

Ives looked hopeful. "So there might be a bit of blood from the Ripper mixed in with all this lot?"

"Possible, but you try finding it when mixed with all of her blood. SOCO have their work cut out on this one. The pathologist might find something under the nails though. Some hair or skin tissue. About time we got a break with this lucky nutter."

Jason wasn't so sure. For all the Ripper's signs of out and out madness, he also seemed to be organised and careful. As the Whitechapel murderer, he'd become known for his daring attacks under the noses of everyone around him. Jason had an idea that he wasn't just lucky though, he was much more than that. Jack was also very calm under extreme pressure; methodical, exacting, careful to the point that it bought him extra time.

The double murder of Elizabeth Stride and Catherine Eddowes within an hour of each other on that September night was audacious to the extreme though. It made the Ripper seem like he was everywhere - striking whoever he wanted with his deadly knives. He had become the bogeyman of London. Indeed, he had been described as such several times during the investigations.

So not only was he methodical, but his calmness allowed him to adapt and make new plans in an instant, for surely he couldn't have planned on killing those two girls in one night. The calmness exhibited a pathological streak that made the Ripper look like he was invincible. So strange then, that he should just disappear off the face of the earth a few months later.

Psychopathic killers do not just give up either. Sometimes they go on for years before being caught, and they certainly do not change their methodology from slaughter to poison as Abberline had originally thought. Some people think that the Ripper must have died, either at the hands of someone else or by suicide. God knows he had read enough theories on the pages of several Ripper websites and their forums.

Pascal showed Ives a passport. "She was Ukrainian, name of Nadia Kurylenko. She's only been in the country a few months." He then jabbed the passport chip into his mobile and pulled out the large polymer viewing screen to reveal a photo page where an attractive brunette was staring into the camera. "Why anyone would come all this way and then take these risks when they know there is a killer roaming is beyond me," he added.

"Desperation I guess. To escape a life even worse."

Both men suddenly went quiet while they absorbed this thought. It made them appreciate living in London a little bit more, even when working on a case like this.

"So where is Bjorkman?" Ives asked.

"Oh, she went home about an hour ago to get a nap before the post mortem later today. She was one of the first at the scene when we were called in at just after four am. A friend of the victim found her like this. She's probably still on tranquillisers now. Hell of a shock she got, could hardly even phone it in."

"I'm not surprised, I'd be a mess too. So do we know how the Ripper found her, did he make an appointment, or do you think he just walked in?"

"Hard to know. The data guys are going through her mobile data details, but they think it will have a high level of encryption on it. Part of the lifestyle of a hooker I'm afraid."

Jason suddenly had a thought about last night. "What time does the pathologist think was the time of death?"

"About 10:00pm, with an hour either side."

Jason stopped in his tracks. While Nadia was entertaining the Ripper and then being murdered, he'd been eating a gluttonous meal and looking over this exact area of London. And when she was being cut open and her eyes pulled out, he'd been drunkenly fucking Samantha as if nobody else mattered. He had neglected his duty. He suddenly felt like shit.

Jason looked out the window at the cordon tape to distract himself. "Hey, I thought you told me Bjorkman was about when I got here?"

"No, I just told you to keep out of her way. I love to see a grown man walk in fear, and thought you deserved it for having nice lie in."

"Ha, you got me." Jason said feebly. Pascal's words cut him like a knife. He was wearing a weak smile, but he was feeling extremely guilty inside. Already his personal life was slowing him down. Yes it probably wouldn't have made any difference this time, but he couldn't let it happen again.

The sooner he works out who this killer is, the sooner they can get on with the task of arresting him, and the sooner the working girls of London will be safe. And what if the Ripper stops being so choosy? What if he starts taking a dislike to any woman on a night out somewhere, like Samantha just a couple of weeks ago? It sent a chill down his neck.

He was going to have to have to live and breathe this bloody investigation with no distractions.

No time off, no fun, no anything until the Ripper is caught.

Chapter 28 – Truce

It was a long, quiet trip back to Charing Cross police station as Jason struggled with his thoughts and emotions. He knew he was being over sensitive about it. He knew he wasn't the only person on this case, and that finding the original Jack the Ripper had foiled thousands of professional and amateur investigators the world over for the last one hundred and eighty years or so, but it didn't make him feel any better about it.

He had been charged with finding this cold hearted bastard as fast as possible, and so far all they had was a hunch from Abberline about a guy called Joe. It was hardly a breakthrough. He wanted to go back to see Abberline straight away and demand answers. He wanted to damn well torture a confession out of him, even though he knew in his heart of hearts that it wasn't him. But he was desperate.

They had to find Eddowes or Kelly as fast as possible. No matter where they were in the world, (if at all) and Jason knew he had to get out there and get some answers, if only to appease his guilt.

He was glad to have the company of Pascal as he walked into the murder investigation team office. He'd never felt so much like an outsider, and now he had to face Bjorkman, the first time they'd been together since the argument in the car. That would have been bad enough, but with his 'off the grid moment' she had a licence to say anything against him that she liked. He'd pushed some serious psychological buttons on her in that argument, and being the kind of person he thinks she is, she'd want some retribution.

That said, if he was going to have to look into every single little clue to catching the Ripper, he'd also have to look into whatever Bjorkman's angle was. He'd seen an incredibly strong anger and sadness during that argument. Something in her past was linked to an Awakening or her early life that had had a huge effect on her. It may even be the reason why she had learnt to block people out so well.

There and then, Jason decided that he was going to use all his skills to try and make amends, to placate and supplicate his way into her good books. Better to eat, drink and sleep with the enemy than to fight them. He then realised that those were the three things he'd just done with Samantha, and felt ashamed again at his thought process. Women trouble on both ends of the spectrum.

Located on the first floor, the office was situated down a series of corridors that appeared as if they had been designed to confuse rather than assist. Maybe it would help in a raid situation. It even had the occasional small window looking out to the tiny yard in the middle, acting like castle arrow slits for hot tar to be poured on invaders.

Pushing through the fire regulation door, he could see that the rest of the team were already in a meeting with Bjorkman at the helm. She gave him a withering look as a warning shot, and then her face returned to normal without missing a beat. Photos from the scene were already up on the wall screens.

Images of Nadia's hollow face, her arms de-gloved (the flesh literally peeled off), and her breasts cut off, left to rot by her media player. There were organs Jason barely recognised because they were in such bad shape. Her spleen, her heart, her liver... all strewn over the bed as he had seen it barely an hour earlier. Carnage without reason.

Isambard had some holographic reconstructions of the original Victorian scenes made up by the graphics team.

They were based on descriptions from the police reports at the time, showing the victims lying on their backs in situ, their knees pushed up and legs open.

By putting them side by side, it was easier to see the similarities. Even with the seemingly frenzied attacks, it looked like the Ripper had a routine, and with each subsequent killing (excluding Liz Stride), he had added to the list of mutilations.

With the last four victims added from 2065, you could see him playing with the eyes. Ranging from the slitted and squeezed eye balls, to the latest stamping. Then Jason saw a mobile scan of the neck... he had at last managed to cut through the vertebrae and decapitate her. Jack's anger possibly giving him the extra strength to cut through.

DS Pascal broke the ice. "Sorry we're late for the meeting, ma'am, once the pathologist finished it took the undertakers ages to collect the body for the post mortem. Did we miss anything?"

Jason felt like ducking on that question, but to be fair to her, she just carried on. "Nope, we've just started actually. As you can see from the photos, it just confirms Isambard's view that we are dealing with the original Ripper rather than a copycat."

She then looked directly at Jason. "Ives, now that you've turned up, can you explain to the team how this might happen? In layman's terms please."

Jason was relieved to be thrown this bone to join in. "Yes, of course. It is extremely rare for anyone's current core personality to be overridden by their past life, with only a handful of cases ever being reported. These events were very low level in themselves, and only of interest because of their rarity."

Jason looked up to make sure he had their attention. He did. "Most of the victims of this past life... er, abduction, were either in a pretty bad place in their personal life, hence wanting it to be taken over by someone else, or they had experienced some recent trauma. And so, experts surmise, their subconscious wanted to escape, hence letting the old identity temporarily come back."

One of the officers at the back put up a hand. Politeness, Jason liked that. "Yes, Carter?"

'Why is it so rare, the world is full of people experiencing tragedies?"

Ives moved a little more into the middle to gain Carter's line of sight. "Yes, that is true, which is why, if you remember through your Awakening sessions, you had the Observer to run you through the Awakening process. Then your guide to basically hold your hand through the whole experience, and of course, several Awakening counsellors to pick up on the slightest deviance from the norm.

"As you know, we pick up past knowledge from our memories, such as languages, or a skill such as engineering... or flower arranging." His audience gave a little laugh. Jason was working the crowd. "And that is normally where it ends. Just because we remember, does not mean we become our past selves again; more that we re-connect with those elements that we choose to.

"If anyone is going through a rough patch in their lives, they are normally screened from having any further Awakenings until they are mentally in a better place. In addition, memories are just past events recorded in our minds when the body is alive. We don't get taken over by our memories within this life, so why should that happen with memories from an older life?"

Even Bjorkman was taking an interest. "So how do we transfer memories from one life to another? I've never heard a plausible explanation."

"Well, let's just say that no one has really worked out

how memories are transferred from body to body. Explanations such as ectoplasmic memory banks or a spiritual version of cloud computing are all still theoretical."

Bjorkman pounced. "Which just brings us back to how the hell has this happened then? How has this person been taken over by their past memory when you say there are procedures in place to monitor an Awakening subject's mental state, and it is just an old memory anyway? If this Ripper ever gets caught, can they be cured and returned to their current core identity?"

"That I'm afraid is the tricky bit. There is so little known about this type of event, that it is hard to say anything with any confidence. I'd say that in this particular case, the Ripper is probably sharing the body with its original owner, as a schizophrenic shares identities. In fact, that is exactly what some people used to believe they were going through not so long ago, with some victims of the mental state believing they were possessed by scores of personalities. A fascinating subject, and with some startling parallels."

Bjorkman didn't look satisfied with the answer. She was agitated, tired looking and in Jason's eyes, looking quite fragile. "So can they be cured, Ives? Surely that is a simple enough question. What do you think?"

All eyes went back to Ives. He was in the guvnor's spotlight and wasn't enjoying the sensation. He threw his hands up into the air in a sign of resignation and shook his head. "I'm not sure, but I'd say that it was possible with the right counselling and therapies. To remove the trauma or alleviate the mental state that is allowing the personality quake to come through."

Silence from the DCI, maybe from satisfaction, or maybe from exhaustion, Jason still couldn't tell. He continued by fielding questions from the rest of the team, all eager to try and gain an understanding into the mind, or minds of the Ripper of 2065.

Bjorkman called the meeting to a close a little while later, and asked to see Jason alone in her office. As soon as her door was closed, she suddenly turned on him, launching into a full attack. "I'm going to say this only once. Don't you EVER talk to me like that again as you did in the car, is that understood?"

Jason backed down immediately. He hunched down to lower his height, he lifted his palms to show they were empty and honest, he lowered his eyes to show no aggression. Hell, he even grimaced to try and show submission to her. He was an open book, a weak man showing regret, who was obviously not going to challenge her authority. Or at least, that is exactly what he wanted her to believe. There are many ways to win a battle, and if running away buys extra time, then run away he will.

"Yes, of course, I'm sorry, Sabina..."

She cut him off immediately. "It's DCI Bjorkman or guv whilst at work Ives, and from now on, I expect the only time for you to not be on duty, or at least contactable on a 24/7 basis, is when we catch this bloody killer."

Ives, quickly agreed. "Of course."

"We've got the post mortem to go to in a short while, but you are not to go. We don't need you there, and to be honest I'm sick of the sight of you. Utilise the time this afternoon to work with Isambard on your side of the case. Honestly, you're both like a bunch of fucking clowns."

It went against the grain to be nice to her at this moment, especially with her being so hostile, but he bit the bullet anyway. "Look, I'm sorry for everything. I know I shouldn't have said those things, and I'm sorry I was not contactable last night. It has just been a tough time for me

too, and I needed a night off, but it won't happen again...
on both counts."

The white flag was up and she had vented her anger. The
healing process could now begin.

Chapter 29 – Vexing News

Jason left Bjorkman's office with his tail firmly between his legs, but in a strange way he felt better. Yes, he was still upset over the death of the Ripper's latest victim, but he felt a few issues had been dealt with in terms of Bjorkman. A bridge was now being built, and he intended on crossing to the other side, if only to help her. This would help him, and thus help the case.

He didn't consider her as a suspect, that seemed too ridiculous, but something about Bjorkman's character was niggling him, so he would just have to keep an eye on her until he had figured it out.

Abberline didn't make much of a suspect either, but it was strange that his handwriting had been analysed as the author of the so-called Ripper diaries. There was also no denying that he'd been in a perfect position of authority and knowledge to carry out the murders. Hmm, the more he thought about it, the more it became plausible, but only from a point that he'd had the opportunity.

It didn't seem right though. Jason still felt he had no reasonable motive, and led a very respectable life till the day he died in 1929. Hardly the mark of a frenzied serial killer. And the diaries were a farce really, with a hand writing expert probably just trying to make a name for himself, by besmirching the name of the lead investigator.

Hell, he'd even considered Isambard for a short while, based purely on his mannerisms and fascination with all things Ripper. If that was the case, they'd have to lock up the entire community of Ripperologists. He must be losing his touch.

Isambard was sitting on the last desk at the back of the

office, as if nesting in the corner. Walking up to him, Jason watched Isambard writing notes with a fountain pen. His writing was beautiful, a long, flowing, elegant script that he imagined Dickens would have had when writing Oliver Twist. Or did he use a quill... or did they have typewriters in those days? His ignorance on such matters made him feel dumb, but to be fair, it was a long time ago.

"Hey, Isambard, what's cooking?" He felt like lightening the mood with a cool greeting, even though his tone was low. As usual though, it was completely lost on the birdlike man before him, who'd look more at home in a curiosity shop than a police station.

Isambard looked up in confusion. "I'm sorry, Mr Ives, I had sandwiches for my luncheon."

Jason had to laugh. He was learning to appreciate this odd character, who, despite his appearance and manner, had a heart of gold. He was just living the Victorian dream in his own way, and it seemed to suit him. Now Jason couldn't imagine him being any other way.

"Er, no, Isambard, I was just asking what you are doing?"

"Oh, of course," Isambard then smiled to show he understood. "I was entering the day's events into my journal; it is of no import really."

"Good, then maybe we better crack on with our side of the case. We have got a lot of work to get through today, and the media are baying for blood, mostly mine. I'm in the headlines again, and they seem to have a love / hate relationship with me. Not surprisingly they can't believe we haven't any more information to give them. But then, if they realised how little we really know, we'd definitely be up shit creek. Did you get any leads on Eddowes or Kelly? I want them both prioritised."

"Then I can be the bearer of some joyous and some

vexing news. Eddowes was discovered in Madrid about fifteen years ago. She was only twenty-one years old at the time. An accountant in the city. But after her discovery of being Eddowes, she left her entire life behind to become a nun on the pilgrim trail of Il Camino de Santiago, in northern Spain. I'd postulate that her experiences either frightened her in the eyes of God, or she is hiding from the world in as private a domicile as possible."

Ives looked a little disappointed. "Oh, sounds like she isn't going to say much then, and probably won't even agree to meet. Can you get me the details of the convent where she is living? I think I may just have to pop in and pretend that I'm passing; that way she'll have less of a chance to say no."

"Your hypothesis is most correct, Mr Ives, as that was the vexing news I had to break to you. I must also warn you, she has been asked on many occasions for her side of the tale, but the requests have always been less than fruitful, even when offered large sums of money. This includes several documentary makers and journalists 'popping in' so to speak, to the point that she has had solicitors involved. I would recommend abandoning that line of action sir, in the interests of all parties."

Jason was glad for the advice. He knew he had a habit of rushing into things, his impetuous nature always eager to get results as quickly as possible. That's what had landed him in a lot of trouble with the Mueller Nazi criminal case a few years back. But it had also started a friendship with himself and Martin Kale, which is incredibly useful in all things Awakening. Sometimes good things can come from mistakes.

He needed to find a way in with Eddowes. "So what do you suggest, Isambard? We can't just ignore that line of inquiry."

"Indeed," answered Isambard with conviction, but with no further contribution.

Ives waited ten long seconds for him to continue, but Isambard was lost in thought again.

Ives ran out of patience. "So... what do you suggest?"

His trance broken, Isambard twitched a little, as if he was re-booting. "May I suggest writing to her mother superior with some news articles appended to your notes? It would inform them about the return of the Ripper, and hopefully that would instigate a most positive response."

"Genius," remarked Jason, trying to build his confidence, "so if you can get her address to start with, and what about Kelly?"

"That is news that will frustrate and disappoint you the most I fear. Mary Jane Kelly has never been seen or recorded, which makes it quite possible that she has never been Awakened, or is still in-between bodies."

"Just our dumb luck," remarked Ives. It made him wonder about that in-between stage. One of the final mysteries of life and death yet to be cracked. What if one day it would be possible to communicate with that spiritual side? Imagine the questions they could ask, the lessons that could be learned. They could simply ask any of the Ripper's last four victims what had happened.

But what of that? Would they then imprison that soul or spirit if they could? As with Bjorkman's view, past life investigations and judgement were bad enough. Could you imagine the social unease of imprisoning people's souls?

Now it was time for Isambard to interrupt Jason's day dreaming. "I could ask my fellow Ripperologists if they have any information regarding Mary Jane Kelly? They are a very resourceful collection of investigators, with many years spent trawling the public and private libraries of the world."

Ives placed a hand on Isambard's bony shoulder. "That my friend, would be fantastic, but it would need to be with a close circle you can trust. We need anything they can think of to track this killer down. In my mind, they are a vital resource that we cannot ignore. There must be thousands of them all over the world. Do you think you can get a few of them to co-operate in confidence?"

"Without question sir, it is in their very nature to dig deep, and we have quite a few members who are serving or retired police officers; a few of quite some repute."

"Good, and I want to see if we can get Abberline to join us in the investigation. Hopefully he'll feel that it will improve his reputation by being involved, and tell us everything he really knows. His knowledge of Whitechapel and the investigation at that time is still as valuable as ever."

Isambard was not so sure. "I will embark on such a course of action if you wish, Mr Ives, after all, you are the boss, but it would be with some reticence to include Inspector Abberline."

"Come on, Isambard, he's just an opportunist. I definitely don't see him as a suspect, but if he is, then I will be able to see it a lot easier if he is kept close to me. Remember, keep your friends close, but your enemies closer. Until we can find Kelly... and I'm still hopeful she's out there somewhere, we will have to work with the secondary players. Eddowes and Abberline to start, and then other police officers and canonical victims when you get a chance."

It was clear that Isambard wasn't happy with Jason's suggestion and was about to disagree, an act against his very nature. "With respect sir, I just don't think we can take the chance on sharing such delicate information with him. Even if Abberline was only a borderline suspect, now as Rochelle, he is also a man of dubious commercial intent."

Jason looked out of the window watching the traffic on The Strand, as if he was looking for the Ripper again. "Okay, Isambard, I respect your view on this, so for the time being we will just do what Bjorkman wants, and keep an eye on this slippery character. But... if we get really desperate, we are going to have to learn to trust him a bit more. Agreed?"

"Irrefutably sir."

Chapter 30 – Post Mortem Details

DS Pascal was busy writing the exhibits down at the post mortem of Nadia Kurylenko. Her once attractive body has been reduced to its key elements, minus the parts they hadn't yet found. One of her kidneys was missing. *What is it with the Ripper and kidneys? Why is he so obsessed by them?* Pascal asked himself.

Dr Bartholomew was adding a few notes to his datacorder to give Pascal a little longer to write each and every sample taken by him. First they start with the body in its white plastic body bag, the ends twisted and stuck down with lots of sticky tape, making it look like a giant sickly sweet in its cheap wrapper.

Then the body is unwrapped and undressed by the mortuary technicians as the officers look on, collecting their thoughts and wondering how long this bloody post mortem will take. Each item found on the body is logged, this time by Pascal. It includes coins, e-cigs, drugs, chewing gum wrappers, etc. It is all part of the story, and may hold the clue to the murderer, no matter how small.

Nadia is stripped naked in a room full of people. Something that in our lifetimes we would feel very uncomfortable about, but here it is routine. The ID tag on the toe completes the loss of any dignity, but this is not the time for embarrassment or nausea, the natural responses to seeing naked or dead flesh.

This is the time for recording evidence, and hopefully for the forensic pathologist to determine the exact cause of death. Even if it does seem obvious because her head has been cut off. He has to find that precise cause, to find the one thing that ended her life on this world before anything else might have.

Such as empty lungs on a body found in a river, showing they had been dead before they were in the water. This means they didn't drown. Marks over or under the skin around the neck, or a crushed larynx, sometimes backed up by small speckles or red marks around the eye called petechia to show they have been strangled. Soot in the lungs and trachea to show if they died in a fire rather than placed there dead already to disguise the murder.

Toxicology to show poisons or drug use. Samples from blood or urine, or even hair, as the pathologist rips clumps out to get the roots. They can show long term drug use. Tricks of the trade, with one or two elements of this particular post mortem even used on the original Ripper victims. A link between these two different times in which so much has passed.

Pascal's hand is feeling cramped. Writing on each exhibit bag the details of the case and the victim's name, before entering the exhibit or sample taken. Blood, vaginal swab – inner and outer, Anal swab – inner and outer, wet and dry, stomach contents to ascertain her last meal (fish and potatoes in the case of Mary Kelly).

Slivers of heart, lung and kidney in a menu of death, until the top of the head is opened up with a spinning electric blade. The technician wedges a small key into the side of the skull to open up what is inside. That sickening crack that releases an intelligence, and exposes the brain in a way that we just don't see in normal life. Then it is sliced calmly and competently by the pathologist to check for any damage or disease, hoping that it is healthy, so as not to complicate the investigation.

In this particular case, they have had to reunite her organs, found strewn across her bedsit flat. After recording them too, they are all placed into a black bin liner, and fed back into her body cavity. All the parts reunited for the funeral. That is very important. The brain is either kept, or put in the cavity too, so a big roll of paper has to take its place in the head of the deceased. Paper made from wood. Wood for brains some might say.

But Pascal doesn't have time to consider all of this. He is too busy with exhibits and dealing with his guvnor's almost obsessive attention to detail. She is watching everyone like a hawk, and it is sending a spiky energy through the room. There isn't even the usual mortuary humour to alleviate the boredom of a seven hour post mortem. All anyone can do, is stand and stare at the Pathologist as he carries out his grisly task.

An hour later Bjorkman's mobile rang. She struggled to press the tiny answer button on her earpiece with her gloves on.

"Yes, Carter, tell me you have some good news for us."

The pathologist carried on, as the rest of the team listened in on her call.

"Aha... yes... really? About bloody time. So what have they found?"

At the word 'found', heads lifted like a herd of gazelles at the sound of a lion close by.

"Hmm, okay... just glove marks? Ah, of course."

Even the pathologist had stopped now, waiting for the conclusion of this call.

"Well that's no bloody use is it! What else?"

Silence in the mortuary.

"Oh, that sounds very interesting."

Silence from DCI Bjorkman as she processes the information.

Chapter 31 – Our Father Who Art in Heaven

Seb stretched out his crooked back as best he could. Sharp stabs of pain rushed from his spine to his hips and legs, but he refused to take any pain killers to ease his burden. His pain is his reminder of his sins, and a small price for him to pay.

As he laid out the song sheets for the coming church service, he reflected on the price that all good people pay to remain on the right path. His path had been as skewed as his spine, but now with his new-found faith and the friends that share it with him, everything is straightening out. Even his back.

He feels stronger and happier than he can ever remember. A peace and calm that is worth more than any money or possession.

Maybe it is time to get back in touch with his sister, his only living relative, and tell her the good news. Maybe he could convince her of the glory of God and get her to give her heart up for divine intervention just as he had.

And maybe one day he should tell her about Jack asking for his help.

But not just yet.

Chapter 32 – A Few Leads

In the end, the post mortem had lasted longer than expected. Complications with the quantity of bruises and cuts, all having to be recorded in a methodical fashion through notes and photography. Almost eight hours, an average working day for most people, spent standing up and looking at a mutilated corpse. Thankfully, the pathologist had stopped half way for a cup of tea and toilet break, but no time to get a meal. Nothing out of the ordinary in that respect, though.

It was now 10pm, and just enough time to drop off the exhibits at the station and have a quick meeting before heading home for a few hours sleep. Murder investigation isn't for lightweights.

Bjorkman rapped on the desk she was sitting on. "Okay, if I can have your attention for a few minutes, and then hopefully we can all Foxtrot Oscar to our loved ones or sad empty homes." She paused, and shot Jason a glance. "Before starting this shit all over again tomorrow morning."

Pascal, Ives, Isambard and Carter were her captive audience, all fighting yawns. "Elaborate on what we have from the SOCOs, Carter."

"Well ma'am, as I informed you at the post mortem, we found a small knife in the victim's bedsit. Unfortunately we still don't know who it belongs to, and it is too small to be one of the weapons used on the victim, but it was probably dropped during the scuffle."

Bjorkman wasn't impressed. "How do we know it's not one of the victim's knives then; surely in her line of work she must have had some for protection?"

Carter pulled out a photo of the knife taken earlier that day. "That's the interesting part. Isambard has identified it as a Victorian pocket knife. It has a very ornate sterling silver handle, dated 1894. I know that's a couple of years after the Ripper, but I'm sure that even he wasn't born with a silver knife in his mouth."

Ives groaned. "Nice... tonight's first Ripper based joke."

"I aim to please," said Carter with a smile on his face. "We then searched for some details and found it was made by the Whiting Manufacturing Co. Not exactly rare, but certainly more identifiable than a kitchen knife."

"Any finger marks?" Pascal asked hopefully.

"No, nothing, it's completely clean. The Ripper may be mad, but he is also very methodical in his forensic process. We might be able to track the knife back to its seller, but it's a long shot."

Bjorkman still looked a little encouraged. "Well, hopefully it's the breakthrough we have been looking for. What else has SOCO got for us?"

"Just the same as at the other scenes guv. Glove marks left all over the place, but no finger marks showing through, which means he is either wearing extra thick gloves, or double gloving. He knows what he is doing, that's for sure. We also found shoe marks from another popular brand of trainer. SOCO says that the mark is very clear, with no wear or tear. They look brand new, so probably bought specially. Problem is, without wear marks it's forensically useless.

"Were there not even any marks in blood?" asked Bjorkman incredulously.

"No not really. In blood we have the outlines of shoe marks, as if they are using forensic overshoes to keep the trainers clean, which means they might be wearing the whole forensic clobber for the mutilation process. It would certainly make it easier to escape undetected."

Ives was curious. "So the killer has very good forensic awareness, which is surprising for someone with a mindset from the 19th century. It probably indicates that their current life may be police related and that there is some interaction between both identities, but they still might not be conscious of each other's existence."

"Not necessarily just police officers, Ives, plenty of people watch crime shows all the time," said Bjorkman sarcastically.

"Yes, true, but then how are they getting the forensic gear in the first place?"

Carter pointed to his computer screen. "Online. Anyone can buy forensic gear from hundreds of sources."

Bjorkman wasn't finished. "Okay, let's just say the forensic suit could be police issue... but the Met alone has over 32,000 officers. Then we have the civil staff such as SOCOs, lab geeks, graphics, admin, techies, catering staff, cleaners, you name it, we got it. Add outside contractors that have access to our buildings and could slip something into their bags, and you have to be looking at over 100,000 people from the Met police alone."

"Oh, I see your point." Jason wasn't going to try and push anything at the moment.

Bjorkman continued. "And so what have you both got to offer? Any breakthroughs?"

Isambard stepped in to answer his DCI's question. "Oh indeed, we have been most industrious, dear boss. We have located the fourth canonical victim, Catherine Eddowes, who is now Sister Carlotta Valdez in the northern tip of Spain."

Pascal laughed. "A nun, I've heard it all now. Blimey, I might be reincarnated as a vicar one day."

"No chance, Pascal, not with your record." Now Bjorkman was making jokes.

Isambard continued. "It is our hope that she will grant us an interview to see if anything she says corroborates with Abberline's thoughts."

"What, we slog our guts out here whilst you both go off on a jolly to sunny Spain?" Now even Pascal was giving them a hard time.

Isambard looked indignantly at Pascal. "This would be an extremely rare interview, a one off in fact. It is invaluable to our collective process until we can determine the current location, or existence of Mary Jane Kelly."

"So still no Kelly then?" asked Bjorkman.

"No, dear boss. She is an elusive one I must confess, but these matters are never easy in our rather complex trail through history. I am also going to call an extraordinary meeting with the London sect of my Ripperologist society to ask for their assistance. I am optimistic that it will bear some fruit."

Bjorkman seemed to switch off half way through Isambard's dialogue. She turned to Pascal and Carter as if the other two were not in the room, but her mood was surprisingly light considering the consequences. "What about house to house, has anyone dug up anything from the neighbours?"

Carter just wanted to go home. "Nothing really ma'am. Yet again the localised cctv signals were screwed up, and being a knocking shop, the neighbours are used to seeing lots of men come in and out. No one admits to seeing anything. If ever there was a perfect victim for murder, prostitutes would seem to be it."

"Careful, Carter, Ives will think you are a suspect if you carry on like that," she joked, but with a stern look on her face. Then her whole demeanour changed as she continued. "Okay guys, this is, on the face of it, pretty depressing.

"Yet another murder and still we have next to no forensic evidence. A knife, that just because it's old doesn't make it his, and neighbours who are both deaf and blind. Fuck, even the Victorians had more than this.

"Find me some bloody cctv that hasn't been knocked out, or someone who saw something, pronto! This is fucking embarrassing, and if we, as a team, don't come up with something soon... we are going to get mullered by the press and by our governors."

Her mood had switched on a dime to perfect effect. None of them were tired now. They had been given a huge wakeup call that the shit was about the hit the fan.

"Okay, meeting over!"

Chapter 33 – A Night in With Libby

She felt awful. Lack of sleep can do that to a person; it affects your mood and your whole ability to function as a normal human being. Mild insomnia had hit her out of the blue as soon as she came out of her teens, which was so unfair. Just when most young people are discovering and exploring the world, hers closed up a little. It had changed lately though, and at first she thought that she had turned a major corner. Now she was sleeping longer, and even during the day sometimes, which was amazing, but she felt more tired than ever!

Her doctor is lovely, always sympathetic about such things, and says it's probably just an adjustment, and that her head is clearing itself. That's why she is having all the nightmares, to clear her subconscious, and that is why she is still tired. Makes sense - sort of. Lucky she works from home; it means she can catch up on her sleep through her naps in the afternoon, but she never seems to fully catch up with being herself.

Jason hadn't been helping the situation. In fact, looking back, it was about the time she met him that her insomnia changed its flow. She had been immediately attracted to the daft sod from that very first date at The Dog and Duck, but had felt wary of him too. She knew she had her baggage, who doesn't, but was he already aware of the skeletons in her closet? Could he really read her mind as was his reputation? It set her on edge every time she saw him, but he had never said anything.

Samantha also knows that she is quite sensitive to things, and her own insecurities are probably the cause of her weird dreams and tiredness. She just has to learn to relax more, take things in their stride. Jason is a catch by anyone's standards, she just has to find a way to make the fledgling relationship work.

Time to put her make-up on, even if it is just Libby coming over tonight for a movie and a few bottles of wine. After all, a girl has to look good, even if it is just for her own self esteem. At least she could rely on Libby for a fun evening. She is such a laugh.

Half an hour late, there was a knock on the door. Libby had never been one for punctuality, but she more than made up for it with stories of her own madcap life.

"So there I was, Sammy, face to face with the biggest tiger you've ever seen, and I was unarmed. I had nothing to protect myself with."

"Oh my God, what did you do?"

"I just walked past the cage and looked at the rest of the zoo."

"Oh you nutter!"

"Yes... but you wouldn't want me any other way would you?"

"Hmm, let me think about that one. More wine?"

The tapas and Rioja were a hit, and they had been too busy talking to watch a movie. Inevitably though, the conversation got round to Samantha's love life.

"Honestly, Libby, I don't know what to do. As soon as he got his leg over, he rushed away saying, in his deep husky voice, 'I have to go,' as if he is in a movie or something. And now he is 'too busy' to meet up ever again, or even vid-link."

"These things do happen though sweetheart, especially when a relationship is new. It takes time to sort out a rhythm... okay, maybe you sorted that bit out quickly, but you have to learn to trust each other."

Samantha took another sip of her wine and reluctantly nodded. "I guess so."

"Come on, Sammy, you said he took you somewhere really nice for your date, so he obviously wanted to make a special effort."

"Oh definitely, he took me to a restaurant on the thirtieth floor of The Shard."

Libby's eyes lit up. "What? You let him take you up the shard!"

Samantha covered her face in embarrassment. "Why does everything that comes out of your mouth sound disgusting?"

"Haha, you should see what goes *in* my mouth," replied Libby, rolling around with laughter.

Samantha hit her over the head with a cushion. "Libby!"

Libby was now laughing so hard that tears started forming in her eyes. Samantha couldn't help but laugh too. The best medicine in the world, and boy did she need it right now.

"Honestly though, Libby, I'm just not sure he's worth the bother."

"Why, was he no good in the sack?"

Samantha sat up straight, in a mock dignified manner, as if they were talking about his driving or dancing ability. "Actually he was very good in the sack, thank you very much for asking. Very loving and attentive."

"Well, you can't let him go then can you?"

"But he is always busy! Oh, you don't understand."

Libby stopped laughing. It was time for a little counselling for her best friend. She got up and sat next to Samantha on the sofa to give her a hug. "Ah, come on,

Samantha, it's not surprising he's busy, he's chasing the bloody Yorkshire Ripper."

"Jack the Ripper, Libby!" exclaimed Samantha in an exasperated tone.

"Yes, him too. So whatever happened about that guy with the scar? Jason was fantastic when he came over to rescue you. I almost dropped my knickers there and then. He was so gallant like."

Samantha rolled her eyes as she smiled. "He called the police and gave us a lift home. He didn't exactly ride up on a white horse."

"You are so fussy."

"Yeah I know, bane of my life. Anyway, the young officer got in touch. You know, the one who took my particulars down. Wink, wink, say no more." They were half way through their second bottle and it was showing.

Libby saluted Samantha. "Aye aye, captain...I love a man in uniform."

"Well, he was more of a boy unfortunately. Anyway, he said that the man with the scar was known back in Liverpool. He has been done for ABH and sexual harassment before, but nothing more serious than that. They had a 'serious' chat with him, but they can't really do any more than that. He was proper scary though Lib, he wouldn't let go of my arm at one point."

Libby rubbed Samantha's shoulders to comfort her. "Which perfectly illustrates why meeting someone nice and trustworthy like Jason is worth the wait. This Ripper will be caught soon and then Jason will be all yours. When are you seeing him again?"

"He messaged me late last night, apologising and saying that he'd like to get together next week. So we are aiming for Wednesday. I'm going to cook something nice."

"Well there you go, Sammy, I'm sure you'll charm his

pants off."

Samantha ignored her smutty remark with a friendly smile. "I know, I know, I'm sure he really likes me... unless he's really a player... or until the next case comes up. I've seen his type before Lib, you know I have."

"Yeah I know hun."

Libby then thought quietly for a moment. "So, Sammy, can I ask a favour?"

"Of course, darlin', anything?"

"If you do dump Jason, can I have him?"

Samantha looked at her friend. She was shocked and dumbfounded... then saw the mischievous grin on her face.

"Oh you bloody fucker!"

Chapter 34 – Packing for Spain

Isambard had worked wonders. Not only had he found the convent housing Catherine Eddowes, but he'd somehow managed to charm his way past the Mother Superior and get Eddowes (Sister Carlotta Rodriguez), to agree to her first ever interview. They were both sitting in the canteen area chatting over a cup of tea.

"How did you manage that?" asked Jason, impressed.

"It was not as difficult as you might envisage, Mr Ives. Indeed, if it were not for the modern minded countenance of the indomitable Mother Superior, we might still be whistling in the proverbial wind. She keeps abreast of the world's news to remind her sisters of the trials and tribulations of the outside world. Thus they appreciate and worship the sanctuary of their quiet and simple life even more."

"Oh, so she knew of the Ripper case?" Jason wasn't sure why he was so surprised. It wasn't as if they were missionaries in deepest, darkest Africa.

"Most certainly. In actual fact, she had already spoken to Sister Rodriguez about the matter so that they could both pray for his capture. Hence, when they received my most humble message beseeching an interview with Sister Rodriguez, they saw it as a sign that it was their holy duty to assist."

Jason grew excited by the prospect of a useful Awakening session at last. "Wow, so she's willing to talk about everything?"

"Oh, not quite dear sir. It will take small and very gentle steps to elicit her full assistance. She has expressly stated that under no condition will she go through an Awakening session again, even if it is by your fine hand, but she has agreed to a witness statement of sorts, or at least, to be questioned for a short period on the matter."

"Okay, I can work with that."

"And with the proviso that she will only meet with you, no one else. She was quite adamant on the matter, and to be honest, the sooner you can meet the better. The Mother Superior feels she may change her mind over time if her resolve weakens. This is a very brave step for her after almost fifteen years of hiding away in the convent."

Jason could appreciate that fact, and was just thankful that she was willing to talk at all. He could get away in the next couple of days, but that would mean rescheduling his date with Samantha. She wasn't going to like that, but there was no other choice. The case comes first, not some silly romantic interlude. That sounded harsh in his mind, but he was trying to remain focussed.

He slapped Isambard on the back, almost spilling his drink. "Thank you for sorting that out. Good job, I'm genuinely impressed. Now get to work and find me Kelly," he demanded with a wink, but he was also half serious.

Isambard beamed. "I have taken steps to accomplish that particular task already. An extraordinary meeting for the London chapter of the International Ripperological society has been duly called, and set for this Thursday, so it would seem we will both be immersed in our investigations of the canonical victims, only separated by geography."

Jason's tea was not quite sweet enough, so he reached for another sachet. "That's great. Any news on the other three women?"

"Alas, very little news. Elizabeth Stride is the only other one of the five canonical victims thus far discovered.

I remember it quite well actually, as it was barely a couple of years ago. She was now a German lady by the name of Amelie Schmitt. She'd only finished her Awakening foundation the year before, so she was still quite young at only nineteen years old."

Jason looked concerned. "Was?"

"Yes. Sadly she was mortally injured in a car accident not long after."

"That's terrible." He was genuinely saddened. Anyone's death being so sudden is always sad, but when it is someone young who has just started going out into the world, it makes it far worse. All her hopes and dreams rubbed out by a freak accident. But then Angela had only been nineteen when the Ripper had snuffed out her life.

"So did Amelie say much about her past life as Elizabeth Stride before she died?"

Isambard looked at his notes. "In actuality sir... no. She had been interviewed on several occasions by different groups, including the German chapter of my Ripperological society, but she was a little reticent to share her experiences, thus her contribution to our cause appears quite meagre."

"Hmm, maybe if she'd have had more time she'd have learnt to share more."

"Indubitably. Fate can strike us any time, and none know how it will touch us."

"Wow, deep words."

Isambard looked up and smiled. "It is most gracious of you to say so sir."

"So what did we learn from Amelie then?"

"Just a stereotypical glimpse into the life of a woman of the night in Victorian London I'm afraid. An unhappy life in some ways, but a strong community of friends through her co-workers and the people who lived around her."

Jason had heard reports like this before. "Oh yes, of course, communities were a lot tighter then than they are now. People knew so much more about each other, which is probably why they were getting a lot more witnesses statements than we are now. It's amazing, we don't even know our immediate neighbours these days."

Isambard looked like he actually remembered them. "So true sir."

"I wish you'd just call me Jason, you nitwit, you're so formal."

"It is my very nature."

"Yes I know, but one day I hope you will learn to trust me enough to relax and call me by my first name."

Isambard looked embarrassed by Jason's warmth towards him, so he just continued with the few details he had. "Thank you." He then gave a little cough to clear his throat. "Ahem, returning to your question, Amelie went on record as saying she had no idea who the Ripper may have been. There were plenty of rumours in those days, but with very little to evidence them. In consequence, they were nothing more than gossip. Typically, she could not remember much of her life, and could not think of anyone on that last evening following her."

"So, a dead end?"

"It would appear so."

Jason was feeling frustrated again. If he'd have known Amelie at the time, he may have been able to help her remember those last few hours in better detail, or even closer to her death. Every avenue they went down, the Ripper seemed to be getting lucky breaks. Well at least they had Eddowes now, and he was determined to get her to remember and share as much as possible. This could be the breakthrough they needed.

That was it. He would get over to Spain as soon as

possible for an interview and find out who Jack the Ripper had been once and for all. "Okay, can you please give me the Mother Superior's details so I can set up an appointment?"

Isambard handed him a note with all the details. "Without hesitation."

Jason took the note. "Good work, Isambard. I'm going to book my flight and pack my bags before anything else gets in the way of our inquiry."

Isambard rubbed his small dry hands together in glee. His whole adult life had been spent in trying to solve the riddle of the Ripper, with records posted online and the assistance of Ripperologists the world over debating on forums.

Now at last, he was involved in a new lead of the investigation with the witness and victims themselves.

This was going to be very interesting.

Chapter 35 – Bjorkman's Bedside Manner

Bjorkman pulled back the covers and got into bed. She lay in her quiet bedroom hoping that she could clear her mind of the thousand issues running through her head, but that just made things worse. Trying not to think of something always does that; it makes it all the more prominent.

So, not to think of the case. Don't think about the Ripper. Don't think about Jason as a damn past life investigator who she is attracted to and repelled by. Don't think about her ex...

Her damn ex... David. *Oh God no. Don't make me think about him now.* Too late, her mind is now running towards that particular hell. *Why did I have to meet him, why did he have to turn out to be such a manipulative bastard and make me do those things?* Tears started forming in her eyes. *"Fuck, I'm still crying after all this time!"*

She got up to get a glass of water. Not because she was thirsty, but to try and divert her mind. She could watch a little TV of course, or try to read a book, but she knew she'd still be reading through half the night. Also that she'd read all the books she wanted to from her collection. Self-help books or bloody detective novels. Why on earth would she read those? But she would on occasion, just to see how authors would solve their perfect crimes.

Their crimes born in their minds. How fucking perfect it all worked out for them. Everything fitted neatly into their line of logic, and although the hero of the story would undoubtedly have their personal problems (some truth there then), they never really seemed to be thrown off course. She'd commented on that to a friend once, and they just said, "Well that's why they are the great detective,

Sabina. They are tenacious, they fight back against everything that is thrown at them, but never get distracted away from the truth. That's just like you. You are a great detective."

Kind words, but really? Just like me? Sabina wasn't so sure. Her life was a mess. Her whole life had been thrown into the Metropolitan police. She had sacrificed everything, and for what? She should have learned from her father's tragic tale. The Met had abandoned him in the end to save their own faces. As soon as there were any doubts to his character they had dropped him like a hot potato. The bastards had deserted him and they would just as likely desert her too.

Pain. Sabina got up again, this time to go to the bathroom. Have a pee and forget. Turn the light on to blast the sudden memories away. Fuck, she might as well do some more work, but she is too exhausted. Too tired to work, and too tired to sleep. On returning to her bed she put the bedside lamp on at its lowest setting; just enough to see a little detail in the room. She would stare at the curtains to try and focus purely on them to empty her mind. It would help her to forget *him* if she concentrated on the fine detail of those curtains.

Oh for Christ's sake, David had helped her choose those curtains!

Chapter 36 - The Convent

Jason had been enjoying the pilgrim trail, even though he'd only picked it up for the last few kilometres. Sister Margarita had kindly set up the meeting with Carlotta, so he could have parked at the convent, but the walk was a luxury. It gave him the time to compose his thoughts so that he was ready for what would be a difficult interview.

The Camino de Santiago (otherwise known as St. James's path) is a series of pilgrimage routes that covers the topmost area of Spain. The main route to Santiago follows an earlier Roman trade route all the way along the Atlantic coast of Galicia, ending at Cape Finisterre. During the medieval period, war and plague had made the pilgrimage very difficult, with numbers dwindling to only a few a year completing the route to Santiago de Compostela. As Jason looked around him, it was now packed with people more interested in the social hiking scene than religious forgiveness.

It had a lovely feel to the place though, with people at their best; enjoying the atmosphere, the scenic surroundings and company of like-minded people. The whole route can take months to achieve. Maybe one day he'd come back to walk part of the route for a week or so, just to sample it properly.

Then way too soon for his liking, Jason reached his destination. La Magdalena, a small and simple convent that has been the home of Eddowes (as Carlotta) for the last fifteen years. Hidden on the edge of the small town of San Zoilo, but just big enough to have a few of the local white storks nested on the roof, as if they'd been there since the time of St. James himself.

The old wooden door had a large knocker in the shape of a scallop shell, the iconic symbol of the route itself, and was just begging to be used in as loud a fashion as possible. Jason fought temptation, and knocked softly out of deference to the Franciscan nuns who live there. The sound still rattled in the empty hall behind the wood, making him wonder how much louder it would have been had he let his childish energy loose.

At last, the oldest woman Jason had ever seen answered the door. She looked at him with half closed eyes, but could still see he was a tourist, or 'Guiri' as the locals call them. She beckoned him in with a vein-lined hand because she spoke no English. A woman from pre Awakening days, and kept that way through her seclusion here.

Through the hallway she shuffled along, until finally pointing to an uncomfortable looking chair. "Here," was her only contribution to the conversation. Jason sat down as instructed and waited quietly as he studied the artwork on the walls, all lending itself to the religious atmosphere. Within minutes a smiling ruddy faced woman came to greet him, speaking surprisingly good English.

"Ah, not all of us have been here forever, Mr Ives," she remarked when he complimented her English. "I was born in Madrid, but studied in London as a young girl. Hmm, such happy times."

A twinkle in her eye made Jason wonder about her history. "Thank you so much for allowing me this visit, Mother Superior. Is Sister Carlotta Valdez ready?"

"Yes, but she is incredibly nervous, so be gentle on her please."

From the hall, Jason was led up a flight of stone steps to an ornate landing decorated with paintings and flowers; the light streaming in through the shuttered windows to add texture to the walls. They then entered the second doorway into a more comfortable looking room, which Jason guessed was reserved for greeting visitors.

"Carlotta will be with you shortly, Mr Ives."

The Mother Superior left him to ponder his thoughts to the sound of a ticking clock.

Chapter 37 - Ripperology

The large hall was dimly lit by the old-fashioned gas lamps burning softly in their glass mounts, illuminating the portraits of the dearly departed alumni. The flickering light gives the surreal effect of movement to these otherwise austere paintings, breathing them back to life once more. On cold winter nights, Isambard loves to place his hands over the glass lamps to warm them. Fire holds an odd attraction to him, as if part of his DNA is related to a moth.

Another meeting had not been due for three weeks, but Isambard had called an extraordinary meeting of utter importance. A good turnout for what was otherwise a grim June evening, still waiting for the overdue summer to properly arrive. The wind could be heard howling outside, along with the rain, battering the newly painted sash windows in its futile attempts to get inside.

He isn't used to speaking so centrally in this forum, an environment that both intoxicates and spooks him in equal measure, but he now has a mission to fulfil. Isambard stood on the small platform, protected by only a small stand and a gavel as he addressed the crowd before him.

"Thank you, fellow acolytes for braving the elements in this miserable weather. Let us get to the crux of the matter as swiftly as possible, so that we can enjoy the rest of the evening with less drama."

Isambard smiled weakly, as if apologising for dragging people from their homes. "Some have been privy to the fact that I have been involved with Scotland Yard in a somewhat desperate attempt to solve our society's newest question... is this the real Ripper prowling our streets?"

Isambard stopped for a moment to review the room. He

had their full attention. "The press have been publishing their hypothetical deliberations with their usual gusto, as to who this new Ripper may be, in whatever form we assume he is in now. Therefore, it is with some trepidation that I have to confirm that their worst fear is probably true. We now believe these to be the deeds of Jack the Ripper himself, by taking over his current identity."

A collective exclamation filled the hall at the confirmation that the very man they have spent so much time investigating, has come back to haunt them in the very streets that they live in. Isambard raised his hands to quieten them down before he could continue.

"Can I remind you all that our vow of confidentiality within these hallowed rooms forbids any of us sharing this information until it has been sanctioned by our ruling committee. I know that you will be eager to share and discuss many of the new facts emerging on a daily basis, but we must remain silent for as long as possible, in a bid to find the Whitechapel murderer before he kills again. Any information we share could put lives at risk if the Ripper has the ear of even just one of us."

A murmur filled the room. Isambard politely let them chatter for a few moments, before banging his gavel to regain their attention. "Even as we speak, Mr Jason Ives, the renowned past live investigator who has been in the news regarding this matter, is in Spain talking to the reincarnated Catherine Eddowes."

Again the crowd erupted into the sound of their surprised reaction. Again the gavel found its mark to regain control. 'Knock knock'.

"Quiet please, so I may continue in a composed fashion. I am sure that you are all aware that this is the first time Catherine Eddowes has agreed to talk to anyone regarding her life, and she is doing it against all her fears because she knows he is killing again. Eddowes has somehow found a courage that hopefully most of us may never be required to do; to delve back into her memories of that most painful of times.

"She is displaying a fine example of that same duty that we must adhere to when needed; which is why I find myself here today in front of my peers and colleagues to ask you to also assist in this same investigation. I am asking you to go to all your groups and friends to ask if they have heard if Mary Jane Kelly is alive again."

The eruption of voices filled the hall once more. This was going to be a long evening. Isambard was relieved to have the use of the gavel but was having to use it more aggressively. 'Knock knock'. The sound of the hammer against the wooden mount abruptly cutting a new path of silence.

"Please, if I could retain your undivided attention for a short while longer to ask for your collective assistance in this matter of the greatest import. Mr Ives and I have good reason to believe that Mary Jane Kelly may have known who the Ripper was, or at least, that she holds information that could point us in the right direction. An interview with her could be the difference that solves this case, which has effectively been our shared case for so many years, and now could be the difference between life and death."

The implications of Isambard's words were sinking in. "I know that there have been no reports of her current existence, and that of course, she could exist betwixt states, or as yet un-Awakened, but we have to hope this is not the case. From our experiences so far, the canonical victims have been so badly affected by their recollections that they usually want to remain anonymous. Either because they are ashamed of their previous position or fear he will strike again. Now, with Jack's return, they will be more frightened than ever."

George Glover was watching from the back of the crowd. A member of the society for over forty years; from the days before Awakening had changed everyone's world and tracing the identity of the Ripper had been his personal intellectual challenge and hobby to pass the time. Now in these crazy days, it seems the Ripper could possibly trace everyone back if he so wished. Time has been turned on its head. Almost anything now seems possible.

He held a hand up to speak. "Mr Smythe, can you elaborate on this matter?"

Isambard knew George Glover. They had debated on many issues regarding the Ripper, and whilst they didn't always see eye to eye, a mutual respect had built up over the years. That is not always the case with Ripperologists. In fact, their forums can be seen bursting with seething posts from every rank and file. The job of working together as a group, without treading on their stubborn egos and ideologies borne of utter conviction, was going to be a difficult task.

"I am sorry to say that I cannot at this precise point in time. Hopefully, as the case comes to a close, Mr Ives and I can disclose more details about the case and our findings."

Shouts suddenly erupted from the crowd. "What, just so you can publish your new findings when it suits you?"

Isambard was taken aback. "No... no, no. This is beyond us trying to make a point in our theories, or trying to make a name for ourselves with a new publication. This is a time for us to set aside our different suspicions and work towards making history together, by doing something truly good. That is how we will catch this felonious fiend. This daemon should not be walking our streets again, and he most definitely should not be allowed to murder any more women.

Glover was moved by this impromptu speech and embarrassed by his colleagues' reaction. He raised his hand once more. "I call aye to, Mr Smythe." He was proposing his agreement to the crowd, supporting Isambard with his position within the group.

Isambard raised his hand once more in the traditional response. "Who says aye?"

Hands started shooting up, the psychology of peer pressure overcoming any petty politics. They all knew he was right, and if making a simple inquiry could make such an impact in this latest chapter of their lifelong investigation, then so be it.

"We say aye." It was unanimous.

Isambard was almost moved to tears by the sheer weight of emotional tension he had felt. "Then I accept aye. My brothers and sisters, from our constables to our commissioner ranks, we can all go out and find Mary Jane Kelly once and for all. I believe discretion and understanding will rule the day, to encourage her to open up and trust us with this most delicate information. Please make it clear that we will not divulge anything to anyone. It is of the utmost importance in the message we are putting across. Confidentiality is the key, and will hopefully earn her trust. As such, all information is to come directly to me."

For the final time that evening, Isambard picked up his gavel to close the meeting.

'Knock knock... knock knock knock'.

Chapter 38 – The Testament of Eddowes

Sister Carlotta Valdez walked into the room like a church mouse; timid, broken, afraid of her own shadow. Straightaway, Jason worked on keeping her calm, using soft tones, no sudden movements, and promises of not pushing her any further than she wanted in the interview. He could see a steely resolve in her though, a small, but solid pillar of strength emanating from within.

Jason could see that she wanted to talk, maybe for the first time since finding out she had been Eddowes and remembering that life of destitution in Victorian London. This was her chance to strike back at the man who butchered her so long ago. Now, as a nun, she was sitting on the chair opposite him, her hands clasped and resting on her knees.

Jason brought her up to date with how the investigation was going so far, and why he was digging up the past to try and catch the murderer roaming London right now. She nodded in understanding, but said very little. Her English was okay, it was just that she preferred to keep quiet unless it was absolutely necessary to speak. It was time to begin the interview.

"Do you mind if I ask you a few questions now, Carlotta?"

She nodded. Yes.

"Great. I know it can be quite painful looking back, but do you remember anything about the night you died as Catherine Eddowes?"

She shook her head. No.

"Nothing?" Jason was surprised.

"A little, not much," her Spanish accent adding sadness

to her brief statement.

"Anything you can remember could lead to a clue, Carlotta, no matter how small you think it is. Do you remember the evening of September 29th 1888, or during the day, if it gives any clues?"

Carlotta looked ashamed. "I had been drinking. I was drunk. I was always drinking. People do not realise how addictive alcohol is, especially when living in rubbish in street."

Jason tried to reassure her. "I am not here to judge on your life, Carlotta, and to be honest, looking at the records of the area, your whole situation in Whitechapel seems to have been very normal. Just relax, take a deep breath and tell me what you know about that day, including who you thought at the time was Jack the Ripper."

She shrugged her shoulders. "I'm not sure who I think it was." She was doubting her own memories. Not surprising after so many years of trying to push them out of her mind again.

Jason glanced at his notes. "Looking at police reports from that time, they say that you came back from the countryside where you'd been working as a hop picker. Apparently you were going to try and claim the reward for information on the Whitechapel Murderer. On 28th of September, you'd been sleeping in a place called... 'The Casual Ward' in Shoe Lane, and during that time, you told the superintendent of the ward that you thought you knew who the killer was. Does that sound right?"

"More or less," she responded in a typically Spanish fashion.

"So who did you think was the Whitechapel murderer when you said that?"

Carlotta shuffled uncomfortably on her hard backed chair. "I don't know, I was just trying to make some money, and I had my doubts about her Joe, so I thought I might point him out."

That phrase again, 'her Joe'. Jason had to tread carefully here; he didn't want to push her down any particular path. "Who was 'her Joe,' Carlotta?"

Carlotta looked confused at the question. "You know, her Joe... Joseph Barnett, he was her man."

Ives thought he'd better try from another angle. "Have you read any of the reports from that time?"

She shook her head and lowered her voice to almost a whisper. "No, I just want to forget it. Wouldn't you?"

"Yes I would. Completely and utterly, but I have to ask these questions, Carlotta, I hope you understand?"

"Yes."

"Well, we have had a look at Joseph Barnett, and we are not so sure about him being a credible suspect, but that is why I am here, so you can put us right. Why did you think it might have been him?"

"Because he had a fierce temper, and he didn't like working girls." She then paused for a moment, and looked him straight in the eye for the first time since meeting. "Is this just between you and me?"

Now it was time for Ives to look a little uncomfortable. "Not quite I'm afraid, but to be totally honest with you, we are desperate, so I am willing to limit the amount of people to the absolute minimum, and if that means just me for certain things, then so be it. We have to catch this murderer before he strikes again."

Again the nod, but this time it was slow and unsure. She had something, Ives was certain of it. He had to get her to confide in him. "Why don't you just start small, and we'll see how much you want to talk about on this matter?"

"There is no 'small', Jason, only big." She then took a deep breath to confront her past, and started talking about herself in the third person to try and create some emotional distance.

"Catherine Eddowes was jealous of Mary Kelly for many reasons. Her youth, her beauty, her living a luxury life with the rich gentlemen. She'd had it all and threw it away because of the booze."

Jason was pleased she was finally opening up. "So you do honestly think it could have been Joseph Barnett who killed you both?"

"No, not now, but I had not thought it through at the time. I just thought he was in the right place at the right times for the earlier murders, but now I don't really think it was him. He had a quick temper, but he was soft really. It's just that..." Her voice trailed off, as if she had lost her train of thought, but was now hearing whispers of new ones.

"Mary had said something to me. She'd told me once that she was afraid of her Joe, that he had a dark side. I'd said something to her about leaving him, but she said she was er, 'mortally attracted to his money'. I remember those words because they were such a funny thing to say. Joseph Barnett had no money." The accents and intonations of Victorian London were seeping back into Carlotta's language now.

"So you think it could have been another Joe?"

"I do not know, we... she and Mary, were both so drunk, nothing made much sense, and Mary could get nasty after a few drinks so it could have meant anything or nothing."

Jason felt they were going round in circles. "Forgive me that I ask, but why did you say you knew who the Ripper was then?"

"I was being stupid and desperate for some money, and if it had turned out to be her Joe, then I'd have been paid well for it." Her English was improving all the time, the link in her subconscious from her time as Eddowes growing stronger as she looked back into her memories of her Awakening.

Jason suddenly wondered if that was why Barnett had left Kelly just before her murder, because he was afraid the police were going to talk to him. But he couldn't stay away from Kelly either, visiting her often and eventually being a suspect after her death; released after just four hours questioning without further suspicion, even though he had a plausible motive in the whole matter.

"Actually, Carlotta, Inspector Abberline who was dealing with the case, now thinks it was another Joe too, not Barnett. Can you think of anyone Mary might have spoken about like that, someone important enough for her to call him 'my Joe'?"

She sighed. "Everyone was called Joe in those days, Joe the butcher, Joe the baker, Joe the tobacco seller, not to mention several regulars of hers."

"But were any of them special to her?"

"No, I think not." Then Carlotta closed her eyes to look into the place she feared most. Ives remained quiet to give her the time to remember. "No, I cannot remember."

Jason knew it was time to employ a few more memory techniques using subtle key words as NLP. It would boost her confidence in her memories as he examined her micro-expressions. Using this method, he could tell if she was really remembering things, or trying to fill in the gaps with her imagination. When he had mentioned the words 'client' and 'special' a tiny glint of recognition lit up, so he asked her again.

"You are doing really well, Carlotta. I am sure you will be able to remember **a special client**. Just let any conversation with Mary **drift into your mind** with Joe in the background, and then **the memory will follow**."

Carlotta stared at her hands for a short while to clear her mind. A couple of minutes passed as Jason encouraged her mind to wander off, then she showed a very small smile. "I remember, there was one client."

This small memory opened up the door. "Yes... yes, it is all coming back to me because she would brag about a gentleman customer who had a thing for her. He was like a lost puppy, and had followed her from the fancy brothel in the West End that she used to work at. She said he used take her around London in carriages, treat her like a lady, even took her to Paris once, but I never really believed her. Once or twice she'd called him *my Joe*, like she owned him."

Jason grew very optimistic. "Was there a second name, or did she say where he lived?"

"No, she never used last names for her gentlemen, but she did say he was from north London somewhere. I am sorry, I cannot remember where."

This was frustrating. Carlotta had categorically stated that she would not let Jason put her through an Awakening, as it was just too painful a memory to explore. He understood her point completely, after all, the Awakening as Eddowes had completely changed her life, pushing her to seek refuge in a convent, but now he had to push her as hard as he dared. Every little detail hanging in the balance and dragged from the darkest reaches of her mind could help.

"You are doing really well, Carlotta, so take your time, think back as much as you can to that memory of Mary Kelly talking to you about her Joe. If you can think of an area, it could really help our investigation... you can remember the conversation."

Tears started forming in her eyes as she started wringing her hands, looking deeper than she had ever dared. "Near Camden I think," she blurted out, relieved that she could run away again.

Near Camden. It was better, but not a lot. After a few minutes, it became evident that she wasn't going to remember more. Time to tackle the hardest question of them all before he lost her cooperation. "So I'm going to have to ask you just once more to try and remember anything that might lead to the identity of the Whitechapel murderer, Carlotta. Don't worry, I'm here to make sure you feel as safe as possible. I am specially trained to recognise traumatic memories and any stress related side effects. I will keep you completely safe on this one, you have my word."

Carlotta looked him up and down, this stranger with words of comfort that had a very trusting face. This was her moment to try and make a difference, to fight back against her past. She began talking again, but this time as Eddowes, taking ownership of her past life once more... God save her.

"It was a day like most. Just surviving in squalor, making ends meet. I remember pawning some shoes to get food, but as usual, it went on booze too. I should have just got on with talking to the police about Barnett, but I was afraid of the repercussions and too drunk to think clearly, so I thought I would just take my time."

Ives was nodding to acknowledge what she was saying. "Go on."

"My head was full of such nonsense. How can a life just take over your mind to the point in which you cannot see all the mistakes you keep making?"

"That is just part of our conditioning, Carlotta, it happens to us all. We all get caught up in the moment, or in the plans we make for our lives." He looked at his notes again. They mentioned a visit to her daughter on that last day. "Can you remember going to see your daughter to get some money?"

Carlotta threw her hands up to cover her face. "She wouldn't open the door, she was ashamed of me, so I went back into town and found another gent to give me money, a regular of mine."

"Could he be a suspect?"

"No, he was a good salt, just his missus didn't understand him, so he'd come to me on occasion. We done the... the... business in an alley, but then he wanted to buy me another drink until he regained his vigour. We both had too much as usual. The next thing I remember is a police officer talking to me in Aldgate high street."

"Can you remember much after that, Catherine?" Ives using her previous name to keep her in the moment.

Her hands were now shaking. "I can't remember her murder if that is what you are asking. I was just looking for a little extra money to pay for somewhere to sleep that night, otherwise I'd end up at The Casual Ward again. They were already unhappy with me because I'd been making a fuss and had a row with one of the other girls.

"Dr Barnardo was there a little while ago, such a lovely man, always helping us and the local children." A smile appeared on her face from the kindness shown to her from so long ago. "My last memory was walking along Mitre Square I think.... or talking to a sailor. He was just messing me around though, he didn't have any money, so I walked off. Oh... everything has gone hazy, as thick as the fog we used to get."

"Sorry, Catherine, but I need you to really concentrate. Visualise the square as you walk along it."

Carlotta had had enough. "For what, Mr Ives? To give me nightmares for another fifteen years, just so I can give you a drunken description of someone who it might not even be? What are you going to do with that? It is unfair of you to come here and ask me these questions. He was just a man who hated women... London was full of them."

She was looking very tired now, and her body language was showing she wanted to leave. Jason knew it wasn't wise to push any more.

"Thank you for your time, Carlotta. Please do seriously consider letting me put you through an Awakening sometime though. I can use a technique that lets you move and talk through your trance, so you would still retain control."

Too much. She stood up and walked towards the door. "Never, Mr Ives. Never again. If I could rid myself of these cruel memories then I would. Surely that is what death is for is it not, to let us forget the pain we have endured?"

She didn't wait for an answer. "I'll get one of the Sisters to show you the way out."

Chapter 39 – Knife Attack

Jack was furious. They had his knife. The Russian tart had distracted him and knocked the knife out of his pocket. He had been weak and stupid. He hated himself. Loathed and despised himself... and his repugnant body that grovelled to its masters.

It was his knife. He had found it in Portobello market in Notting Hill. The stallholder had been naughty selling it to him really, as it should have been licensed, but antiques can be sold under many different categories, and lost in a general description of Victoriana. He'd had one just like it back in the day. It wasn't sharp enough to be a killing tool, but it was small and compact enough as a second line of defence. It cut his fruit nicely too.

At least they'd get nothing from the knife. He'd cleaned it good and proper before leaving home, so no prints on it. Jack looked at his hands and tried to focus on the lines and ridges on his fingers. The loops and whorls as the experts like to call them. He must have left plenty behind in 1888, and it amazed him that even with these unique marks, and the blueprint of DNA, they still hadn't managed to track him down from exhibits seized at the original scenes. Time had taken care of that side of things at least.

They didn't know who he had been... and they'd always been wide off the mark, but now... now they were getting a little closer. Apparently they were questioning Abberline and his old victims, with that Eddowes girl hiding in Spain. *What's the point of murdering them if they are only going to come back and talk?*

Maybe he should go to Spain and sort her out once and

for good. He liked the idea of that. And now they are looking for his Mary too. The idea threw lots of different emotions into his head. If they found her, it might give him the chance to make amends; to plead for her forgiveness. But she would never accept him like this. Maybe he should find her first and get her to agree to a suicide pact. The both of them could die together and come back in their proper bodies; true love conquering all.

He banged his head against the wall in frustration. Even he knew how mad that made him sound. True love, what did she know about true love? If she was thirsty enough for another drink she'd sell her dainty box to any sailor who had a pretty penny. It was her ruin and had been the death of her in the end. Not him, he was just the blunt instrument that fate had picked out to complete her bloody task. Maybe that is why he'd been made into a monster in the first place.

All these people from his past walking the earth again, it made him think. Could his mother or father be out there too? Or Jenkins the school bully who'd punched him in the face on the last day of term? Father O'Brian had touched him up many a time when he was too small to say anything, and told young Joseph that it was all very normal, just God's way of giving a little innocent pleasure... but a secret nonetheless. Surely he should still be rotting in Hell?

But no, if Father O'Brian should be in Hell, then surely so should he. Unless these really were God's words running through his mind, tempting and coercing him to find yet another girl to butcher. A message to whores the world over to change their ways. Down with all whores! The message he'd seen in those fake letters. Yes, people had agreed with him, they knew he was on the right path and all added to the smoke screen with letters and postcards to confuse the Yard and the committee.

The voices had been pulling him in every direction lately. He wanted to stop his mission for a while, if only for a little peace and to let the path run cold, but he was still hearing orders in his head to kill. His mother's voice was dominant for the moment though, and she was ordering him to stop. How could his mother's voice have followed him through time, and possibly be alive in another body at the same time? Would you know if you met them? Even before this damned black magic called Awakening had arrived... would you know? Or would you end up courting your mother, brother, daughter, sister, etc. It made him feel sick just at the thought of it.

That last murder had been difficult, and who knows what they might find from the knife, but it had made him feel better for a short while. Watching their life fade away has a very calming effect, as if he is transferring all his guilt into the girl at that very last moment, and as executioner, he is purging his own sins so they die with her.

The urge is building up inside him again. He is confused; the angel and devil sitting on each shoulder offering advice.

Time for a thrill?

Time to sit still?

Time to kill?

Chapter 40 – Shadows

Everyone had left the great hall; back into the night from whence they came, leaving Isambard to close everything up. He set the controls to turn off the gas lamps, and chuckled to himself that health and safety required computers to turn off a gas lighting system. In a way though, it reflected the marriage of old and new, much like the society itself, with its faux Victorian themes, kept alive in 2065.

And he hadn't been surprised by the lack of information on Mary Kelly either. She had always remained a mysterious character, with little more known about her than the Ripper himself. In fact, if it had not been for the statement from her lover Joe Barnett to the police after her murder, then even less would be known. But even his details in the statements are held with a great deal of caution. Odd that they should not trust his words, and yet he has never had a convincing case brought against him by the thousands of Ripper investigators over the years.

The storm had blown itself out, leaving the air very still. It seems strange after all the noise earlier in the evening, as if the wind has been frightened away, leaving an eerie atmosphere with a tale to tell. Just the alarm to set now, before he can return home to his family, a welcome relief after such a long day. But then Isambard heard the sound of footsteps by the main entrance doors. Crisp, quiet steps, as if someone were trying to creep up on him.

Isambard froze as the hairs on the back of his neck stood on end. Usually he wasn't so easily frightened, but the whole setting lent itself to unsettling his nerves.

"Hello?" he called out. Always such a polite way to ask if someone is either friend or foe.

No answer for a few seconds, then a shape came out of the darkness.

Chapter 41 – Tough Decisions

He'd postponed seeing her again. Yet another emergency had cropped up, and a lot of excuses have been used lately. Meetings, research, too tired, and now a trip to Spain! Samantha understood, she really did, but it doesn't mean she has to just accept it. She'd asked herself so many times over the last few weeks if this was what she really wanted, and in her heart of hearts, she knew it wasn't. It was just a case of the right guy at the wrong time, that's all. It happens, she knows that and accepts it, fate just playing its hand once more.

She'd tried keeping herself busy with work, or seeing Libby, but now Libby has met someone and it is going really well for them. Samantha was very happy for her best friend of course, but she was jealous too. Libby hadn't had to juggle her diary or had the disappointment of countless dates postponed at the last moment; they were in sync. They'd seen each other almost every day last week, and Sammy was wondering when her friend might come up for air.

Apparently the sex was brilliant too. Hearing that was like being kicked in the teeth. All Samantha wanted was to have someone to come home to and have a family with. Not right now of course, she wasn't some desperate bunny boiler with a five year plan. Samantha just wanted someone reliable, good looking, sexy, funny, financially strong, and good in bed. Was that too much to ask?

And, like it or not, the clock is ticking... hickory dickory dock and all that. She isn't getting any younger and it is driving her mad. The stress is affecting her sleep patterns and she's been walking around like a zombie these last few weeks. Is Jason really worth all this?

When she was feeling strong and independent, it was a firm no, but then doubts would creep in, the ebb and flow of her subconscious swaying her to and fro. She was feeling dizzy from it all and just wanted some form of resolution, even if it meant ending things. For now though, she'd have to keep distracted by finding another box set to watch, something with six or seven seasons would be good. Is this what finding the right person entails though, waiting for them to have enough time to fit you into their life? It doesn't seem right.

Samantha gestured at her wall screen to flick through her media player.

"You better hope I find something Jason Ives, or you are history."

Chapter 42 – Downfall

Jason was having a bad day. He was already unhappy with the lack of information he'd gathered in his interview with Eddowes, and now he was having to deal with the security nightmare of customs in Spain. Amazing after all these years that they still haven't forgiven the UK for leaving Europe, so now he has to jump through hoops just to pass through the green zone. The guy at passport control hadn't been very helpful either.

He read the name on his passport and gave a sarcastic laugh. "Is this true, you are, Jason Ives?"

Jason was used to the occasional comment about his name, but not at this level. "Yes, is there a problem?"

"Hmm, not for me, but for you... maybe. The news says you have been trying to catch this Ripper, out of the past?"

"Yes, that's right."

"So how does that help with the now?"

Ives, gave a big sigh, nothing worse than a guy who has a little power and abuses it to ask stupid questions. "There are many different reasons. I'm sure you are too busy to hear them all."

The man in the tiny kiosk glanced over at the crowd behind Jason. A crowd that rarely disappears no matter how fast he works. He was bored. "I'm sure they can wait a little longer, just explain a little more. That is the reason for your visit here in Spain is it not, for business, not pleasure?"

What a tosser, thought Ives, and hoped he had clearly let that show on his face. "Okay. We can build a profile with the information, which can help; but more importantly, we are hoping that there is a record somewhere of his past identity linking to a current one."

Passport man thought about it for a second, and gave that annoying smile again. "I guess, but the press don't seem to see it that way. Maybe you would like to stay here a little longer, take a vacation?"

The thought had crossed Jason's mind as he walked a little of the pilgrimage trail. His life had been very busy all year, and this case had only escalated things. How great would it be to invite Samantha over for a few days? Too soon maybe? He was daydreaming now. He didn't even have time to read the stupid news, never mind take a few days off.

"Chance would be a fine thing," he replied.

∞-∞-∞-∞-∞-∞

"DCI Bjorkman, Superintendant Wilson will see you now."

Sabina had been summoned to a meeting with her commanding officers to answer a few questions about the case. From the tone in his voice over the phone, it wasn't going to be much fun. On walking in, she noticed the empty coffee cups and half finished biscuits lying on the saucers. They'd obviously had a pre-meeting meeting to discuss elements about her. Not a good sign.

Superintendent Wilson held out his hand to welcome her. "Ah, come in, Sabina. DCS Briggs and Commander Pashmali wanted to be included in this chat, I hope you don't mind?" A request, but with no choice in the matter.

"Of course not," she lied.

"Good, because to be quite frank, things are not going well with the investigation are they?"

"Oh I don't know sir, progress is slow, but we are

getting there." A brave attempt to appear positive, but she knew it wouldn't work.

Commander Pashmali wasn't as patient as the other two. "Really? Then maybe you could bring us up to date with the progress you have been making, so that we can start answering our critics in the media about why we haven't caught this man after four murders?"

∞-∞-∞-∞-∞-∞

Samantha couldn't find anything that grabbed her attention, so she asked her wall screen to find the news channel reporting on the Ripper case. For some reason they had temporarily given up on blasting the police for their ineptitude in failing to catch this killer, and now decided to focus on the inclusion of Jason Ives. It seems to be a love hate relationship with him and them. They absolutely love the fact that he is tracing the Ripper's past, but are also concerned with it being a waste of police resources.

They then started talking about his background, with successful cases brought by families of those affected by war, and even interviewed a few of his ex clients who'd been murdered in the past and he'd won cases for. It seemed quite balanced at first, until they brought in his infamous Mueller case. Described by them as one of the worst examples of entrapment ever recorded in past life crimes.

∞-∞-∞-∞-∞-∞

Now they'd lost his luggage. Who loses luggage in this day and age? He hadn't wanted to put his hand luggage in the hold anyway, but as usual they'd run out of space and wouldn't let him take it on board. Hopefully it was just

213

waiting on the tarmac in Spain to be flown over, and luckily there wasn't anything of too much value, but he did have a present for Samantha. He'd found this beautiful necklace in the local market and knew she'd love it. He was hoping it might make her feel better about him having to cancel yet another date with her.

He'd have to try and charm her with a bunch of flowers now.

∞-∞-∞-∞-∞-∞

Bjorkman had been waiting for something like this to happen. It always does when the media start attacking the Met. The commissioner starts shouting at his subordinates, and they just carry on shouting down the chain of command, like a very unpleasant and loud game of Chinese whispers. She wondered if you were even allowed to call it Chinese whispers anymore. Now it is probably just... whispers.

"Well sir, we are still looking into the cctv footage we had from Brick Lane, with several possible witnesses saying they think they saw him, including a bus driver. So we have built up an ID photo and are just waiting for the right time to release it to the press. We also have a partial shoe mark, and most recently, we recovered his pocket knife."

"Have you brought anyone in for questioning though? Pashmali was not going to let her off the hook on this one. He'd already had his bollocking from the commissioner at 7:30 this morning. It was not a good way to start the day.

"Not as a suspect sir, no."

"Then what the devil have you got, Bjorkman?"

"Well, as you know, he is incredibly forensic aware and takes great strides to cover his tracks. We have been left very little to work with here sir, but we are working night and day to try and get more."

∞-∞-∞-∞-∞-∞

Samantha couldn't believe this was the same man she had been dating. The press were calling him irresponsible and self serving to the point in which she felt like she didn't really know who he was anymore. Apparently Ives had been heavily involved with the war crimes unit and had been getting good results. He was also gaining a reputation as a Nazi hunter, which had its good and bad connotations, but then he took it a step too far.

They ran a report, describing that by using his unique body language skills and a knack for pulling detail out of old records, he had managed to trace down a man in Paris called Pierre Leconte using old war time biographies of Julius Otto Mueller, a well known Nazi war criminal who had escaped to Argentina just before the end of the Second World War. The difference in this case lay in the fact that Leconte had no idea that he had been Mueller because he had never had any Awakening sessions.

Ives had posed as a professor of Awakening, opening up a new academy near to Mueller. He then managed to convince him to take some cheap sessions under the pretence of Ives getting back into field work rather than teaching. Ives went on record as saying it had been a huge gamble, as he had never been more than twenty percent sure, but after three months of sessions he hit the jackpot. Pierre Leconte was found to have been Julius Otto Mueller and duly put on trial.

Mueller's defence team pointed out that it was entrapment, that Leconte had not known he had been Mueller until Ives had tricked him into his sessions, and therefore, he could not be guilty until he knew his past. Ives had acted before his guilt was known, and lead him to his guilt through his revived memory. Suddenly, Ives found himself in the dock, with the press and the organisation for People Against Past Life Crime as his judges.

Leconte was not only released, but given a new identity so that he could live his new life in peace. Then the founder of Awakening, Martin Kale, got involved to help write up new laws in this area, but took the step of involving Ives, who he recognised as someone who could make a difference if given the right guidance. It was no secret that the two had become good friends over the years, as they shared a lot in common.

Samantha realised that she had heard elements of this story before, but never linked them all together.

∞-∞-∞-∞-∞-∞

The shuttle from London Heathrow had been smooth enough to get Jason to the Uber pod. Now all he needed was a taxi for the last leg of what should have been a simple journey. As the auto-cab pulled away from the curb, it automatically flicked the tellycast on with the latest news, lest anyone die of boredom looking at the journey.

Jason groaned as he heard his name mentioned. He'd only been out the country for one night, and yet it seems he is now the villain of the piece.

Must be a quiet day for news, he figured.

∞-∞-∞-∞-∞-∞

Superintendant Wilson had joined in now. "What do you mean the Ripper is forensically aware? You should be more aware. You should be scouring every single lead we have... and yet we have nothing!"

Bjorkman felt like walking out. She even felt like crying under this attack, but she wouldn't give the bastards the satisfaction. She was stronger than that, and made of much sterner stuff than these three fat fucks who couldn't even remember what it was like to run a murder inquiry, or risk your life working on the streets of London. They were typical of the politically minded twats that come from university and climb the rapid promotion ladder of the Met. They might be clever, but in her mind, they were most definitely not police officers.

Sabina zoned out for a few seconds, as an image of her pulling out her Met issue gun from its holster and shooting them in the face flashed before her eyes. She blinked, discarding that disturbing image straight away. It makes her realise that she has become very aggressive over the last year. The stress is making her angrier, and her language is now worse than ever. She's been hardened by the whole experience and doesn't like that fact. It makes her feel less feminine and less human. She refocused to fight her corner.

"We are doing the very best we can with the resources we have been given gentlemen. We have several leads on the knife that we are working on... and Jason Ives and Isambard Smythe are also following leads." She stopped herself saying any more. She couldn't believe she was using those two to defend her case, but she was throwing anything she could at them to shut them up. It didn't work.

Detective Superintendent Briggs turned red with rage. "Those two idiots? Have you seen the news lately, Bjorkman? The press are having a field day with them both at our expense. People want results now, not finding out who did this almost two hundred bloody years ago."

Superintendent Wilson went quiet. Sabina guessed that he hadn't mentioned to the other two that it had been his idea to bring them onto the case, but she also knew that it was more than her career was worth to put him in the frame now. She looked down at the floor.

"I know sir, I'll take them off the case immediately."

The three officers looked at each other before Pashmali broke the silence. "Not so hasty, Sabina. By all means, give them the third degree, but let's play out this stage of their enquiries under the proviso that they have to come up with some useful information in the next two weeks.

We don't want to be throwing the baby out with the bathwater now, do we?"

∞-∞-∞-∞-∞-∞

A tear rippled down Samantha's cheek. This was the final straw. Jason is always too busy to meet up, and when he does he is always vacant or tired, usually both. And now she wouldn't want to go outside with him anyway, through fear of idiots calling abuse or the press trying to get new photos.

Samantha sat on the sofa for a few moments before picking up her mobile.

∞-∞-∞-∞-∞-∞

Jason collapsed onto his sofa as soon as he got through the door. Well, at least he didn't have any luggage to unpack just yet. His mobile rang as soon as he got comfortable, as

218

if it had been waiting for the worst possible moment to disturb him.

It was Bjorkman. He was tempted to just let it ring but answered anyway.

"Hello."

"Ives, get to the station tomorrow morning as soon as you can, we need to talk."

"Oh, okay, what about?"

"Your future on the case. I'm sure you must have seen the news lately. I'm sorry, but I warned you that the bastards would drop you in it as soon as the shit hits the fan. Well that time has come."

Jason buried his head in his hands. He wanted to give up. What is the point if no one wants your help anyway? He looked at his watch. It was getting late and he was tired. "Okay, I'll be there at 8:00am."

He finished the call and was completely fed up. It seemed like he was fighting against everyone now, and even he wasn't sure what he could do anymore. He was tempted to just let them get on with it. Hell, maybe he could even have some semblance of a normal life if he stopped now... but he knew he couldn't just sit back whilst the Ripper was still out there.

His mobile rang again. Jason flung it into the armchair next to him not wanting to answer it, then saw Samantha's name on the screen. He grabbed it quickly.

"Hi, Sam."

"Hi... I'm sorry to drop this on you, Jason... but I can't do this anymore."

Chapter 43 – Accusations

It had been a long night of little sleep for Jason. He'd tried to change Samantha's mind for a few minutes, but all through the conversation he knew she was right. He was not in the right place for a relationship right now, and the press regurgitating his background had only made things worse. She apologised for not being more patient, but felt she needed to be moving forward in her love life, not sitting in stagnation at home, waiting for this whole Ripper thing to be concluded.

She also apologised for not being strong enough to ignore the press coverage he was getting now, but she wasn't used to being with someone who attracted that much attention, and it just made her anxious. Jason knew she was being kind in a way. He knew that none of this was Samantha's fault. She hadn't signed up for this when they first started seeing each other, and he'd known that he was too busy. It had been playing on his mind a lot over the last few weeks. So they both said goodbye, with the small proviso that when this case is over and forgotten, they could get in touch and maybe meet up for a coffee.

This was certainly not new territory for Jason, but it still hurt like hell. Not just because he really liked her, but because of the guilt that comes along with the package; the questions haunting him in the early hours of the night, making it almost impossible to sleep. Could he have tried harder to make it work, should he have called more, should he have warned her when they first met? All nonsense of course, just the guilt burning him from inside. Ironically, if he wasn't such a decent person and didn't care, then he wouldn't be hurting so much, but then, that's life.

And now he had his meeting with Bjorkman to attend to. It was going to take a considerable effort not to lose his cool. She had been on his back right from the beginning of this case. In fact, she had been making his part of the investigation harder by her bickering and noncompliance. He still could not work her out, which in any other circumstance would be beautifully refreshing.

Ha, beautiful - to think I thought she was so attractive when I first saw her, but it turns out she is ugly on the inside. His thoughts were running away with him. The ice maiden who changes her mood at the drop of a hat. Almost always cold, but sometimes she would melt a little, like a delicate frost covered flower on a warm spring morning.

He decided to hold onto that thought as he knocked on the door of DCI Bjorkman's office on the first floor of Charing Cross police station.

Bjorkman was sitting at her desk. The blinds were half closed to avoid any harsh light entering the room. "Ah, Jason, thank you for coming over so early."

Jason was a little taken aback by her politeness, then smiled a little to himself. *Ah, nice cop routine this morning then.* "No problem, I wasn't sleeping anyway," he said sarcastically.

"You and me both then," she answered sympathetically. "Hopefully I'll remember how to sleep properly when this is all over, but I doubt it. Look, Jason, I'm sorry for all the shit that has been going on. I know I'm not always the easiest of people to deal with."

"You're not bloody joking", replied Jason implying humour, but actually meaning it. He wasn't in the mood for niceties this early in the morning.

Bjorkman smiled weakly. "I know, but then you don't know half the things that I have to deal with on a day to day basis. You might not be such a nice person either if you were in my place"

"No I don't, but then maybe you should be sharing that with someone, DCI Bjorkman." He said her title officiously, to show that he was complying with her instructions from when they'd had their argument last week.

Bjorkman looked like she was going to get defensive again, and then stopped herself just in time. "Look, Jason, I'm trying to say I'm sorry here, just give me a chance... and you can call me, Sabina when it's just you and me, okay?"

Jason raised his eyebrows in surprise. "Okay... thanks... I guess. So what is happening, Sabina?"

"The idiots upstairs are piling on the pressure even more I'm afraid. They want results from all of us, including a name from you for his original identity to keep the media distracted, and a suspect brought in for questioning, if only to show we are following leads."

"What, anybody?"

"Honestly? Yes. Anyone as long as we can just about justify the questioning for a few hours. What happened with Eddowes?"

Jason, looked at his feet. "Not quite as much as I'd like I'm afraid. She won't go through an Awakening, and her memory of her time as Eddowes has faded. I used every trick in the book to eke out every detail, but still would have liked more."

"You must have something?"

"Yes, but not much. The only thing that correlates with Abberline is the use of their term, 'My Joe'. It seems that there was some confusion over Kelly and Eddowes using that term, and that might be another reason why Kelly's lover, Joseph Barnett was interviewed by Abberline.

"I managed to establish some other good points though,

as it turns out Kelly did have a special customer called Joe who she was involved with. He was rich, and even followed her from her plush brothel in the West End to the slums of Whitechapel. He must have been very fond of her, possibly even in love, as he could have quite easily stayed where he was. There were even a few witness descriptions of rich gentleman types wearing expensive clothing at several scenes. Which is noteworthy, as Whitechapel was not a rich area, so they'd obviously come over specially."

Talking of someone else's affections made him think of Samantha for a brief second, leaving a tinge of sadness in his gut. Bjorkman looked interested though, so he carried on.

"It also looks like this 'Joe' may have lived somewhere south of Camden. Isambard has already addressed his Ripperologist friends, asking for their help to try and find any details relating to Kelly to try and trace her. Hopefully, they can work out any suspects called Joe or Joseph who may have lived in the area. It is a long shot, but it takes time to trace any of these people."

Sabina still didn't look happy with this news. "Jason, I have to be honest here and say that I think you are wasting your time on this wild goose chase over a simple term like 'my Joe'. Why aren't you interviewing known suspects?"

"Because that would take even longer, Sabina, and if you think about it, they have either been questioned already by the police at the time, or investigated by Ripperologists for the last 180 years. We'd have known from them by now if there was any tangible evidence to their guilt.

"So you are just ruling them out?" She was getting angry again.

Jason was also getting frustrated. "No, I am just prioritising this particular route, but of course, I will follow any credible lead on a suspect."

Bjorkman's eyes darkened. "To be honest, Jason, looking into a client relating to Mary Kelly only deals with Kelly's murder... not the other victims. It holds no logic. I'm telling you to stop wasting your time looking at the victims and start interviewing the high profile suspects. You should start with Joe Barnett, or that royal surgeon or the wife poisoner who was Abberline's prime suspect. Bloody hell, Jason, you have loads of people who have the finger pointed at them, and yet you are playing stupid games with the victims."

Ives was trying to keep his cool, but was getting annoyed at once again being obstructed by Bjorkman. "For God's sake, Sabina, just try and show some trust in my judgement."

"No, Jason, I won't. You may well have built up a career with your past life crime antics, but I'm not having it. Stop this line of inquiry now... that's an order."

"An order to stop what I feel is right? What is wrong with you, why are you getting in the way every time I feel like we have a lead?" That was it; the gloves were off, his temper in full gear. Ives was going to go with a wild hunch of his. Bjorkman just stared at him with those deep blue eyes that seem to hold no soul.

"In fact, DCI Bjorkman, I'm going to ask you a question right now. I'm going to lead off on another enquiry based just on a hunch of mine. I have a new suspect and I am going to ask them directly."

"What are you talking about?"

"Sabina... are you Jack the Ripper?"

224

Chapter 44 – Honeymoon in Paris

July 1887 – Royal Veterinary College, London.

Joseph sat patiently in his tutor's office waiting for his latest assessment. By all accounts he was doing very well in his penultimate year as a student of Veterinary science. It has been a long period of study, but at least it keeps him away from home, and is thankful for that small mercy. He promised himself that London would be his new home when he sets up his new practice, away from his mother's loving, but sometimes heavy hand. He misses the smell of the sea air though, and the weather was infinitely more tolerable than the smog ridden capital, but it offers almost nothing in comparison to the delights of its nightlife.

The theatre shows in the West End, the art galleries and the world leading museums at his doorstep. They all satisfied one's cultural wanderlust, but truth be told, it was the less salubrious entertainment that had often caught his eye. His fellow students and friends had wasted no time in regaling him with stories of their sexual conquests in the homes of careful madams. In that they ran classy and safe establishments for procuring young and healthy girls, just waiting to be handpicked by gentlemen privileged enough to be able to afford them. That is where he had met his Mary last year.

The beautiful Mary, with skin as white and smooth as milk, and lips that were full and soft, and would open to his command, to do all sorts of acts that he'd never dreamt of in Bournemouth. She had entranced him with her sexual witchcraft. His heart had become hers to the point in which he it felt it would break if she was not happy. He had not planned this of course, his mother already has him betrothed to another, which at least works to his advantage when writing to his fiancé.

He'd write to her as if she was 'his Mary', professing a love exclusively reserved for another, but a love that would be impossible to realise. A man of his standing could never be seen with an impoverished girl from Ireland, never mind a prostitute. But he would dream of it from time to time when he felt lonely. He'd even taken her to Paris once; Paris, the city of Love.

For a few brief days they had been able to play the role of a gentleman and his wife on a short holiday, and secretly pretended that it was their honeymoon. She seemed to enjoy it for a while, but then he had been stupid, and actually proposed to her as if she were a lady of equal standing. It had been the champagne really, or at least that is what he had told himself, the delicate wine giving him indelicate thoughts. She had been upset by it all. Quite understandable really, for she was clever enough to know that it would never happen, and that he was already betrothed. The act had removed the veil though, the reality setting back in that she was there on a wage, and he was there as her employer, paying her for sex and to tell him she loved him.

And my, did she get nasty when she drank too much alcohol. This beautiful flower would transform into a screaming banshee before his very eyes, and this latest upset had caused her to drink more than usual. Joseph had had to endure the embarrassment of being this banshee's 'husband', and then suffer the further indignity of being asked to leave the hotel the following morning. It had caused a rift at the time, but he still loved her anyway. To him, it was just the result of the hard life she'd had to endure over the last few years in London. To him, she was a lady no matter what different sides she had to her nature.

He recognised that nature. He had the same volatile temperament that could be switched by gin or opium or tiredness. It was a cruel gift from his father's side, whether he wanted it or not. Only last month he'd read a novella by Robert Louis Stevenson called, 'Strange Case of Doctor Jekyll and Mr Hyde', and it made him think of himself and his Mary.

In fact, he'd joked with her about it, how they had this common daemon residing in them both. He thought it made them perfect for each other, but she thought the opposite. She feared his dark side, and knew her own would drag her down. She'd even remarked once that the drink would be her undoing. "It'll kill me one day Joe, just you mark my words."

"I'll look after you Mary, you know I will," he had replied, and he'd meant it. He'd follow her to the end of time if need be.

The Paris trip had been the final straw for them both though, at least for a while. She didn't want to see him anymore, said it hurt too much, that she'd got too close. And then a little later she got kicked out of her brothel for a lack of ladylike behaviour. How strange that they should both end up in Whitechapel in the end.

He'd lost his reason for a short while after being rejected by her, and decided to throw himself upon the saggy bodies of the Whitechapel floosies. He knew the risks, and that is what had lured him in - but he didn't care about his life anymore. Mary was still refusing to see him and had moved in with a man, which pained him even more. He knows she will relent one day though. The further she falls from grace, the more desperate she will become. One day they will be together again, he can feel it in his bones.

His bones... He doesn't feel very well today, quite stiff

actually. Maybe he has caught a summer cold, but nothing a rum toddy couldn't fix.

His tutor came in, apologising for keeping him waiting, and sat down on the other side of the imposing oak desk as he fiddled around with the tiny spectacles on the end of his nose. Then he opened an envelope marked *J.R.* specifically for his pupil.

"Now, Joseph, I'm very pleased with your progress this year. Carry on like this and you'll make a name for yourself."

Chapter 45 – Lead Us Not Into Temptation

Bjorkman looked shocked, the blood rushing from her face to leave her looking temporarily frail. "What? "Are you mad... are you stark raving mad, Jason?"

"No, maybe I'm just coming to my senses. You have been putting a spanner in the works all along, so either you are a rubbish detective, which from your record I seriously doubt, or you have some huge secret reason for wanting this case to fail."

"Fail? You think I want this case to fail? I was the stupid idiot who pushed to take over this case. I somehow thought it would do my career good; biggest mistake of my life... and now, you... you come in here and start accusing me of being the Ripper? You are either desperate or you are playing some kind of mind game with me."

"No mind games, Sabina. Just give me a reason why you have been so negative with my involvement."

"This isn't all about you, Jason."

"No? Is that really true? Tell me, open up to me, because I know you are holding some kind of secret and it is affecting the case."

Bjorkman quickly stood up and closed the door tight. She motioned Jason to keep quiet for a moment until she recovered her composure.

"Okay, but this goes no further than you and me, is that understood?"

Jason's dig into her past was paying off. "I can't promise you that if it compromises the case, Sabina."

"Oh for fuck's sake, Jason, I'm not the bloody Ripper. Do you want to me to try and explain my position to you or not?"

Ives had been put firmly in his place. "Well, yes."

Sabina sat back down, she was visibly shaking. Her wall was beginning to crack, her defences crumbling before his very eyes. "The problem is not with catching the Ripper, Jason, it is not even with you as a person, but what you represent."

Jason leant back on his seat, visibly giving her more space. "I know you are very against past life crime, lots of people are, but to this extent? You are a police officer. It is your duty to look into every avenue of evidence that might come up, including past life crimes. And to be honest, you must have known that someone like me was going to get involved in the case. This is Jack the Ripper for goodness sake, of course a past life investigator was going to get involved."

"Yes, and I knew that, I'm not stupid, but I hoped it would all be kept in-house with our team doing it. That way I would have more control. Look, I know I'm not making much sense, and you are right, I have been awkward and a tough bitch at times. But I have never tried to get in the way of the case, you have to believe me on that."

"Okay, so tell me what's going on and I'll try to believe you."

Tears started running down Bjorkman's cheeks. She was crying silently, as if she was trying to hide her tears.

"What is it, Sabina? Honestly, forget what we have spoken about in the past, let's just get this problem out of the way right now."

Sabina screamed. "My father was killed by a G-eye!"

"What?" It was now Jason's turn to be shocked.

"Not directly... but in effect he might as well have pulled a gun out and shot him." Sabina took a bottle of water out from her desk drawer to take a drink. She smiled.

"I wish this was whisky. Isn't that what they usually do in the movies in moments like these?"

Jason gave a sad smile, "It usually works for me. So, what did this guy do?"

"Just his job I suppose. He'd been charged with finding the murderer of his client from the mid 19th century. During his investigation trawling through his records, he found my father. My father, who had been a good man and an excellent police officer, who had gone through Awakening in the good faith that it would make him a better man.

"He had been recorded as killing this man, the G-eye's client, but it wasn't being actively pursued until the victim started pressing charges. After a long and arduous trial, he was found guilty and sentenced to five years in jail. My brother and I were only eleven years old."

"Jesus, I'm sorry to hear that, Sabina. It is a terribly complicated area in our laws. Did he serve the whole sentence?"

"No, he didn't. He could not stand life in jail as a police officer, or the shame of losing his job. The Met dropped him as soon as he was found guilty from so long ago. Guilty from a past life... tell me what makes sense in this whole mess?"

Jason didn't know what to say. It was the worst scenario, and something that crops up from time to time. "No it doesn't make much sense really, but they are getting better with giving out these sentences, Sabina. I'm sure that would not happen now. It was all so new then, no one really knew how to deal with past life crimes in the early years."

"He killed himself, Jason!"

Jason was lost for words. "Shit... I'm sorry." He felt cold inside.

"My mother could not cope, she felt so betrayed by the whole system. She ended up like a zombie on powerful anti-depressants. My brother never recovered from it either. He turned to drugs and burglary, then spent time in prison himself until he launched himself off the second floor of a cell block. He must have known it wasn't high enough to kill him, but he did it anyway. He was in hospital for five months to try and repair his spine, which has left him hunched up. He went completely off the rails. He even tattooed a web on his face. He looks like a fucking freak now!"

Jason felt awful, he'd pushed her to this, and now the truth was finally coming out. No wonder she had wanted to keep quiet about it all. It was the trail of a tragic life that no one would want to admit to, and it was a good bet that if her managers knew any of this, it would put a series of obstacles on her career path.

Suddenly he was full of admiration for this strong woman who had overcome such a terrible beginning in her life. She had turned it around and faced her fears to become a police woman herself, just like her father, and she had risen through the ranks to DCI in what was still a male dominated profession.

Now he felt awkward for pushing her so hard. He put an arm around her to show he was sorry and she collapsed into his arms. The tears just flooded out. This was probably the first time she'd been able to let go with someone in years, and he knew the value of these moments, to let go of your anguish, if only for a short time before facing the world again.

"I'm so sorry, Sabina, I had no idea."

She looked up at him, her lapis blue eyes staring straight into his, her pupils dilating, letting him into her deepest personal space. Jason brushed away some fresh tears gathering on her cheek. Sabina took his hand, and leant in to kiss him. He didn't know what to do. There was no doubt that he was attracted to her, but he had only just split up with Samantha, and to be honest, he knew kissing her back would be a huge mistake, but he kissed her anyway.

How could he not? How could he reject her at her lowest moment that he had triggered? His mind was racing in every direction warning him of the pleasure and pain this could lead to; her soft salty kisses just echoing those faults. Sweet and savoury, to be devoured, cherished and feared.

On impulse he pushed her gently away. "I'm sorry, this is probably not a good idea. It's not that I don't want to, just that it's bad timing." Those words again. It was always bad timing.

Sabina nodded, but didn't want to listen to logic. "I know, not a good idea I guess, and I know you're in a relationship..."

Jason rolled his eyes, "was... until last night," and then instantly regretted saying it.

She smiled softly with an impish grin on her face. "Then fuck common sense Jason, I need you with me right now." Sabina stood up and walked over to the door to lock it, taking full charge of the situation.

"So fuck me instead!"

Chapter 46 – A Step in the Dark

The shadow loomed.

An old, but smart dark suit walked out from the darkest part of the room, worn by an Afro American with strong features tinged with grey sideburns. It was George Glover, looking right to left, making sure Isambard was alone. Isambard nearly jumped out of his skin.

"Good heavens, Mr Glover, you gave me an awful start."

"I apologise, but I had to make sure it was only you here. I have some news that might help your plight. Would you mind if we went into the lounge for a quick chat?"

"But of course." And with that, Isambard led the way to the oak panelled room across the hall and invited George to sit on one of the generous burgundy leather sofas, usually reserved for reading or discussing new lines of Ripper inquiry. George looked nervous, which in all the years Isambard had known him, he had never seen him like this.

"Isambard, I feel I have to set the scene a little before we get started. As you may know, I moved over from the States when I was still a child. My father worked for one of the banks in the City of London, and by the time he retired and moved back to America, I had grown up and found myself married. I had completely embraced the way of life here in London, as it has always seemed like home to me. And, during that time, I immersed myself in some of the culture and history of London, including the mystery of Jack the Ripper."

Isambard sat silently, nodding acknowledgement when appropriate.

"So, imagine my surprise when I finally went through

my Awakening foundation, only to find that I had lived in London during the time of The Whitechapel Murderer. I was older than the kids that go through Awakening now of course, God knows how they deal with the secrets and lies that spring out from their past at such a tender age. I remember reading with sorrow all those years ago about the nun who'd been Catherine Eddowes and could not cope. Completely understandable of course, she had been so young, and with her strict Catholic upbringing it must have been distressing in so many ways. I sincerely hope she has found some peace in her solitude."

Again, Isambard nodded, "I believe she has found a little sir, although she still finds it very difficult to talk about our topic. Tragedy visits us all in different ways, and we respond accordingly. She has been very courageous in talking to my esteemed colleague."

"Yes, indeed she has. If I had been younger, I might have crumbled myself on several experiences, especially as their techniques were so rudimentary at the time."

Then Glover lost his train of thought for a few moments, his nervousness making him forgetful.

Isambard prompted him on. "You were saying that you were in London at the time of the Ripper... did you know any of the victims? A realisation then drew on Isambard. "Did you know Mary Kelly?"

George touched Isambard on the arm. "I'm glad you are dealing with this, Isambard, I feel I can trust your confidentiality.

"By my honour sir, you can trust my silence on this matter."

"Thank you, it will be good to talk a little about this after so many years. Maybe it is the fact that I was already in my mid forties when I started my Awakening, or maybe it was that I was married with children that helped ground me so well. Or maybe it was because I was already a keen Ripper investigator at the time, that it gave me a solid knowledge of all the surrounding details, and therefore, the fortitude to remain calm under the circumstances.

"I honestly thought it was pure chance at the time that I was living in London when I was Awakened, but if you read some of the latest reports on Awakening, it does seem fairly common that people are reborn in or near a geographical region that they have a connection with. Not always of course, sometimes we are thrown all over the world, but we have some form of link that brings us back to people and places. Hence my feeling of knowing London when I first arrived."

Glover was stalling, and could see a little frustration on Isambard's face as he waited for the key part of the conversation, so decided to get to the point.

"Isambard, I have kept quiet about being Mary Kelly for over twenty years now, and it is a secret I would prefer to take with me to my grave."

Isambard was dumbfounded. To think he had been in so many Ripper conversations over the years with Glover and yet he had never guessed. It made times where he had tried to argue his point seem ridiculous, after all, how can you argue with someone who has lived through it all?

Glover put his hand up to stop any questions. "And before you ask me anything, I fear I must warn you that as soon as I had my first Awakening as Mary Kelly, I knew how the implications of looking back into that life any further might affect me. I also knew from my Ripper studies where it was going to end, but I was of course, curious too. You cannot imagine the balance of my Ripperologist curiosity fighting against my fear of seeing my own gruesome murder, but I think we all know that we have to tread carefully with our past."

Isambard was certainly curious now, and thoughts of getting home had left him at the door. "So did you have any more sessions?"

"A few, but it always seemed quite difficult. My observer was very kind as she patiently tried to take me back through my life, but a fear was always keeping me back. It is difficult to even know what is true anymore. Our memories are all shaped by our experiences, and our perception of them can change, even within one lifetime."

A thought crept into Glover's head. "I'm sorry, Isambard, but you have to keep the Kelly inquiry you started this evening going as if nothing has changed, at least for a while longer. I don't want anyone wondering who you met or heard from that ended your search so quickly."

"Of course, I will even put fresh messages out to our group tomorrow."

Glover nodded. "Good. It's foolish I know, we should be able to speak freely about our past, but it was always the constant questioning that I used to fear the most. Unfortunately, I now fear the Ripper's knowledge of me too, as I also feel there was some form of relationship going on between us at the time. I honestly don't know much though."

He then paused for a moment to voice a decision he had obviously made that evening. "I am willing to have a few Awakening sessions with Mr Ives as long as he agrees to respect my feelings in this whole matter, and let me remember only what I am willing to undergo."

"You can trust Mr Ives, dear sir, he is a man of great skill and honour. I can set up a most confidential meeting that will meet any stipulations you set."

"Good, then I suppose we should arrange a meeting as soon as possible given the circumstances. I don't want to read about another victim finding his bloody knife."

Isambard thought he'd better bring Glover up to date with what little they knew. "I fear I cannot say much about the interview with Catherine Eddowes for the moment, as I must extend the same level of discretion to her as I will to you. However, I must share a morsel of information to see if we are treading the right path thus far. Both Eddowes and Abberline have mentioned that Kelly appears to have had a relationship with another Joe or Joseph other than Barnett that might seem pertinent, as it may have been more than just professional.

"It would seem there was a client of Kelly that resided south of Camden who had known her for some time. He even followed her from a high class brothel in the West End to the slums of Whitechapel; and as you know, there was talk of a gentleman visitor on her last night, possibly bringing her a present. Do you remember any details, such as where he lived?

Glover looked uncomfortable. "I do know the details of that evening, of course Isambard, but every detail fills me with such foreboding that I rarely study them. I believe Mary did have a special customer called Joseph though. I can't remember much, but I'm sure it is in there somewhere."

He pointed to his head when he said this, indicating that strange area that Awakening has still not explained, of where the ethereal memories are kept from body to body, lifetime to lifetime. "He lived in..." His eyes drifted up, dragging the memory over the coals of time. "Where was it?" he asked himself rhetorically. "Oh, I remember, he caught a carriage from there to collect me once, we went to the theatre... I think. I am sorry, Isambard, the memories are from sessions I had so long ago. Hang on... Yes," Glover lifted both hands in the air as he punched through,

"Mornington Crescent."

A tear started forming in the corner of Glover's eye. An unconscious reaction to the memories being delved into again after such a long period of time. Isambard noticed but said nothing. The investigation had so far been slow, with traditional methods of forensics bearing no results, and scant witnesses seeing this shadowy figure. Somehow this Ripper was just as elusive as he had ever been, even though technology has transformed detective work to new levels that they could never have dreamt of in the Victorian age. Now it is time to move forward. They have Abberline, Eddowes and Kelly involved in the investigation now.

How odd, that asking the original victims and officers could lead to the Ripper's past identity. Not through some gadget or forensic science, but through a natural process of past life regression.

A process that may one day unlock secrets older than time itself.

Chapter 47 – Awkward Silence

DCI Sabina Bjorkman looked at Jason with a mixture of embarrassment and annoyance. This morning had definitely not started out as it had meant to, and she now felt she had been cleverly manipulated into opening up about her personal life. The following... engagement had been awkward too, and was going to be difficult to gloss over in a professional manner.

Jason looked at Sabina with a thousand thoughts running through his head, and he didn't know which one of them to deal with first. Her opening to him about her father and her brother had touched him in every way possible, and made complete sense in terms of her emotional wall and her hate of past life investigators. It had solved the riddle and quashed his hunch to smithereens, which was good in a way, as it was a tenuous line of inquiry, and a persistent, nagging feeling that he could now lay to rest.

Then he thought of her sexually; the words, the face, the taste of her lips when they kissed. He wished it hadn't happened, even though part of him had always wanted it to. He stopped his thoughts right there; the memories of that interlude in her office only an hour ago, on this quiet Sunday morning at the station.

It was now time for their meeting, with a confused look on Pascal's face when he turned up and felt the odd energy in the air. Isambard had arrived too, and noticed nothing at all, much to the relief of Jason. Bjorkman started the meeting with a little less gusto than normal, but recovered to her normal level quickly as she switched into professional mode.

Again, they had very little to go on in the traditional

policing angle, with next to no forensics and witnesses that were hard to find, sketchy or not very reliable. The Ripper seemed to be able to vanish into thin air, leaving some of the media agencies to comment on a supernatural element to boost sales. He was scaring a lot of people, with many women afraid that he might get bored with prostitutes and pick on them instead.

Men were being pointed out all the time by suspicious members of the public, scared of their own shadow and therefore wasting a lot of the police's time and resources, but no stone could be left unturned. This was becoming one of the biggest investigations in Scotland Yard's long history, but it was also looking a lot like the original Whitechapel Murders investigation in terms of being undetected and casting fear over London.

Isambard was shuffling around even more than usual, giving Jason the impression that he had something new to add to the mix, and he wasn't wrong. "I have some most illuminating news from my meeting two nights ago, which will hopefully cast a different light on this whole investigation. I apologise for not announcing this earlier, but I had to win the confidence of my source before he felt he could fully trust my pledge of confidentiality. As such, I can only share this with our small team here in this room for the time being."

Everyone looked at each other, then nodded in agreement to Isambard. They were getting used to his manner now, but were still unsure of what he was about to disclose.

Isambard continued. "I can now divulge that not only have I learnt the current identity of Mary Jane Kelly, but I have his permission to allow Jason to put him through an Awakening session."

The room went quiet as everyone digested this

information. Bjorkman looked confused. "So she is a man now, is that what you are saying?"

"Yes, dear boss."

Ives had a coy smile on his face. "It's not that uncommon to have a different gender from time to time, even though we do tend to stick to a certain sex."

Bjorkman still looked unsettled. "Of course, but it still always surprises me for some reason. It just seems so odd."

"Me too, ma'am, being a boy always gives me the willies." Pascal could always be relied on for the corny office jokes, but it was only Carter and Jason laughing with him this time.

Now it was Isambard's turn to look lost. He blinked twice, and then smiled to show good faith. "Very droll sir, but the matter at hand still awaits. Kelly wants to come in and expedite the matter with some urgency, which marries our own agenda at least. When can we set things in place?"

Jason was also enthusiastic to get started. "Isambard, I can do today if that suits everyone? What can you tell us about him?"

"Well sir, I don't want to say too much, the walls have ears so they say, so I'll keep to the bare minimum if you do not mind. His name is George Glover. A sixty-eight year old American solicitor originally from Boston, but he has lived in England since childhood. It is by amazing coincidence that he is also a member of our London chapter of Ripperology."

Jason didn't look so surprised. "I have been involved in many cases where the suspects or witnesses or even family were fairly close at hand. It is called 'The Unfinished Business Principle', as if our souls need to clear some type of cosmic energy to right our wrongs. It is how I originally found Mueller... in 'that' trial, and why some people believe very strongly in past life crime detection. Martin

Kale also believes in it very strongly and has been working closely with his new protégé Adam Capello in trying to answer some of these questions from Awakening."

Pascal looked bemused. "Yes, I've heard of this Adam Capello working with Kale, he looks very young. What's the connection between them?"

"Capello just completed his Awakening foundation last year," answered Ives. "Apparently he has had some form of future life experience that gives him a unique insight into projects Kale is working on. He won't say much about it at the moment, only that it is part of some greater plan. You might have noticed something in the news, but apparently someone has been hogging the headlines lately," he said with a wink.

"Ah, go on, Jason, you must know more than that, what with you being mates with Kale."

Jason laughed. "Ha, I know you too, but you don't tell me everything you get up to with Mrs Pascal."

Pascal looked deflated. "That's because nothing much ever does happen with Mrs Pascal anymore... probably because I'm at chuffing work most of the time. Hmm, a future Awakening memory; I didn't even know that was possible?"

"It shouldn't be, hence him working with Kale now I suppose. Martin is still keeping tight lipped on the subject though."

"Ooh, Martin now is it?" Pascal joked.

Isambard coughed loudly to break up the impromptu conversation. "Ahem, if I may interject once again, gentlemen. I will contact Mr Glover and ask if he is willing to come into the station later today for the said session."

Jason looked at his watch. "Great, anytime after 3pm, that will give me time to get my equipment together. I'm sorry, but I should really do this interview by myself to avoid any distractions, but I will record it all for us to watch afterwards. In the meantime, I suggest we put together a set of questions. What does he remember from his original Awakenings, Isambard?"

"Very little I regret to say sir. Mr Glover had his first sessions not long after Awakening really took off in the 2040's, so it was very rudimentary. Apparently he had some very strong flashbacks as a woman in Victorian times, which was disconcerting enough by itself, but then he recognised certain details from his knowledge of the Ripper. He thought it was his mind playing tricks with him at first, his imagination throwing in these stark images for some reason."

Bjorkman was taking notes. "So how did he keep it all secret from the rest of the world? In fact, why did he even keep it secret at all? Surely a Ripperologist would be over the moon to find themselves involved in the case. It doesn't make sense."

"Oh no dear boss, for him it was quite the opposite. At the time of finding out, he had a young family and had just set up his own solicitor's practice, both of which were infinitely more important to him than the society. That has always just been a hobby. So suddenly becoming famous as the last, and possibly most written about victim of the Ripper did not appeal to him in the least. Undoubtedly Mr Glover's interest grew more, but he never felt the compunction to share his secret until my meeting earlier this week. He was also very lucky with his original Observer, who kept his secret too."

"He was lucky, I've heard all sorts of stories being leaked by Observers," commented Bjorkman.

Jason could see her going off on another Awakening rant. "True, but a lot of that has changed. In fact, the latest reports show that a lot of lessons have been learnt since the early days. Confidentiality is a lot higher now."

Bjorkman didn't look convinced. "Yeah right, that must make your job a lot harder, she muttered sarcastically."

He let it pass over him."What matters right now is getting Kelly to come in this afternoon."

"I will orchestrate that right now dear sir." Isambard was happy to be pushing the case along.

Ives looked at everyone in the room.

"Good, because if we draw a blank from this, we are right back to square one."

Chapter 48 – Penance

These are the weirdest dreams of them all. Visions of cradling a baby fighting for its breath are mixed with views over the sea from a window seat. Seb can hear screams coming from the room at the end of the hall, but he dares not look inside it.

Crying. So much crying from loss and sorrow. A dead toddler is lying in a coffin, the smallest he has ever seen, and yet he feels like he has lost his father, not his son. Emotions are overwhelming him to the point of madness.

Why did his father have to get drunk so often and pick fights?

Why did his... husband, have to screw pox ridden whores?

These sights, sounds and feelings are so foreign that he feels that they are not his.

Someone is telegraphing their pain to him.

Sebastian hopes he is just the receptacle.

Chapter 49 – Mary Jane Kelly

Jason double checked his equipment for the Awakening session, and asked George to make himself comfortable on the nicest couch they could find in the police station. Strict instructions had been given and signs posted, warning of the consequences if they were disturbed. Ives hoped that George was going to be an easy subject, as his advanced age gave him a certain calmness. But as soon as they started, George started fidgeting.

His heart rate had risen to 130bpm and adrenaline levels peaked at fight levels a few times, keeping him very alert, so Jason employed a few tricks he'd used before on other unsettled clients. He pretended to turn some of the equipment off for a break, and started talking about classic cinema, one of Jason's passions. From the days of the silver screen with 'Citizen Kane' and 'Some like it Hot' right up to one of his corny favourites from just a couple of years ago, 'Return From Hell' which tells the tale of a psychic G-eye.

Listening to someone talk about their passion can have a distracting and soporific effect, especially when laced with NLP... otherwise known as 'sneaky bastard hypnosis'. Within half an hour, Glover's resistance had worn thin. The Awakening had finally begun, and George was now going into a deep trance. This was no ordinary deep trance though, as Ives wanted to give George the full ability to talk back to Jason, so that questions could be asked and answered.

Once in, Jason quickly started calling George by his previous name. "Mary, I need you to tell me a little about your time in London when you first arrived."

"Ooh, it were lovely at first my darlin', so many people and I seemed to land right on my feet." Glover then stopped, as if remembering something else. "Well, not quite at first. For a while I was scrubbing floors for the nuns in Crispin Street to earn my keep. They could be right nasty on occasion, but I kept my head down until I learnt from my new friends that I could sell my fancies to fine gentlemen in the West End. Odd innit, that I can make money so easily in one way, but struggle in the other?" Mary let out a big sigh full of sorrow. "It fair messes with my head. I was a decent girl back home."

"I'm sure you still are, Mary, just that London has a habit of doing that to a person if you have no money. We all have to eat and sleep somewhere safe after all, and it was tough in those days."

"Ha ha, it was a terror at times, but then the lovely gentlemen gave me far more attention then I'd ever had in my life before. It all but took my breath away."

Jason decided it was a good time to ask about her time in the West End brothel. "Were there any particular gentlemen that you became fond of in your nice brothel, Mary?"

"I was fond of them all, dear. They could be quite silly sometimes, but always charming. They'd take me to the theatre on occasion, give me fine dresses to wear, and I'd have to pretend to be their niece. If any of them got nasty, they'd be barred from using our services. Well, that's what Madam would say, but I heard she had special girls for that."

"There must have been a client you became especially fond of though?"

"Not really, I was so giddy with excitement at first, but the drink got to me I think. I seem to remember being kicked out."

Tears started flooding down Glover's face. "Madam told me I was being too disruptive. I had to leave that lovely place. I didn't realise how hard it was going to be after that, or I would have gone straight back home to Limerick."

"What about your trip to Paris? Who was the gentleman you went with there; he must have been quite special?"

The tears suddenly stopped as Mary rolled back the months to happier days. "Ah, that was quite an adventure. Joe took me as if we were newlyweds."

Bingo! Now they just had to hope that it was the right Joe that they'd been pinning all their hopes on, and that he had some relevance in the whole story.

Mary Kelly continued."He loved me you know, but I just didn't feel it with him. He would have married me in earnest if he could, but he was betrothed to another, and his mother would never have accepted me. We even had a few quarrels on the matter, with him saying he'd have lost his allowance and be written out of her will if he openly declared his feelings for me. He was so weak willed when it came to his mother. Spoilt our trip into Paris it did, and I kept him away for quite a while after that episode."

Jason was treading very carefully now. "Mary, what can you tell us about your gentleman Joe?"

"He was a funny one, seeming as you're asking. Lovely in so many ways, but touched by a sadness that no one could ever solve. He'd have been all right on his own in terms of money I think, although he was still attending some form of college. He told me he was an animal doctor once. I laughed so much, said that we couldn't even afford a doctor for our own ailments never mind our livestock or pets, but he was deadly serious."

"Can you remember his family name, Mary?"

"No... he never told me that, and I never asked. Not good for business to pry too much into their affairs. I only knew the rest because of our trip into Paris. He would open up from time to time about his cruel father. He was fair affected by it all, but would never leave the family. Odd isn't it, that in some ways I was freer than he was? I'd have married him like he wanted, but we both knew it was not to be, so I just enjoyed the lovely food and clothes and champagne. You can keep the caviar though, horrible stuff. Did you know it's fish eggs? Just give me a slice of fried roe anytime, much more honest."

"Can you describe him?"

"Ooh, you are a nosey one. He was about the same height as me, mousey hair, bushy moustache and that thing where their eyebrows meet, always made him look shifty, but he was alright really. I'm awful at describing anyone though."

Jason thought he'd try things from a different angle. "On the contrary, you have given an excellent description. Now I need you to travel further through your life though, Mary. I'm going to give you a date to visit. It is near the end of this story, but it is being told in a very safe place. I am here as your observer, to watch and protect you. In some ways I'm holding your hand through this all."

Mary smiled. "You boys always want more than that, you can't fool me."

In spite of the situation, Jason had to laugh. "Ha, trust me Mary, I'm more like a big brother than most of the men you are thinking of."

"Aw, that's so nice... big brother... looking after me." Glover seemed to be fading away, going too deep, too relaxed to the point of almost falling asleep.

"Don't go away Mary, I need you to stay awake just

enough to look into the 8th and 9th of November 1888. Can you do that for me please?"

The smile disappeared, replaced with a sullen expression. "Don't want to."

"I thought you might say that, but remember, you are going to show me around and introduce me to all the characters in your story."

"Oh... all right then, my sweet, we'll go together then, shall we?"

"Thank you, Mary. So, please tell me about the 8th of November, I'm really interested."

"Horrible day to look at, so grey, and a bitter wind whipping up, don't know why you want to look at today?"

"I know, but just humour me."

"I'm missing my Joe a little, but we don't half quarrel a lot over money, ain't even got an honest couple of pennies to rub together since he lost his job. He does visit though. Loves me he does, so I know he'll be back. I'm sick of this life though, sometimes I just feel like giving up, but then I grow fearful. I'll probably meet my maker soon anyway. It's a race between the cold or drink... or that awful Leather Apron prowling around Whitechapel. He's already butchered Long Liz last month, such a terrible affair. I'm going to give up this whole business as soon as I get enough money together to get back to my ma."

Do you mean Joe Barnett when you say 'my Joe' on this occasion?" asked Ives.

A little laugh again. "I might do."

"Can you tell me who is who, Mary, it is really important?"

"Hm, all right. Yes of course I meant Joe Barnett, but sometimes I miss my other Joe too. He has been very attentive as of late. He might even be my ticket out of this misery at long last. He has changed. He's so carefree, and says he does not care about his inheritance anymore. He is due to complete his animal doctor studies next year and thus stand alone, but he don't look well. I fear he might have consumption, but he swears he ain't."

The hairs on Jason's neck stood on end. Something was prodding his subconscious with all the clues that had been swimming around his head these last couple of months. His hunch was becoming very strong, matching Abberline's from all those years ago. "Did you meet either of the Joes that evening?"

"Oh yes. My proper Joe came to see me as he does every day since we split, but I had Lizzie with me. She's another one of the girls forced to earn a shilling. He came around just before 8pm, but didn't stay long on account of my company. He hated the fact that I was helping out my friends, but I was getting thirsty by that point, and wanted some supper, so I went to the Ten Bells to find something."

The Ten Bells. A pang of fear and sadness passed through Jason as he remembered back to that night when he came charging to the rescue of Samantha and her friend. "Did you meet someone, Mary?"

"Oh yes, had to really, on account that I was brasic. Always easy to get a fella to buy me a drink. Billy was there, he was only too happy to buy me drinks, trying to get me fluthered he was, and I think it worked. Oh my, it is all so hazy from here on in. I can't really see too well."

"Don't worry Mary, that's just the beer making you feel a little drunk. Who is Billy?"

"Oh, he's a harmless one, a market trader. He's got such a soft spot for me, too. Mm, he even bought me fish and potatoes for supper, but then he knew he'd be getting his reward afterwards; just a quick blowsy this time for walking me home, but enough to keep him happy. Nice man."

Jason looked at his Ripper notes prepared by Isambard, outlining what was known about her last night on this earth. "Was he wearing a Billycock hat by any chance?"

Glover was laughing again, as if he was drunk now, and in the past. "Ha ha, yes that's right, that's how he first introduced himself to me, said his name was Billy, and that his hat was named after him. He was all Billy and no cock if you ask me, silly sausage. He had so much red hair I just started calling him Billy the Carrot in the end."

"And then he left?"

"Oh yes, no point in keeping him around, and I still needed some money. I've had enough drink to forget my fears now my lovely, time to go on the street again. I so hate the cold though."

"Who did you meet next?"

"A few people, but they were just wasting my time. I even asked my friend George for a shilling when I saw him, but he says he's skint too."

Suddenly Mary's voice got higher and louder. "Oh, my heavens, it's my Joe, my gentleman friend, he's all togged up this evening. I'm telling him, it's too dangerous to walk around like that, but he doesn't seem to care, says he's ready to confront anyone who takes him on. I must say, his bravado is quite becoming. I wish he had been like this on our honeymoon in Paris."

"What is he wearing, Mary?"

"Oh I don't know, ducks, I'm not really concentrating, if you know what I mean?"

"Try looking at him very carefully and telling me what you can see."

"I don't feel very steady. His face seems to be cloudy. He has a moustache, but they all have a moustache these days. Why do you need to know what he looks like?"

Ives didn't want to worry her. "I'm just interested to

meet your Joe."

"Oh my word, why are my eyes not working properly, what's happening to me?"

Mary was nearing death, the fear of the situation clouding her mind.

Chapter 50 – Family Ties

It has been a fair while since she last saw her brother, but Sabina is glad that she has, even though it can be upsetting sometimes. Her argument with Jason and confession regarding her family has reminded her that she is not alone, even if Sebastian does have huge problems of his own. Well usually; he is looking a lot better than she has seen him in a long time.

He found God just over a year ago and it seems to have given him peace. If that is the case, Sabina feels she could do with a little God worship herself. If only she could give in to something like that. How wonderful it would be to just walk into a family of believers, with the right supportive network to help you on your journey. But she can't fake something like that, no matter how tempting.

And his group have found him a job, in spite of that hideous tattoo that he still refuses to have removed. He seems different this time though, calmer, as if he has worked through some of his daemons, and is actually considering laser treatment.

Sebastian thinks that maybe he has served his penance at last, and that it is time to change his outer personage, now that the inner person feels purer. A small part of him feels absolved from his sins. Sabina is not so sure, but at least it makes him feel better about himself, so she is happy for him.

They went for a walk and she broke down in tears... the second time that day. Once the floodgates open, it is difficult to shut them again, but she felt better for it. She explained to him about the pressures of work and the huge case they were working on, and he was showing some interest. His bible group have been discussing this reincarnation of Jack the Ripper, and debating what God's purpose in it all must be. Is he really attacking these prostitutes as a message to clean up the streets of London? Is the message so powerful that it would go further out into the world? He seemed curiously obsessed with the Ripper, and some things he said worried her, but she didn't want to push it; too complicated by far.

And whilst Sabina didn't agree with everything he said about God, she was just glad that it was working for him. He looked taller and healthier with this new found purpose, as if touched by the Holy Spirit itself. Even discussing the case was therapeutic. They hadn't had a proper conversation in years.

She mentioned Jason Ives, and tried to humanise him a little by saying that he was a good person doing a difficult job, but Sebastian said that he still had not learnt to forgive what had happened to their father. One day he would though, and then he would be truly free, for they were both trapped by their bitterness towards their past.

"We have had a good lead though, Sebastian," she said, "Jason is interviewing a victim called Mary Kelly, and I think it will at least lead to the identity of the Ripper from 1888. Maybe it is time for people to know who he was at long last."

Sebastian looked at her with those same lapis blue eyes; twins, peas in a pod, identical in so many ways and all but telepathic; the chaos of their past haunting both their minds. "Has Kelly not endured enough?"

"I would have thought so, and she is a he now... and a Ripperologist. Honestly Seb, the world just does not make sense anymore."

Sebastian darkened, his faith being tested by modern events in a world that was changing faster than anyone could truly comprehend. They talked at great length about this point; all the players in this theatre of life, converging to tell such a sorry tale. Sabina said more than she should have, but hell, he is her brother, and it was so good to talk.

It reminded her how much she loves her brother, and he loves her.

The twins are bonding again...

...some good coming from chaos and madness.

Chapter 51 – The Parcel

"Don't worry Mary, your eyes are working fine, just that your memory is a little muddled. Use your older memories of what he looked like to break through the fog." Ives was using every trick in the book to keep her on her last memories. "Freeze the moment you see him in the light and describe what you see to me."

"Ooh, I didn't know I could do that, my dear. Hmm, let me see. He's wearing a soft felt hat and a long dark coat with some fur on the trim."

"That's very good, carry on."

"And he has a white collar with a black necktie that's fixed with a horseshoe pin. Oh I like his shoes, so smart, but they are getting dirty in our streets, not like the West End. He's wearing dark spats over light button over boots and has a huge gold chain sitting in his waistcoat and a red stone hanging from it. He'll get done over if he's not careful, just mark my words, but as I said, he don't seem worried for some reason, bold as brass he is. 'What are you doing here?' I says. He says he's got a present for me... how lovely. He used to buy me such lovely dresses, but that was so long ago."

"Is it in a parcel?"

"Yes it is, sweetheart, how did you know?"

It was all written down for him, the witness statement from her friend George Hutchinson, who had been worried by this stranger hanging around her. He'd even followed them to Miller's Court to make sure she was alright, but gave up as the clock struck 3 o'clock in the morning. Hutchinson described a gentleman wearing kid gloves and carrying a parcel. Hutchinson probably never got over the events of that night; the time when he could have caught the Ripper, or at least, saved Mary's life.

"Oh, just a guess." Jason said cheekily.

"You are a clever one. He's been hankering on coming back to my place, but it's a frightful mess. Hmm, but I want to know what the present is now, and he says he's getting cold. He's been so nice, so I says, 'all right my dear, come along, you will be comfortable'. Then he puts his arm around me and gives me the sweetest of kisses, as if we have been married for years on end."

Mary stopped for a moment, looking into the scene. "Oh no, I've lost my handkerchief, which is upsetting because I've got a cold coming on, so he gives me his red hanky. It's so soft, and he tells me it is a token of his love. He's always saying soft things like that to me; loves me, he does."

"Did you go back to your lodgings then?"

"Oh yes, he's suggesting we get a fire started to warm ourselves up. He seems carefree and serious at the same time, his manner is very confusing, but then it might just be the ale talking. He is promising to take me away from all of this mess. I owes so much rent, almost 30 shillings of arrears, but he says he'll pay that too. He wants me to move to Hampstead with him to set up a practice. I'll be his governess to guard his respectability, and means we could be together. It sounds too good to be true."

"Are you going to accept his offer, Mary?"

"I don't know, it's all so sudden, I can't think straight, everything is so muddled. **Oh murder!**"

"What is it Mary, are you okay?"

"Oh yes dear, I just screamed out when I saw the initials on his hanky. They have JR sewn in, so I says, 'that's Jack the Ripper's initials', but he just laughed. He says, 'you silly girl, they are my initials, JR... Joseph

Ride'. I was fair faint when I saw them at first."

Jason tried to remain calm, but he was very excited. At last they have the full name of either the last person to see her, or the Ripper himself. Now they can go through records to see if this Joseph Ride is on any type of database they can gain access to. Awakening, genealogy, police or public records... any type of record held for any kind of reason that could leave a trail to his life now in the 21st century. But the interview isn't finished yet. Mary is still seeing into her past, far longer than Jason would have hoped, but then this had not been a quick killing as with all his other victims, this was a social visit and a promise of love and a new life.

"What was in the parcel, Mary?"

"It was some fine lace and some documents showing lodgings in Hampstead, and he also brought a small bottle of London Dry Gin for us to enjoy. I'm so happy, I can't stop singing... Oh, wait a minute. What is happening, his face has changed, why does he look so strange?"

"How do you feel?"

"Feel? How do you think I should feel? I'm scared... why are the walls moving?"

"It's okay Mary, I'm here remember, and can bring you back at any time."

"Then bring me back, I don't think I like it here anymore."

The Awakening interview had reached that awkward point again, just as it had done with Elizabeth at his last Session. Once again he found himself having to promise safety, but take her right to the edge too. Every detail gleaned could be what makes the difference. Yes, he had a full name now, but would that be enough?

"I will, don't worry, just give me a minute more to look around. Describe the room."

"Do you promise?"

"Of course, everything is in control." A guilt ridden answer, even though he knows he can pull her out of 1888 in an instant.

"Okay, but only a quick look. Joe has lit the fire with a few old clothes and rags. I didn't want him to really, but he says I can leave all my old clothes behind. We'll go shopping in the morning. It'll be lovely, and the fire feels so warm now. Honestly, the damp had worked its way right through to my bones, so we are sitting by the fire and chatting as we drink the gin."

"What is he saying, Mary?"

"Same old... He says he loves me of course, but I know that. This time seems different though, I believe him and his promises, but then I must admit that I want to escape this vile life so bad. I think I'll give him a kiss... I actually want to, and he kisses me right back. Oh, I don't think I should tell you what's happening next; it is a little indelicate, if you know what I mean."

"Don't worry, just tell me as much as you can, Mary, as it is quite important."

"Why is it important?" Mary didn't sound so happy.

"We need to find Joseph Ride, and you can help."

"Feels odd talking indelicately to my brother."

"Ha, I'm sure it probably does, but I'm not really your brother am I, just someone you can trust as if I was your brother, or someone strong to protect you, but I do need to know as much as you can tell me."

"Hmm, I've heard it all now, sweetheart. Well, we just start kissing, soft like, but his passion is strong. His coat is off now and I'm trying to open his shirt, but he won't let me. He was always so strong, but now he feels thin and sallow and I'm getting worried about his health again. I'm pulling his shirt open... Oh heavens!"

"What can you see, Mary?"

"He has the pox, and he has it real bad, terminal like. I'm scared Jason, I can't scream though. His hands are around my neck, his eyes wild. Get me out of here... please, for the love of God!"

Jason used the safe word of 'Resolution' to bring Glover out of his trance. A change from woman to man, from 1888 to 2065. One hundred and seventy-seven years passed in an instant. Ives had heard enough, and knew they had been very lucky in having someone who could see that close to their own death.

Maybe the Ripper had just strangled her enough to make her pass out. Maybe he wanted to say more words to her. Ives had to wonder what anyone might say to someone they love as they murder them. Love and hate are both sides of the same coin after all. Do you say sorry as you take their life? Do you try and revive them when the red mist has passed? History may never know what happened over the next couple of hours between Mary and Joseph Ride.

According to police witness statements from neighbours, a Mrs Cox said she'd heard someone go out at a quarter to six in the morning, so that would have given the murderer a couple of hours to burn her gifts of lace, and maybe the documents he'd brought with him.

Now Jason knew that this man called Joseph Ride was Mary's killer, and in his mind, was definitely the Ripper.

His initials of JR might have given him the idea to send a letter to the Central News Agency and invent the name Jack the Ripper to boast his kills. Or just to put them off the scent, or as a warning to all the women of the night to change their ways. They didn't seem to have a choice though. Certainly Mary had not on that cold night. They all needed money, even though they drank a lot of it when they could. The drink drove out the cold and made them forget the terrible world they were living in.

Joseph Ride, a veterinarian student with only one more year till he graduated. Same height as Mary Kelly, so about 5 foot 7 inches, and riddled with the pox, so Mary had said. To the point of it being terminal. It made sense, as the killings seemed to stop from that point, although many would say that they didn't. Mary was the last of the five canonical victims, and had been the victim mutilated the most; her face completely disfigured, and her heart was found to be missing at the post mortem. She had stolen his heart, and so he had finally stolen hers; a lover's retribution.

Ives hated keeping anyone in an Awakening trance so close to their death, but yet again it had proved invaluable. For the first time since this damn investigation had started, he felt they had a good chance of catching this tortured soul.

At long last, Jack the Ripper had been unmasked!

Chapter 52 – Retribution

Eyes wide open. Daylight filtering through the lens, hitting the retina and landing upon the rods and cones that sense light, and turn the resulting impulses into signals that reach the brain. A brain that converts the billions of signals into an image that it can understand, and instantly 'see' what is happening outside of the body. Until that point the brain is visually blind, relying on its other senses of touch, taste, hearing and smell to move around its alien universe. Everything in the mind and within the body are that person's personal universe, and is interpreted accordingly.

This brain is slightly different. It would appear that there are several universes held within the same space, the same body, all vying for the top position of conscious thought. Jack has fought his way to the top right now, using another sense... pain. Physical and emotional pain illuminate his particular universe right now. It is how he 'sees' and interprets the world; a world that is growing more insane than he is. He has heard news of Mary Kelly and he cannot understand a word of it.

She is alive, but she is now a man! This abomination layered upon his own abominations where they are both in fucked up bodies, as if that is the price for coming back at all. Until this moment, he had hoped that she would be out there somewhere, waiting for him to rescue her from this strange alien world in which they are both very much the outsiders. But he cannot love her now... not like this. Is this his retribution? Does he have to suffer for his sins even if he is being bidden by God himself? It makes some kind of sense in his muddled head. So this must be the ultimate sacrifice, to do the Lord's bidding no matter what the price.

It would be too easy otherwise.

There is only one course of action to take now, it is clear. He must find this George Glover holding the spirit of Mary within him, just as he is held prisoner in this body. He must then convince her to enter a suicide pact with him, so that one day they can meet again in their rightful bodies, and away from this accursed city.

Now they must both die...

Chapter 53 – The Lodger

Time is moving very slowly for Isambard today, but then time has always been an odd element for him to grasp. His passion for all things Victorian makes him feel like he is living a double life sometimes, with his modern day life existing underwater. Every now and again, he is allowed to rise to the surface to take another breath of air before submerging back to the depths.

He is lucky that he has found a soul mate who understands his peculiar obsession. Indeed, he met her at a Victoriana fair almost twenty years ago when he'd had more hair and vigour, but it had been his peculiar pattern of speech that had intrigued and entranced her in the end. That and their shared past, lost loves from a time gone by, reunited by chance and Awakening.

But right now he is happy to be in the present day, even though it is related to the past. He is trying to patiently wait for Ives to finish his Awakening session with his friend Glover, to see if they have gleaned any fresh details that could free the logjam of information that has been blighting the Ripper investigation since Abberline's day.

It is only five o'clock, but it seems a lot later in the day than it really is. Time for his second, and final large cup of coffee of the day. He knows he is a creature of habit, but it gives him little points in his routine to look forward to, and right now, the bittersweet taste of hot coffee on his tongue has been a craving he's put off for the last hour. He's been very patient and obedient to his time keeping, so feels he deserves his treat at long last, as he carefully measures out the filter coffee to make a fresh brew.

Ives emerged from the corridor with a big smile on his face and grabbed Isambard's bony shoulder. "Hey, I've got great news, my friend. You got time for a quick meeting in the sergeant's office? I want to chat with you about it before we see Bjorkman and her goons."

Isambard looked at his coffee with a sad longing as it sat brewing in the corner. It will be cold by the time he gets back to it, but can't bring himself to say no to Ives in this enthusiastic state. "Of course sir, it would be my pleasure."

As soon as they entered the office, Jason closed the door and sat on the desk to make himself comfortable. "Isambard, I have a name for you to run a check on. Have you ever heard of a Joseph Ride?"

Isambard looked stuck. His face froze as he tried to locate the name Ives had given him in his memory bank. "The name does seem most familiar, Mr Ives, but I would not have the presumptuous temerity to suggest in what context. Is he a suspect or witness that you have happened upon?"

Ives slowly translated Isambard's words. "He is a suspect. In fact, he is the 'my Joe' that we have been looking for." He paused for a second to let it sink in. "Mary Kelly had a special client that had followed her from her better days at the Mayfair brothel. It would seem that he was besotted by her, and was the last person to see Kelly alive."

"So Mr Glover was able to remember Kelly's killer?"

"Yes, he was amazing, so calm and collected, the perfect subject to put through such a harrowing Awakening. Kelly was picked up by Joseph Ride just after 2am on the night of her death, and matches the description given by George Hutchinson, the last witness to see her alive. They spoke at some length before Ride followed her back to her lodgings. Ride was very relaxed and confident, talking for another hour or more before murdering her. She must have been terrified."

Isambard pulled out the large polymer viewing screen from the side of his mobile, and punched in several details related to Joseph Ride and the Ripper for an internet search as Ives continued.

"It would seem that Joseph Ride was calm because he knew he was dying of syphilis. He already had a death sentence that was far more painful and terrifying than the rope."

"Oh indeed sir, the pox was rampant in London at that time, and so painful it could most literally drive a person insane."

Ives looked at Isambard as the penny dropped. "Of course, it all makes so much sense now. He catches the pox from a prostitute, maybe even Mary herself, and it drives him insane. Who else would he take his anger out on, but one of the girls who'd passed it on to him? And with his lack of fear, and seemingly good luck, he was able to commit these audacious crimes right under the noses of the police and public of Whitechapel."

"Indubitably, Mr Ives, I think you have knocked that particular nail on its logical head." Isambard then saw something of interest on his screen. "Oh my word."

"What?"

"The lodger theory... it has some truth to it after all."

"The what?"

Isambard explained his thoughts. "The artist Walter Sickert has been a suspect since his death in the mid 1900's, and then again in 2002 when the crime author Patricia Cornwell claimed to have DNA evidence that linked him and one of the Ripper letters. Sickert was obsessed by crime, and especially by tales of the Ripper. Indeed, he once claimed that lodgings in which he had once rented had also been inhabited by the Ripper."

Ives shook his head, dumbfounded by this sudden

news. "What, really? If we knew where the Ripper lived, surely that would have led to his identity?"

"Not in the case of the Ripper, sir. As you may have realised by now, his trail is full of red herrings created by hoaxers or misguided investigators. It makes it very difficult to know which avenue to walk down. Walter Sickert was also suspected of being caught up with royalty and Masonic plots, much the same as Abberline was. Most curiously though, he painted several scenes believed to be Ripper related, and one actually called 'Jack the Ripper's Bedroom,' which has had a lot of examination, but still gives no clear evidence."

"But what about the DNA evidence you just mentioned from Patricia Cornwell?"

"Yes, it gave a match, but it was from such small quantities and so old that it could only put Sickert into a genetic group of people who could have done it, rather than an exact hit. Even if it had been a direct hit, it would only prove Sickert had written a Ripper letter. It has been estimated that over six hundred letters were sent after the murders. Two women were even prosecuted for sending them. By all accounts, Sickert's Ripper obsession and character would agree more with this, than him actually being the killer."

Ives had to remind himself that he now had the name of the man who murdered Mary Kelly, although it would still take some work to link him to the other murders. To know with confidence that he had been the Whitechapel murderer, rather than a copycat killer. Sickert could still be a suspect. Hell, it would seem anyone could have been a suspect in those days.

He still needed more information. "What else does it say in that 'lodger' report?"

Isambard scrolled down the page. "It would comply

with the geographical clue we had earlier. Apparently Walter Sickert's lodgings were in Mornington Crescent, Camden, in a house owned by an elderly couple. It was several years after the killings, but it was them that told Sickert that they had lodged the Ripper. They'd been suspicious due to the odd activities of their tenant going out at all hours, and burning his clothes from time to time."

Ives could feel the pieces coming together. "Kelly's killer burnt items in her fireplace... it has a definite link and is a good story, but is it to cover Sickert's tracks, do you think?"

Isambard was still reading from his screen. "A plausible theory I must concur, but I have just found notes from a book called 'Noble Essences: A Book of Characters' by Osbert Sitwell, published in 1950. Apparently Sickert had told Osbert of this strange tale, many years later. I'll read this excerpt."

With that, Isambard found where he wanted to start from, cleared his throat, and read aloud.

"Some years after the murders, he had taken a room in a London suburb. An old couple looked after the house, and when he had been there some months, the woman, with whom he used often to talk, asked him one day as she was dusting the room if he knew who had occupied it before him. When he said "No" she had waited a moment, and then replied, "Jack the Ripper!" . . . Her story was that his predecessor had been a veterinary student."

Ives suddenly interrupted the reading. "Kelly told me that Joseph Ride was a Veterinary student! It looks like Sickert was telling the truth after all."

"It would appear so, which will be a surprise for many of my colleagues." Isambard then looked back at his screen.

270

"After he had been a month or two in London, this delicate-looking young man -- he was consumptive -- took to staying out occasionally all night. His landlord and landlady would hear him come in at about six in the morning, and then walk about in his room for an hour or two until the first edition of the morning paper was on sale, when he would creep lightly downstairs and run to the corner to buy one. Quietly he would return and go to bed; but an hour later, when the old man called him, he would notice, by the traces in the fireplace, that his lodger had burned the suit he had been wearing the previous evening. For the rest of the day, the millions of people in London would be discussing the terrible new murder, plainly belonging to the same series, that had been committed in the small hours. Only the student seemed never to mention it: but then, he knew no one and talked to no one, though he did not seem lonely. The old couple did not know what to make of the matter: week by week his health grew worse, and it seemed improbable that this gentle, ailing, silent youth should be responsible for such crimes. They could hardly credit their own senses -- and then, before they could make up their minds whether to warn the police or not, the lodger's health had suddenly failed alarmingly, and his mother -- a widow who was devoted to him - had come to fetch him back to Bournemouth, where she lived. . . . From that moment the murders had stopped. He died three months later." Isambard stopped reading and looked at Ives.

Ives was ecstatic. "It all fits. What was simply a tale from an artist obsessed by the Ripper now looks like a witness statement."

"To be honest sir, it could well have been this occurrence that started Sickert's obsession."

"You could be right Isambard, it would certainly arouse

my curiosity, especially if I had the type of artistic temperament that Sickert seems to have had. How does Ride's name feature in all of this, though?"

"In a very tenuous link I'm afraid to report. He goes on to say that the landlady told Sickert the lodger's name, which he then supposedly wrote down in the margin of a very rare copy of 'Casanova's Memoirs'. He then gave this valuable book to a gentleman called Albert Rutherford. Unfortunately, Rutherford could not decipher Sickert's handwriting and the book was lost in the Blitz. Osbert Sitwell finished by writing, 'My friend Mr. Rutherston informed me that he lost the book only during the bombing of London, and that there had been several pencil notes entered in the margin, in Sickert's handwriting, always so difficult to decipher."

Ives was now the one jumping up and down. "The Ripper always seems to be able to lose himself in history or scandal or folklore. I can't believe the book was lost in the war."

"You have to remember, Mr Ives, the Blitz destroyed large areas of London. Many people lost their belongings... and their lives."

"I guess so, but you still haven't told me how they got the name Joseph Ride in this report?"

"Oh, that was through the work of a Ripperology journal called 'Ripperama'. One of their editors by the name of N.P. Warren researched this whole affair to find that there was only one student who failed to follow a career beyond 1888, and who came from Bournemouth. His name was Joseph Ride and he was twenty-seven in 1888, the average age of suspects given by several witnesses at the time."

Ives had heard enough. All the pieces of the puzzle were finally coming together.

Chapter 54 – The Name Game

DC John Pascal said little in the meeting. He prefers it that way. You can learn a lot more by listening than talking, and he had nothing to add anyway. Bjorkman had been shocked by Ives's news of the Ripper's identity, as she'd really had no faith in their methods at all; and yet here they were, discussing his name. A name that has eluded some of the best detectives in the world for so many years.

Such an innocuous name, thought Pascal. Joseph Ride... so English, so unassuming, unlike many of the other characters involved in the world of the Ripper. Frank Abberline is a strong name, and Walter Sickert, sounds like Sick Heart, perfect as a mentally disturbed artist obsessed by murder. Osbert Sitwell, Sickert's friend... now that's very Victorian. Then there was Prince Albert Victor, Montague John Druitt, Hyam Hyams, Francis Tumblety, Fogelma, Carl Feigenbaum. All interesting names, but then maybe that is the point, the 'grey man' is always harder to find; they just melt into the crowd.

Pascal still didn't trust Abberline for some reason, but then it probably had to do more with his staged French accent and manipulation of the truth than him being the Ripper himself. Shame really, Abberline had been an officer he'd respected when he first read about him, an officer who knew his patch like the back of his hand. Never meet your heroes, they say.

"Pascal, what the hell are you daydreaming about?" Bjorkman was now forcing him into the conversation.

"Sorry guv, I was, er, formulating a secondary plan of action." He always had been good at thinking of excuses.

Ives looked at him knowingly, but decided to help his

273

friend out. "Yes, I've asked him to make some checks into the artist Walter Sickert just in case we need to find and question him too," he said with a wink.

Bjorkman looked at them both for a second with a scowl, then moved on to the next plan of action. "So what databases do we have access to for this kind of thing?"

Ives had been thinking about that too. "Well, we obviously have the UK national police records, and I have contacts for Europe and North America in a pinch, but probably won't need those. We'll also use Google Generations, of course, it's amazing how many people post their past life links on there. Past life reunion sites are also a fantastic mine of information, but first port of call is the Awakening records. I have special access privileges for past life investigators. I just have to complete the paperwork first."

"Then what are we waiting for, gentlemen? I've told the Chief Super about your miraculous find, and it has bought you some more time, but it has been almost three weeks since the Ripper last struck, and if the past is anything to go by, he'll be due another murder soon." It was a stark warning from their DCI to not waste any time.

"Can I mention Joseph Ride's name to my Ripperologist contacts, dear boss, as they also have databases and forums going back decades that may be of some assistance?" asked Isambard.

Bjorkman wasn't in the mood for taking chances. "No, it is just too big a risk to give his name out at the moment. If the Ripper knows that we know his original name, he might ramp it up a gear or two."

"I understand your reticence to divulge his name ma'am, but I could do it within the small select circle that has already sworn an oath to guard our details with their honour."

Bjorkman was not so sure. "Really Isambard, do people still say that kind of thing?"

"Most certainly, and I think you would find our collective cooperation very helpful. Speed is of the essence here, you have just said so yourself."

"No, not yet, ask me again next week."

Ives disagreed. "I'm sorry but I think Isambard is right. I know it is a tough decision to make. After all, if the name gets out to the press via this group, then it could have grave repercussions, but so could waiting to release it. We need to use every tool we have to catch this maniac. Please don't slow this down any more than is really necessary"

Bjorkman looked at him. She could see his determination and knew he had a point, but she was between a rock and a hard place with this one. "Okay, but it is against my better judgement."

Jason and Isambard nodded in acknowledgement.

"I'm going to make this clear though, if anything happens as a result of this getting out, your heads will be on the block, and I will be the one holding the axe," Bjorkman warned.

Pascal looked at Ives with a smirk on his face. It was so nice to have someone else absorb her frustration and anger for a while. It also gave him a chance to deviate the investigation to some ideas of his own whilst she was distracted. "It might also be useful for me to interview Glover from our side of the investigation, Jason, so if you could give me his details?"

Ives was a little surprised. "Really? But he's only a past witness."

Pascal nodded. "Yes, as far as we know, and that is probably the end of it, but he is still a prime witness in the whole case; and as such, he should be interviewed from the more traditional side of things... or are you afraid of plod getting more out of him than you?" He winked at Ives to show he was teasing him.

Bjorkman took charge. "Good idea. Isambard, set up a meeting with Pascal at his home, he'll feel a lot more comfortable there."

"Of course, dear boss, but I must inform you that he has just flown out to the United States of America for a family visit. I shall endeavour to arrange a meeting as soon as he returns."

Bjorkman rolled her eyes. "And they wonder why it takes so long to get a case investigated. Really, would it have harmed him to delay for a short while?"

"I believe his niece is getting married," offered Ives.

Bjorkman looked a little jaded. "Oh, well at least someone's happily in love. Some of us are just too damn busy to contemplate such a thing. Okay Isambard, do what you can do, and do it fast." It was quite a personal statement from someone so private, and took everyone by surprise, but the small chink in her armour quickly disappeared as she rallied everyone together.

"Okay gentlemen, it's getting late. I suggest we all finish for the evening, and then get cracking through all the databases we can get our fingers into tomorrow morning."

Everyone was happy to be calling it a night. They grabbed their things and started to leave. Bjorkman stood by the door of her office seeing them off.

"Oh, not you Ives, we still have some issues to go over."

Chapter 55– Personal Issues

Jason entered the lion's den. He'd been wondering when this might happen. They hadn't really spoken about 'that moment' they had spent together in her office last time. The moment when it could have been so much more. He'd been offered sex with this beautiful and sometimes frightening woman, but his guilty conscience towards Samantha had stopped him, and for what? Samantha had been the one who'd broken off the relationship too early, and he hadn't heard a word from her since that day.

He closed the door as he went in, then noticed with interest that Bjorkman had opened a few buttons on her blouse to expose those generous breasts of hers. Jason's rather unique mind then reminded him that his attraction to large breasts was just from a very primitive instinct, but it didn't make it any easier to look her in the eye.

"Have you thought any more about 'us', Jason?"

He was still taken aback, her swing from professional ball breaker to sex siren in such a short space of time was a keen reminder that women are the masters of multiple emotions. Without waiting, Sabina pressed her body against his and started kissing him. It would appear that she wasn't going to take a 'No' this time, as her hand strayed down to his crotch.

There was no way he could pretend that he wasn't interested any more, especially with his tongue rolling around in that dirty mouth of hers. Logic jumped ship, his pulse racing at the prospect of having this Scandinavian sexpot forcing herself on him.

With an almighty effort, he pushed back, reclaiming some of the dominance by slamming her against the wall for a moment, his left hand rising up from her waist to the bottom of her breasts... teasing himself whilst teasing her, delaying the moment just a little longer.

He kicked her foot further to the left, spreading her legs just that little bit more. Sabina let out a loud guttural groan, worrying Jason for a moment that someone might hear outside, but he knew it was pretty much empty at this time in the evening. The excitement of maybe getting caught screwing the boss did start kicking in though, all adding to the overwhelming sense of lust coursing through his veins.

Jason felt his animal instinct take over his ability to think with any reason; this... sexual red mist, over-riding everything else in pursuit of the ultimate pleasure. As he felt his body twitch, he knew that she had won this particular battle.

But right now he didn't give a damn!

Chapter 56 – Pillow Talk

Silence for just but a few seconds. Beautiful, delicious, unmitigated silence that breathes a certain stillness into an overactive mind, as if it is pure oxygen. Hmm, beautiful, but deadly by its purity.

Sex. After so long. Sex. Reclaimed, reinstated, re-bloody-markable.

It has been way too long since her last positive encounter, and for that Sabina lies in her bed full of gratitude for the break in her otherwise chaotic life. A life full of so many problems that it sometimes gives her reason to think of ending it all, but she could never do that to her brother, not after all the shit he's already been through in his life. Her twin brother, her boy, her love.

And just like that, the silence is over, interrupted by the inevitable sound of a siren weaving through the London traffic. Then the freezer kicks in, its low hum vibrating through the floor, and the neighbour's dog beginning its night time routine of barking for half an hour before being whisked back into its cramped apartment.

And now she has added to the chaos by 'sleeping with the enemy'. God knows what 'he' will think of that. No doubt there will be hell to pay, but she is dammed anyway, of that she is sure. Well, almost sure. Is there really any Heaven or Hell anymore now that Awakening has arrived? Or is life on this earth some form or purgatory, with billions of years to work out the karma and thus pronounce your sentence?

Her mind starts racing again, so she pushes everything

aside to replay her evening with Jason, the first selfish act she has done for herself in what seems like forever. The feel of his body, his touch, his warmth enveloping hers. After their encounter, he held her for a few minutes in an embrace. The feeling of being protected and... well, love would be too strong a word, but... wanted, it had almost overpowered her to the point of tears, but she couldn't let that happen.

A smile swept across her attractive face, revealing a dimple that rarely sees the light of day in these troubled times. Then she grabbed a large pillow in her near empty king size bed, to hug, and be hugged back. This has been her love life for so bloody long, but now the pillow has a face, and a touch of warmth to it.

Now is the time to cry. To sob and wish things could be different, but still she can't scream out, that is a luxury for people with large houses in the country with no close neighbours. If she wants to scream, she'll have to bite the pillow and clench her fists, screaming out and screaming in at the same time, as she usually does.

Now she sees Jason's face on the pillow though, as she entwines her legs around the bottom part... dancing horizontally in slow motion, her sadness briefly dispersed by a little happiness. A face that she's loved and loathed in equal measure. He is her loving oxymoron; the best and the worst person she could ever be with. She knows she is being silly, but she is alone after all, so she puts out a hand to stroke his imaginary chin on the pillow.

She even looks into his eyes which are smiling back at her, and can't resist the urge to kiss its cotton cover. As she pushes her tongue out against the dry fabric, she imagines that kiss again. Warm, wet, sweet...

Suddenly the taste turns incredibly sour and starts burning the back of her throat as if she has brought up some sick in her mouth. Repelled, Sabina pushes back against the pillow to see the face of Jack the Ripper snarling at her; spittle spraying in her face as he launches into a vile series of insults.

Pure unadulterated hate, emanates from his evil eyes.

∞-∞-∞-∞-∞-∞

It's late, but Jason cannot sleep after the events of the day. His time with Sabina in her office had been amazing in a way, but he knew there would be consequences. She is beautiful, intelligent and strong, but she is also very messed up. Part of him sees the brutal reality of such a relationship, but another part of him looks a little into the future to guess what might be, if only she had someone like him to help her through those problems.

Really, you're actually considering going down this route again? It didn't help with Karen, did it, that fucked up bipolar... He suddenly stopped his angry train of thought, not wanting to give any more energy to the woman who had almost destroyed him with her love and hate routines. A cycle of idolise / demonise that holds little logic and taken almost two years to see sense. But he is a different person now, stronger through his ordeal, wiser, a better person in so many ways.

He flicked the wall unit on to check his string of database searches for the name Joseph Ride. Then added the words Ripper, Bournemouth, Current identity, Awakened state, Observer, 2050-2065... and anything else that might be linked, then ran it through a personal algorithm he'd devised to rank and organise in terms of word importance, against number of hits. He'd already gone through one level of searching, but it was beginning to look pretty certain that there was going to be no official record of a Joseph Ride from 1888 being Awakened and identified.

It didn't surprise Ives. After all, just like fingerprints and DNA, unless there is a reason for disclosure it wouldn't necessarily be made accessible, even at his security clearance level. Unlike fingerprints and DNA though, if it has happened, it will be recorded somewhere, even if just a footnote in a routine report. He has to hope that some little detail has slipped out somewhere that could lay a small clue to finding the right file.

They have found the Victorian Ripper's identity at long last, which is an amazing feat in itself, so surely now they can find the link to who he is?

∞-∞-∞-∞-∞-∞-∞

"You dirty whore, you Jezebel from the pits of humanity."

The Ripper was angrier than ever before. Can he really see everything that she has been up to? Sabina was horrified by this sudden apparition. She has seen him before of course, and knows about his existence; her shameful, disastrous secret that has burnt her soul. But can he really see what she does when he is asleep?

"Don't talk to me like that, Joe! What would you know about humanity anyway?"

Jack's face was everywhere she looked. "You disgust me. I see you cavorting with this oddity of an investigator. I see your memories, mother of mine, can you not understand how sickening that is to me?" His voice had risen higher and higher to the point of despair, interspersed with sobs. His pain was evident.

"I am not your mother!" How many times has she

screamed this at him, but the alternative is no better. To know that you are the Ripper himself, his reincarnated form thrust upon you in the prime of your life. A troubled life that had just begun to settle, the calm before the storm.

The 'mother' of all storms.

∞-∞-∞-∞-∞-∞

Jason checked his messages. His contacts and friends may be of little use in this particular case, but you never know. Cody might find that the new Ripper had been born in the United States, or Jasmine from Interpol might find a more international option. He'd put out his urgent request to all of his contacts but one. That would be his last resort, the card up his sleeve to use only if absolutely necessary. He'd give it a few more days first to get all his replies back from his web of investigators, garnered from assignments all over the world.

And now he also had Isambard, who might be his best chance yet. He'd certainly come up trumps with finding Mary Kelly... and to think that he'd even wondered about him being a suspect at first. Jeez, something had spooked his usually good senses right at the start of this investigation, what with Isambard and Sabina featuring on his initial silly list.

He must be really losing it.

∞-∞-∞-∞-∞-∞

Right now, Sabina was literally losing her mind. He was taking over again, stealing her body, but this time whilst she is still awake. Is he getting stronger, or she is getting weaker? She really can't tell. She's tried screaming at him, pleading with him, begging him to lie low, telling him that she cannot protect them both much longer if anyone else should die.

If only she had reported her mental state right at the beginning, but she had been too afraid to talk, especially in light of what had happened to her father. She knew Scotland Yard would ditch her without a second thought. They'd say some kind words, but as soon as her back was turned they would be stabbing her in it. She would have lost everything, and it would have finished off her and her brother. Oh God, what will happen to him?

She had been a victim from the absolute beginning thanks to David, her bastard ex-boyfriend and Observer, blackmailing her from the start.

David had been the catalyst.

The trigger that fired Jack back.

Chapter 57 – Ripped Out

8 Months earlier.

November 2064 - Sabina's apartment.

The headaches are getting worse, but Sabina can handle that for the moment. The real problem is with David. The bastard is really taking the piss now.

"David, you know I hate that you are doing this to me. This is blackmail, don't you realise that?"

But David takes no notice of her words; in fact, it only spurs him. He loves the power he has over her; it is intoxicating and he is addicted. He crept up behind her and cupped her breasts with his large hands that end with grimy fingernails.

"I know you don't mean that my little strumpet."

He is her ex-boyfriend and ex-Awakening Observer, who had convinced her to have more sessions. To regain extra past skills that would help her in her new promotion at work and allow her to be more 'aware' like everyone else. She'd known in her heart of hearts that it was probably a bad idea, but she had been trying to face her fears.

Jack the fucking Ripper... She hadn't known it was him at first, she just thought she'd been a murderer called Joe. If only. A normal murderer might have been okay, after all, things seem to have changed since her father's day, but it still would have caused problems with work.

She'd heard of some good officers losing their position due to unfortunate discoveries, and most people find this sort of thing out early on in their Awakening Foundation when young. It seems more acceptable and they plan their career path accordingly, as long as they were not a psycho serial killer.

But Jack the Ripper - he was exactly that, a vile psycho killer of unfortunate women.

David was just as shocked as she was at the time, and kept it off the record. He'd been pretty good originally, but then when she had wanted to end their relationship he turned really nasty. He threatened to tell the police, so she threatened to tell his wife. It was the turning point in which they both suddenly hated each other.

Now he is blackmailing her for sex, knowing full well that she doesn't want to be physical with him. How ironic that she is now the one effectively prostituting herself, to save a prostitute killer. If it wasn't so sad it would be funny.

The evenings are dark already, and a bitter wind is howling through the gutters. Sabina feels trapped by her situation, and the weather is just making her feel worse. It's only 10pm, but it has been dark for almost five hours. She is shattered and just wants to go to bed, but without David hounding her. She just wants him to leave.

Maybe it was because her period was due that tipped the balance, or that she was on her fourth glass of wine to try and block her life out of her mind. Maybe everything was just coming to a head, combining to bring all the elements into play that create a monster. Or maybe it was just fate, something that she would never have control over. Whatever the case, she would have to live with the consequences for the rest of her life.

She pushed him away. "For fuck's sake David, leave me alone. I'm not your plaything. It's time for you to leave."

David was also drunk from too much wine. He just

laughed in her face. "Aw, stop playing hard to get, you frigid bitch, you know you want it."

"All I want is for you to get out of my apartment, don't you get that?"

David took hold of her arms and pushed her against the wall. He licked her face then pushed his hand between her legs. "I love it when you play hard to get, you know that? The more you say no, the more I want you."

"Leave me alone."

"Come on, I'm trying to give you a clue here, you cold cow. Tell me you want me to shag you and I'll get bored." David loved playing mind games with her.

"Fuck off." She tried pushing him away, but he was too strong. He was literally pinning her to the wall by her neck and her crotch.

"Tell me to fuck you and I'll let go," he snarled.

She was exhausted. She just wanted him to leave. "Fuck me David," she said sarcastically.

"Better, but not good enough. Say please as if you mean it."

Sabina tried to stay calm. She felt that if she was going to lose it now, she would never stop being angry, so she done what he asked, hoping he'd leave her alone. "Please fuck me."

Unsurprisingly it didn't work. Instead he just became more aggressive. "About time too. I'm going to give you a right seeing to that you'll never forget." He kicked her feet from under her, and pushed her to the floor. Sabina screamed out.

"No, get away, leave me alone."

"And now I want you even more," David said, relishing the control. He was pulling her jeans off now, with her trying to kick and scream. He put his hand over her mouth and whispered in her ear. "I think someone needs to tell the police about your dirty secret."

Sabina stopped kicking. It was pointless fighting, he was in total control of her destiny. He could use and abuse her as he wished. Tears welled up as she softly pushed against his chest, but all her strength had suddenly deserted her.

A smile crossed David's face. "Nah, I want more than that. Put up a little bit of a fight at least. I want our fantasy rape to feel real."

She looked at him incredulously. "What? You are raping me you bastard, don't you get it?"

Slap! The back of his hand against her face.

"Ow, stop."

Slap! The taste of blood in her mouth from her cut gum. "Please, stop," she screamed.

He held her again by the neck as a rage took over him, strangling her to the point of blacking out... everything turning dark.

As Sabina begins to pass out, she finds herself dreaming of a snow covered hillside. Beautiful thick snow from a Disney movie; from the days before global warming had taken that treat away in England. Running and shouting and throwing snowballs at a little boy called Joe wearing a funny Victorian outfit. She feels so happy playing this game, especially when they go sledging.

"I want to go first," she shouts as she grabs a sled and runs up the hill. The cold air fills her lungs from the exertion, but it is worth it for the view at the top. A beautiful snow covered landscape that goes on forever, just begging for her to ride down.

Then the scary man next to her cuts the skin off a rabbit, and the blood spurts out into the snow as if its heart is still beating. Blood soaking into the snow like wine into a tissue, eventually turning her whole world red. A blood covered landscape... a blood covered floor... that leads to a corpse next to her.

It is David with a chest full of holes from multiple stab wounds. Even in her confused state, Sabina knows from her professional experience that such a frenzied killing implies extreme hate, and that hate is surging through her body. It feels good. It gives her strength. It gives her a short burst of freedom.

Freedom from David. The only person to know of their clandestine meetings, and the only person to know of her past. Then the horror of it all suddenly hits her. She is a police officer, a detective chief inspector of the Metropolitan police and she has just committed a murder!

She will have to use her police knowledge to dispose of his body – acid probably, and flush him down the toilet where he belongs. And apologise to neighbours if they say anything about the noise. It wouldn't be the first time they'd heard rows.

With the horror follows a period of madness. Her mind had been searching for an answer, and Jack had come to the fore. He had seized the opportunity to break through when she had been at her weakest point. She was all but finished until the Ripper had come to her rescue.

Jack had saved her life.
Jack was her saviour.
Jack was now her.
Jack was...

Back...

Chapter 58 – Dear Boss

Ives was frustrated by the endless dead alleys presenting themselves. Three days have passed since their last meeting, and yet no one is making any kind of headway with the new information. It seems as if Joseph Ride is a ghostlike figure himself, when looking at the scant details of his life in Bournemouth and London. A quiet man, unassuming and mostly forgotten.

No records of his Awakening in the last thirty years either, almost as far back as Awakening itself, giving the false impression that it just didn't happen. But logic dictates that he must have been Awakened somewhere, otherwise they wouldn't have a problem now.

The atmosphere with Sabina was odd too, as if she was trying to forget that 'they' had ever happened. She blew hot and cold, and was even more erratic than ever. Jason decided to just let it lie. She was probably on extra stressed mode with this turn in the investigation, and just wanted to concentrate on finding Jack. They'd have plenty of time to talk once this nightmare was over, and in a stupid way, it felt good to have to second guess this woman, even if her damn wall could be infuriating at times. It was fresh and unpredictable, which appealed to a darker side of him.

DC Carter received a message on his mobile, read it and turned white. Suddenly everyone was getting messages, filling the room with an annoying mix of tunes, and sounding like some form of awful jazz tech fusion. Carter looked at Bjorkman, then lost his nerve, turning on Ives instead.

"Er, Jason, it would seem that the Ripper has left a message for the press."

Carter flicked the wall screen on, and asked for 'News with Ripper letter' as a search. Already the web was full of entries. Carter scrolled down to the BBC site and selected the appropriate link to find an image file of a letter sent to the press purporting to be from the Ripper himself.

The huge screen displayed the letter for everyone to read:

Dear Boss,

I feel love and pity for you, but then you know that dont you? I keep reading that the police are close, but they wont fix me just yet, cos I'm cleverer than they likes to admit. I have a new game to play this time though, are you interested? The next job I do will be my most daring venture yet.

I want Jason Ives dead!

It makes me laugh just thinking about it. I want to Rip him proper, foot to face for what hes done to my poor Mary. Let the world know that he has trapped her in some black fellas body, and to think that they call me the sick one!
And you Dear Boss, I think you are a dirty trollop, no better than my whores, so maybe I'll fix you next. I have not thought it through yet.
Cant chat all day, I've got work to do. My knives wont sharpen themselves.

Yours Truly,
    Jack the Ripper

PS: Tell that Glover fella that I'm gonna let Mary Kelly out of her cage soon enough. She'll be alright by me she will.

Ives let out a loud groan. "How in the hell?"

Even Bjorkman wasn't strong enough to hide her dismay for a few seconds. She closed her eyes to block everything out, took a deep breath and decided to press on as if this was a good thing. "Okay, so he's made contact to start rumours, sling mud and issue some threats. Sounds like he's running scared if you ask me."

Pascal didn't know what to think. 'Dear Boss' had to be aimed at Bjorkman, but what did he think he had on her? And how did the Ripper know about Glover being Kelly? And then there was the use of the term 'Dear Boss'. He knew it was a Ripper introduction of course, but it is also what Isambard always calls her, and now it sounded more wrong than ever. In his eyes, Isambard had suddenly turned from being a harmless eccentric, to a seriously freaky stick insect who knew too much about the case.

Everyone started looking at each other, wondering where the leak had come from and then settled on the pale face of Isambard, who blinked back at them with memories of his school days returning to haunt him.

He tried to explain the letter. "May I be so bold as to suggest that the Ripper has surreptitiously planted this communiqué to divide our unit?"

Still silence.

Isambard pushed on. "It seems quite apparent Dear..."

Pascal started shouting. "If you call her dear boss once more I'm going to ask everyone to look the other way whilst I smash your face against the wall."

A few more moments of silence.

"I apologise profusely. It was most insensitive of me. As you know, my particular vernacular is just a skewed element of my sometimes unorthodox nature; but it is fairly innocuous, I mean no harm." Unfortunately, the more nervous Isambard became, the more he got lost in long words.

Ives put a hand on his shoulder. "Don't worry about it."

"Don't worry about it?" ranted Pascal, "how the hell does the Ripper know about Glover? There must be less than twenty people involved in this case that know about him, because we were too afraid of the repercussions. So guess what? The Ripper already knows, so who told him?"

Bjorkman joined in the fracas. "I have to admit, Isambard, that your Ripper terminology and choice of words are creepily similar to what you might expect the Ripper himself to use, and you and Ives are the only outsiders. We've been working as a team for over four years now, and never a hint of a leak."

Jason stood his ground. "Hey, just because we aren't police officers doesn't make us press informants, and just because Isambard's language is different, doesn't make him a Ripper suspect or snitch. Don't forget, Glover may also have said something to someone he thought he could trust. Or someone we might have asked to 'quietly assist' us... didn't keep quiet."

"Oh I doubt they would sir," ventured Isambard.

Ives shook his head in disbelief. "Not now, Isambard. Look, maybe someone has seen a note left around this office, or the board on the wall with Glover written all over it! We could all be to blame." Jason was trying to diffuse the situation, but it was only getting worse. Now Carter was having a go.

"Ha, so you think the Ripper has been cleaning our office so he can spy on us? That would take some balls. What next, maybe you'd like to implicate Commander Pashmali, or the guvnor? What do you think, guv?"

"Shut up Carter, I've got enough idiots to deal with in this room without you adding to the burden."

"Yes guv, sorry guv."

A look of anger was firmly etched on Bjorkman's face, but she was fighting it. "Let's calm down and set a plan of action. Glover lands back at Heathrow tomorrow morning, so Pascal and I will go pay him a visit later in the day to see if we can get any more information from him regarding this whole mess. Pascal, you'll be on grovelling duty whilst I try to reassure him of his safety and our crap professionalism. Think you can handle that?"

"Yes ma'am."

"Good. Carter, I want you to contact the press to see how they really got this f'ing message.

"Yes guv."

"And that leaves Tweedle Dee and Tweedle Dumber to get a fucking name from some database... or maybe try asking the right questions."

Jason didn't think the warning in the message was being taken seriously enough. "Er, okay, but aren't we also going to deal with the fact that this letter issued a death threat to me?"

Bjorkman screwed up her face. "Man up Ives, you're not the only one implicated in that stupid message. Isambard can protect you, or maybe get one of those pretty police officers downstairs to shadow you."

Ives suddenly had a shameful epiphany. He realised that despite her terrible background with her family, her rare sensitive moments, and their shenanigans in her office, he didn't really like her very much. He made a firm decision that no amount of sensitive secrets told, or sex in taboo places was going to ever change that. He looked straight into those beautiful blue eyes and put up his own wall.

"Yes ma'am."

Chapter 59 – Fighting Talk

Sabina practically kicked the door down in an effort to get outside the station. She needed some fresh air to deal with the situation, but it didn't seem to be helping much, even when she reached the park at the end of the road.

Get a grip, Sabina, he hasn't won just yet. Something is bound to go my way soon. She was hoping against hope that she could think her way out of this problem, but then of course, **she is the problem**. It had taken all her strength to shut Jason out, finding that the best way was to be as horrible as possible, even when she wanted nothing more than to surrender herself up to him. Would he really understand though? After all, it was he in his professional role as Jason Ives, past life investigator, who'd tricked that poor man into finding out he was a Nazi war criminal only a few years ago. Why would he treat her any differently?

And what of Joe's motives towards Jason, (she refuses to call him Jack) is it a bluff that he wants to kill him? Surely she should know what he thinks... but there are so many blank spaces in her memory. At least the revelation of the Ripper knowing about Mary Kelly being interviewed has caused a rupture in the team. Hopefully that will buy her more time. Hopefully she can get to see Glover, and, in some weird way, they could both bring back their past selves to talk to each other. Would that settle Joe down?

Joe was the one who had wanted to send the letters, even though the risks were so great. In the end he, she, they, it, or whatever she could think to call the both of them, had printed the letters on fresh untouched paper, and then placed them in generic untouched envelopes, using double latex gloves. Yes, the talc powder in the gloves would probably leave a little residue, but nothing that could leave a trail back to her.

Ten copies like that, all posted from an anonymous post box in a leafy lane in Essex to different news agencies in London. Detection was unlikely, but she'd still worn her excellent male disguise from Angels, the film and theatre costumiers near Soho, just as she had when out murdering. The devil is in the detail so they say, and her police forensic knowledge had kept the bastard out of everyone's reach so far. She'd also taken a few risks in covering some of her tracks away from her team's eyes.

Come on, you are a fighter Sabina, there has to be a way out. Maybe that note to Jason will help.

Silence... **blank the mind**... he might be listening!

Chapter 60 - Television

Another 24 hours have passed... another day spent dealing with the press enjoying this rollercoaster of a story. It is getting in the way of the investigation by sapping what little time Jason has to work; but now the media have the letter in their hands, they want to know how he feels about his death threat from the Ripper. The first man ever threatened by this sadistic wolf, walking the streets in sheep's clothing. It has gone global, forcing commander Pashmali into giving him 24/7 protection, to show that the Met are protecting their man. Unfortunately, he was also pushing Ives to comply with the press at the same time.

So the letter was doing its task magnificently in breaking the team apart, and slowing everyone down. If ever there was a time for the Ripper to strike another prostitute, it would be now, whilst everyone is looking at the police rather than the victims. Sabina was also being watched over, but she'd already taken the wise step of self appointing Pascal's brutish figure to watch over her. If anyone could do that, it was her protective sidekick, who's worked alongside her for far longer than any other officer in the team.

So that is how Jason found himself sitting in the BBC studios at 7.45am, talking about the case to their popular news presenter, when all he wanted to do was get a proper night's sleep to attack the day with a fresh outlook. It has been chaos though, with news agencies all over the world asking for sound bites from the man that has rattled the Ripper. Apparently putting in a breakfast-time interview was going to be the most time efficient way of answering some of those questions.

Jason looked to the side of the presenter to see Carter hovering by one of the automatic cameras. He was guarding Ives today, but at least he could relax more in these surroundings. Surely the Ripper wouldn't attack him on live TV... but who knows what this shadowy killer with no fear of being caught might do next.

∞-∞-∞-∞-∞-∞

Jack was looking straight at Jason Ives, watching every little movement with the trained eye of his mother's knowledge. Jason was projecting the confidence of a calm man in control whilst talking to this grey haired fool asking him questions, but Jack could now see past that. He could see tiny glimpses of a man under pressure, and it made him feel warm inside. Creating fear in someone gives an immense feeling of control. You are dominant in their mind, and the more you can ramp up the fear, the more control you gain.

This is how he had gained more control of this damned female body; attractive to many, but weak and grotesque to him for so many reasons. He had loved women in his Victorian youth, only to learn to despise their drunken ways. Often selling their virtue for a pocket of change, even when living with men that they would call their lovers.

Sluts and trollops, all of them. So how ironic it is, that his only way back into the world of the living is through one of them. Sabina is strong in so many ways though, and he'd get confused when he had to lurk in the back of her mind, oppressed by her strength. He'd hear her voice and sometimes think that she was his mother, her domineering voice sending waves of fear and love to his blackened heart. It is clouded by the dreamlike state that he finds himself inhabiting most of the time though, making rhyme and reason untenable. So who is the voice then? Where is it coming from?

And then with an almighty effort, he would rise to the surface, when the hunger to kill gave him the strength. But what of that transition, from subservient son to dominant force? It only leaves him feeling hollow inside, because through all of it, he still loves his mother. Is she just as confused as he is, and sacrificing the use of her body to let him roam the streets once more? To touch and taste? To participate in the world of the living, to feel heart-ache and pain?

∞-∞-∞-∞-∞-∞

The producer had been lovely, making sure they have plenty of fresh hot coffee and things to eat in-between interviews. Carter was enjoying the sudden glimmer of celebrity hospitality, but then he isn't the focus of the attention. He is very much on the periphery, dipping his toes in the experience without total commitment to the cold water.

Next stop the ITV studios to placate them for snubbing their breakfast show. All part of the Met police press publicity machine, to make sure that they are seen in the best light possible. Fighting crime is done in many ways, and propaganda is still high upon the list for management at the Yard.

No doubt Carter would enjoy the lunch and tour of the studios. Jason thought of Isambard working back at the office by himself. He'd pretty much been made the scapegoat for the revelation of Mary Kelly, based on no evidence at all. It wasn't a good example from the team; they should know better.

∞-∞-∞-∞-∞-∞

Jack is flitting in and out with Sabina, a skill he is learning to perfect. It gives him the ability to keep a tighter grip on her whilst at work, not that she's taken a step wrong so far. Then anger suddenly rages through him again, as he remembers her time with Ives. Yes, she had been faithful to him by not handing herself in, and she has protected him all the way, but she also dirtied herself on Ives, and the thought makes him feel utterly sick.

It would seem that the bitch had been playing some type of game with everyone, himself included. Saying that she'd had no option but to open up to Ives, because he had suddenly suggested that she was sabotaging the case, and maybe even be the Ripper herself. Normally the best place to hide is in plain view of everyone. It is why Sabina had pushed so hard for the case in the first place, but Ives was different.

His professional instinct had been slowly putting the pieces together. Most people least expect those around them, even if they hate them, because they still see them as human, and they still think they could see it in your eyes if you were a killer.

So Bjorkman had screamed in her mind that she'd had no other option but to open up about her past; her family, her father, her brother, and it had certainly thrown him off course for a while.

Was that really the reason though, or had she seen something in him that might help in her plans? Did she really have to offer him sex just to further confuse him? True, he was already in a vulnerable moment in his relationship with that tart of his, and it did throw him off the scent, so it was difficult to deny.

She had managed to fool this so-called professional for a while, but in the end, she had wanted more of him and taken it, forcing Jack to the back of her mind to obscure the view. It had been a step too far, and he wasn't going to let it happen again.

So what of that letter? Yes, he hates Ives, and maybe he will get to kill him along the way, but his main objective now is to see Mary. The threat was just a ruse, a distraction to set things in place. He will find her, talk to her, tell her she is being held hostage in this American black man's body, and hopefully she will give her blessing for him to set her free.

He will rip the man's rib cage open wide, to let her soul fly out once more.

Then, soon after he will take his own life – he will destroy the body he is using, and it will free himself and his mother in one fell swoop. Justice will be restored in another lifetime, free of the madness of owning or sharing the wrong body. One day they will be sweethearts on equal measure, with his mother watching from the sidelines, finally proud of everything he has managed in balancing this sad affair.

He looked at Ives once again and then walked across the room, moving closer to the screen. It was a loop of an earlier interview, so he switched to another channel to see Ives being interviewed by someone else. This time it was a blonde bimbo showing too much cleavage.

∞-∞-∞-∞-∞-∞

1:15pm, and Ives had just finished his last interview. He was looking forward to getting back to the office to try and push on. It will be interesting to see if the team has managed to trace any of the letters to a source. To see if they have any forensic value at all, or even try and see where they had been posted from, if that helps.

As they left the building to get a cab, a gentleman in a smart suit stopped playing scrabble on his sleeve screen and walked over to them with a big warm smile. Carter quickly pushed his arm in front of Ives, so that he could position himself in the way.

The man suddenly stopped on seeing this, and lifted his hands to show that they were empty, as a magician would to a crowd. "Oh I do apologise gentlemen, but I have been asked if Mr Ives is free this afternoon?"

"For what?" growled Carter, taking his job very seriously for the first time that day.

The gentleman flipped a card from a special pocket in his sleeve in one fluid motion. It displayed his credentials and ID.

"Mr Martin Kale would like to talk to you about your case, Mr Ives. He hopes that he may be of some assistance."

Chapter 61 – Kale and Capello

The man in the suit straightened his Oxford tie, as he graciously thanked Jason for agreeing to come along at such short notice. Carter was only too happy to extend what had already been quite an eventful day, but even he couldn't have guessed that it would end by him meeting the founder of Awakening.

Jason had once visited his country home near the edge of Godalming in Surrey, but never to his London address. Sitting on the banks of the Thames, the main atrium afforded magnificent views of Tower Bridge on one side, and St Paul's on the other. It reminded Jason of his ill-fated date with Samantha close by, high up in the Shard.

Parker, the man in the suit, asked Carter to remain in an adjoining room for a few minutes, so that Jason could have a quiet moment with Kale first. Normally Carter would have objected strongly, seeming as he was officially guarding Ives, but it seemed too ridiculous to even question his request. Not because of his fame, but because Kale had been assassinated himself in the early days of Awakening. It meant that Kale was only too aware of the threat to Jason's life, and his own security was very high. In fact, it was his death and resurrection as a ten year old boy, that had finally cemented people's belief in the new science, and from that point on, the world was never the same.

Jason entered the room through the large walnut inlaid doors, to find Kale sitting on a sumptuous mocha coloured sofa right by the plate glass window. Sitting on an armchair next to him, was a young man not even twenty years old. Ives had never met this person before, but guessed it must be Kale's mysterious protégé, Adam Capello. He took a mental snapshot of Capello to try and read as much about him as possible before the conversation started. Most people do it subconsciously, the well known 'first impression' formed within seven seconds, but can take a lifetime to correct.

Jason hadn't been surprised that he couldn't read Kale when they had first met, a mentalist can rarely read another, but it was a different experience from Bjorkman. Hers was a strong wall built through her early formed trauma. It was rough around the edges, akin to using a hammer to smash a walnut. Kale's signals worked more like his own, so that, if truly relaxed, Jason's body language would just mirror the people around him to build up an instant rapport without thinking about it. It makes all the difference in those seven seconds. So two people mirroring each other only led to false signals bouncing around like crazy, but virtually invisible to anyone else.

Capello was different though. Quiet, but very self assured and wise beyond his years. His body language was a completely open book, resembling more a hall of mirrors, than a single one, and displaying thousands of personalities. His persona was one of the most interesting Ives had ever seen. Impressive, but not imposing. Even a person normally blind to body language would pick up the very positive signals he was transmitting.

Kale stood up to greet him. "Jason, it's good to see you again. This is Adam, I hope you don't mind him sitting in on the meeting?"

"Not at all," he replied, as he shook Adam's hand and looked into his eyes.

They looked back at him as if they could see everything; his life, his secrets, his soul.

∞-∞-∞-∞-∞-∞

Bjorkman was getting ready to meet up with George Glover at his home address, just thirty minutes from Charing Cross police station. Her mind was running at a thousand miles an hour, fully aware of what lay ahead, but unable to do anything about it.

Pascal grabbed his jacket nonchalantly to follow her to the car. As far as he was concerned, he was just following her to what he assumed was a fairly routine interview, in what had been an unusual investigation so far.

Little did he know how much more unusual it was going to get.

∞-∞-∞-∞-∞-∞

Jason looked around the tastefully furnished room, illuminated by the late summer sunshine bursting through the windows. Large framed photographs of historic moments in recent history adorned one wall, offset by another crammed full with traditional paper books perched on hardwood shelves. A modern library in its simplistic design, but right in the centre was a small wall screen, the size of a modest monitor. Jason guessed it was a lot more than that, probably a computer dedicated solely to accessing library files in every format from every resource available. Next to it, a bespoke instant book printer and a 3D printer completed the package. In one wall, a library of the world in all its physical dimensions.

In the centre of the room was a large globe next to a beautiful wooden desk. Documents were strewn all over the left side from some recent work, and a map of Egypt on the right side, with a large crystal skull acting as a paperweight. A curious mix of cultures on one table, but then Jason would have expected nothing less. Kale smiled as he saw his workspace being scrutinised.

"Adam and I have just returned from Cairo, a little project that we have been working on. I'd love to talk to you about it one day, but for now, we have more pressing issues."

"Yes, your man said you might be able to help with my inquiry. To be honest, I was thinking about getting in touch, so to hear from you first, especially under the current circumstances, is very welcome."

"I could hardly ignore the news, Jason. Your investigation into Jack the Ripper has put you in some jeopardy. A fascinating turn of events in any context, but I have to say, I have been feeling a little guilty about the whole affair," said Kale.

Jason raised an eyebrow. "Really, why?"

"Simple. Without Awakening this would never have happened. I'm fully aware that whilst my process may help our fragile society in a lot of ways, it has also introduced a lot of problems too. I liken it to a powerful drug that might save your life, but it can't escape the fact that there are unavoidable side effects. It is a responsibility that I take very seriously."

"Oh, and there I was just thinking you were worried about me," Ives joked.

Kale laughed. "And that of course. Our work together in the past has always been interesting, and I'd like to think that we have become friends in that time."

"Of course, me too, and I'd appreciate anything you think you can help me with."

Adam Capello moved next to Kale to enter Jason's line of sight. "Oh I think we can do that. It would seem that you have discovered the original identity and details of Jack the Ripper? This would be most useful for us."

"Not much more than his name I'm afraid, Adam. His actual character and background are still very vague. All we know is that he was a twenty-seven year old Veterinary student from Bournemouth, but living in Mornington Crescent in London at the time of the killings, with the name of Joseph Ride. He had a widowed mother who was devoted to him and may have known his secret. His relationship with the victim Mary Kelly went back a lot further than just the night of her killing, though. If anything, it would seem that he was in love with her, but circumstances, including him contracting syphilis, may have driven him mad with pain and eventually killed him."

Again, Jason could feel Adam soaking everything in. Not only his words, but his pitch and tone, intonation and timing, even his movement. It wouldn't have surprised Ives if he could see his aura too. After a few seconds, Adam looked at Kale to give a little nod before Kale patted Ives on the shoulder.

"Okay Jason, would you mind waiting outside for a short while?

∞-∞-∞-∞-∞-∞

Traffic was a nightmare. One set of road works after another had turned the half hour journey into the full hour, but at last they had reached Glover's address. Bjorkman looked around the street and saw a cafe at the far end. She touched Pascal on the arm, gripping it slightly tighter than she had intended. "I'm going to go and see Glover alone, John, it will be a lot better that way. Grab yourself a late lunch and I'll join you for a coffee when I've finished."

Pascal looked confused. "But guv, I'm meant to watch over you."

Sabina rolled her eyes at him as if he'd just made a stupid comment. "Don't be such a wet blanket. Pashmali is only playing the political game to try and show he cares. We all know nothing is going to happen to me. If anything, it's Carter who is going to be the busy one babysitting Ives... that's who the Ripper really wants."

Pascal objected for a little while, but he knew it was pointless arguing against his boss, and lunch did sound good.

She must have heard his stomach growling.

∞-∞-∞-∞-∞-∞

The skull glowed on the desk as Adam channelled his thoughts into it. The combination of his knowledge from thousands of his past and future lives, when combined with this ancient artefact from a lost civilisation, gave access to almost any event at any time.

The scant information that Ives had supplied should be enough to provide the link. To find a name for the Ripper lost in the past had been a difficult task, but now it would provide a point to focus on.

Adam concentrates on the details, looking back at his own time as a pioneering photographer in 1888, and uses that as a base to listen to the echoes of future voices in his mind. They take him down to the south of England and the beautiful coast of Bournemouth. Then past its shiny new pier, before locking onto a six bedroom house with a white picket fence. Now Adam can see the tortured energy of Joseph Ride as it leaves his pain-riddled body by the sea. This energy, spirit, life-source... soul, moving towards the in-between stage; awaiting its next body.

Born again 1919 and named Jose Luis Martinez. He struggled to survive just 18 months before giving up his mortal shell.

1936, born Michael Kline in Stuttgart. He showed musical promise as a schoolboy before a friend set off an unexploded wartime bomb which damaged his hearing. He died in a bar fight in 1959, leaving a young wife and small daughter behind.

1974, born Stephen Smith in Bradford. A sensitive child who never really took to the world. He left school at 15, working in various dead end jobs and stealing to pay for his addiction to drugs and alcohol. A lifetime spent on the streets until he died of HIV related pneumonia at the age of 42.

2031, born Sabina Bjorkman...

∞-∞-∞-∞-∞-∞

Jason waited patiently outside with Carter, though curious about what they were doing in there that they didn't want him to see. Did they really have a secret database that showed everyone who had ever had an Awakening? It must be possible, if a little too 'Big Brother' for his liking. That said, if they could just give him a lead to follow he would be eternally grateful.

He glanced at his watch. Bjorkman should be in her meeting with Glover by now.

∞-∞-∞-∞-∞-∞

George Glover hurried his dog away to the kitchen so that he could answer the door without her jumping up and down at his guest. He'd already had to deal with the press ringing him up and asking stupid questions every five minutes, so he was extra cautious, and looked through the security spy hole before opening it. The tiny fish eye lens gave a distorted view of an attractive blonde woman holding up her police identification. He was still very angry about his name leaking out to the press, and was ready for a bit of a show down.

Someone was going to pay for letting his secret out, and right now, he was planning on venting his spleen to her whether she wanted to listen or not.

∞-∞-∞-∞-∞-∞

Sabina was staring at him very intently from the moment he'd answered the door.

"Thank you for letting me pop over this afternoon Mr Glover, I know you only got back from America last night. I hope you had a pleasant trip?"

All smiling and polite, but there was something wrong in the air. "Er, yes, thank you. Can I offer you a drink?"

"No thank you, I'd rather we just get down to business if you don't mind. Do you live here alone, Mr Glover?"

"No, I'm still lucky enough to be married, but who knows after this whole business is sorted," he said sourly. "I'm going to be honest and say I will be putting in a formal complaint."

Bjorkman shrugged her shoulders. "I don't blame you, Mr Glover, a complete balls up if you ask me." She was looking left to right, surveying the surroundings... getting ready to pounce. "Where is she?"

Glover was a little taken aback, but had to admire her honesty. "My wife is still in the States seeing her family...

...Now let me ask you a question DCI Bjorkman. Do you know how my name got to the press?"

Bjorkman ran her fingers across the fireplace mantle as if checking for dust, then smiled at him coldly.

"Yes, I told them."

Chapter 62 – Abduction

Crash!

The noise made Jason jump out of his skin as the huge doors were flung open at great speed. Capello came rushing out, quickly followed by Kale.

"The detective in charge of your investigation, am I right in thinking that it is a chief inspector Bjorkman?" Capello was almost breathless, as if in shock.

Jason looked worried by this sudden change in tone. "Yes, why?"

"I have good reason to believe that she is Jack the Ripper."

An awful sick feeling took hold of Ives, as if his gut was shouting at him for not listening to his instinct. If it really was her, how could he have been so stupid? "What? How could you possibly know that?"

Kale beckoned them back into the room and sat Jason on the sofa. "We have a specialised and very confidential database that we can gain access to when absolutely necessary. By using the name you found for the original Ripper, we were able trace certain... steps which led to Sabina Bjorkman."

"Steps? Why hasn't her Awakening Observer come forward with this news? Why didn't we know about this?" Questions were swamping Jason's mind.

"We are working on a way to trace the life-energy that makes us who we are, but it is very experimental, so I must ask you both to keep it confidential. For the time being, we can only see some of the basic stepping stones through lifetimes, but not many of the whys and whens. We'll also try and find out who her Observer was, and work from our more traditional records."

Jason bolted upright on his chair. "Oh Christ, she's with Mary Kelly right now!

∞-∞-∞-∞-∞-∞

"Mary, I've come for you..." Her voice was suddenly a lot lower and very menacing.

Glover's heart sank. Somewhere in the back of his mind he knew that tone.

"You?" Was all that he could utter.

"Ah, so you remember me, my love?" Bjorkman leant over and ran a finger down the old man's face, that look of obsession stronger than ever. Without thinking he recoiled, completely bewildered by this normally attractive woman, suddenly looking so ugly. "We need to talk!"

"I don't remember much about Mary if that is why you are here, only scant details from a few Awakening sessions, so I can't help you." Glover was scared, but not so much that he couldn't start formulating a plan of action. Try to put her off, distract her, and then maybe run and grab that 9 iron by the door to use as a weapon."

"Oh, I'm sure I can get you to remember me properly... I'm your special gentleman, your Joseph waiting to take you home.

"You... are... Jack the Ripper." Glover was stating the name, hoping against hope to be corrected and find that he was wrong. This had to be a sick joke.

Bjorkman stopped for a second. Her eyes started filling with tears at the name of this killer that Joseph had become. "Not to you. Never you. Remember that last night we spent together? We chatted for hours about starting a new life. You wanted to escape the horrible mess you found yourself in. The squalor of your bedchamber, your sad solitary room that you called a home. I released you from all that Mary, and I should have followed you there and then, but I grew confused, my illness was affecting my mind, and seeing you gone sent me on a downward spiral. I gave myself up to my mother, told her everything and she hid me away to die in agony in my personal prison."

Glover was aghast. "Do you expect me to feel sorry for you? You murdered and butchered my body. I don't know much about her life because I have always been too afraid to look back. You stole a life from me."

"I did not steal your life, my love, it had already been robbed by your surroundings. You were drunk most nights, selling your body to pay for rent a night at a time. You had nothing, not even your dignity."

"How dare you! I had my friends and I still had hope." His anger let his knowledge slip through.

Jack laughed, he was in full control now. "So you do remember. Come closer, let me whisper in your ear."

∞-∞-∞-∞-∞-∞

Parker had his foot down, speeding as fast as he dared along the crowded London streets. No doubt Mr Kale was going to receive quite a few fines this evening. At this rate, even his own license might be at risk, so he really hoped it could be straightened out later.

Jason was on the phone to Pascal whilst Carter called the office to see what was happening from their end. "Pascal, tell me you and Glover are safe?"

Pascal sat looking at his steak and kidney pie growing cold in front of him with a touch of trepidation. "Yes, I'm fine, the guv just told me to get a spot of lunch cos she wanted to speak to Glover alone, you know, add a little feminine charm to calm him down?"

"Fuck!" It wasn't like Ives to swear, so it grabbed Pascal's attention even more.

"Why, what's happened? Is the guv okay? Oh God, something's happened to her hasn't it, and I'm sitting here scoffing my face. She told me to come here."

"I don't know how to answer that one. Just let's say I know who the Ripper is now."

"Fantastic."

"Not really... Bjorkman is the Ripper."

Silence at the other end as Pascal thought this over, followed by a loud roaring laugh. "Oh fuck off, you really had me going there. I almost had a heart attack."

"Pascal"

"Yes?"

"It's not a joke. Get over to Glover's house now, but do it quietly. We don't want to scare her into doing anything rash."

Silence again as Pascal's world came crashing down around him. He banged his head with his spare hand. "What the hell does she want with Glover?"

"At best I'm hoping her identity as Jack just wants to talk. At worst... I really don't even want to go there at the moment. Just get going, I'm on my way."

"Will do. What's your ETA?

∞-∞-∞-∞-∞-∞

Glover lunged for the golf club by the door, his adrenaline fuelled body giving him the burst of speed necessary to reach his target. As soon as his fingertips touched the leather handle, he found himself swinging it round to hit this unwelcome visitor.

Jack moved in swiftly to get very close, left arm

315

meeting him at the fore arm to block the blow at his weakest point, then kicked out at the old man's shin with his heel. Bjorkman's police defence skills were proving very useful.

"Sit down!" Jack's voice through her vocals gave a very eerie tone. Instantly frightening and never to be forgotten. Glover collapsed in pain, dropped the club and crawled over to the armchair to recover.

"What do you want?" Glover was almost sobbing now, he knew that had probably been his only chance.

"I told you, I want to talk."

"I can't remember much, I told you."

Jack was growing impatient. "I don't want to talk to you, I want to talk to Mary."

"I can't do that, I keep telling you, I only had a couple of sessions."

"Then I better rip her out of you."

Glover put his hands up defensively, even though Jack had moved no closer. "Wait! Let me see what I can do. What do you want to know?"

"I want to talk to Mary, not ask you questions. Now shut down your idiotic mind and let her come to the fore. I wish to converse with her and her alone, not have you chaperoning our conversation."

"I don't know how. Listen to me, I can't just let my previous life come back, it doesn't work like that. I don't have the training, it is impossible."

Jack stood up and walked over to Glover. He brought Bjorkman's face so close to his that he could feel her breath. She looked lovingly into his eyes. Tender, sweet and vile. Without warning, Jack slapped Glover hard across the face with the palm of his hand, then back again.

Slap, slap, slap until Glover could take no more. He quickly grabbed her left wrist, twisting it round.

∞-∞-∞-∞-∞-∞

You can track my car. It says I'll be there in fifteen minutes. In the meantime, approach the address quietly, and try to snoop through a window. The last thing we want to do is spook Bjorkman into doing anything stupid."

Pascal was still in shock. "Really? My boss who has been leading a hunt for Jack the Ripper, turns out to be Jack the Ripper. I don't think it could get any more stupid, Jason."

"Good point, but we'll talk about that later. Get going and give me a call once you have assessed the situation."

Jason hung up, leaving Pascal to start running like mad. Twenty years ago when he joined the force he'd have been over there like a whippet, but the sudden exertion and half a steak and kidney pie were taking their toll on his big frame. A gym membership was looking like a wise investment if he wanted to keep his job right now.

At last Pascal could see the car they had arrived in, parked by the curb just ten meters from Glover's front door. He was forced to slow down so that he could get his breath back, but acutely aware that lives could be lost in a matter of seconds. As he crept to the window on the left, he held his breath, but he could still hear his own heartbeat and was sure it would give him away.

Nothing, just a view into the kitchen.

Hunched over, Pascal then trampled over the pretty border of flowers in the well kept garden to get to the window on the right.

Slowly... ever so slowly Pascal raised his head to bring his eyes level with the bottom of the window frame.

317

∞–∞–∞–∞–∞–∞

Jack grabbed Bjorkman's police issue Glock from its holster and placed the muzzle straight into Glover's eye socket. "Let go or I'll shoot your fucking face off."

Glover let go instantly, there was nothing he could do. He felt powerless, old, weak and afraid. Part of him would have preferred to take the chance in still attacking than feel this wretched, but his natural survival instinct had stepped in automatically. Better to survive for now, and maybe fight another day.

"Mary... I'm so sorry, but you always knew how to get me worked up. Jack reached out with both hands and cupped Glover's face, staring straight into his eyes, trying to see past the Afro American man sitting where his love should be.

A kiss, just with the lips, but given with such tenderness, her left hand caressing his face, the right hand unconsciously ruffling his hair with the gun. Glover's heart sank. He could see the sadness in this all, wrapped up in the madness that can so often follow loss and regret. But what could he do? Should he try and fake being Mary?

Tears were now running down Bjorkman's face. The penny had dropped. "You really are not there anymore, are you Mary? I wanted to talk to you so badly, make you see that we could make good all the mistakes of the past. Yes, I know we both made mistakes, and I know I hurt you, but then you did steal my heart!

Anger.

Jack suddenly screamed with complete abandon, as if his soul was finally being dragged to Hell... but not just yet. He grabbed Glover by the chin with his right hand, and pointed the gun at his heart. "You and me are going to go on a journey, my darling. We are going to travel through time once more, but on this occasion I will do you right. This time we will both die at the same moment. This time we will travel along the same path on a new adventure. Man and woman in our correct bodies, and one day we will be man and wife as God has always intended.

Finger on the trigger...

Chapter 63 – Negotiation

Isambard was dumbfounded. He had just heard the news from Jason regarding Bjorkman and was now having to rush to an address to help with an urgent task. Jason didn't have time to explain, but it was imperative that he do it as fast as possible without any questions.

A huge pang of guilt rippled through him as he realised that he had inadvertently put his friend George Glover at risk the moment he had asked for his help. Then told the very person that George was most at risk from. No wonder the Ripper had been so hard to trace. Bjorkman knew how to protect herself forensically, and was also able to cover her tracks and deviate the investigation onto the wrong course at every juncture.

As Isambard's squad car raced through the traffic on emergency response mode, the sheer number of people made him feel very claustrophobic. Millions of people were living and working in London right now, completely unaware of what was unfolding only a few miles away. No doubt the media would be letting everyone know over the next couple of days.

Soon, all their lives would be on display.

∞-∞-∞-∞-∞-∞

Bjorkman's mobile suddenly sprang into life, almost panicking Jack into pulling the trigger, but he wasn't ready just yet, and was irritated by how much the ringtone was nagging for his attention. He took the mobile out of his pocket and answered it without seeing who it was.

"Sabina, this is Jason."

"She's not in at the moment."

"Then I'd like to talk to you Jack, I want to help.

Jack had to laugh in spite of his pain. "You, help me? You disgust me."

Jason paused for a second, his time with Bjorkman in the office was already coming back to haunt him, and made him feel quite ill just at the thought of it, but he had to find a way to calm Jack down. "I'm sorry Jack, but I didn't know who you, or Sabina were. Let me make it up to you, let me help."

This time there was a short pause from Jack as he looked at his beloved hiding in this man's shell. "I want to talk to Mary, but this idiot won't let me."

This could be his way in. "He can't Jack, he does not know how to. Most of us are not as strong as you. We are bound by our current bodies and the personalities that come with them."

"Abberline could!"

"Abberline is well trained, and like you a very strong character. I am able to get Mary to talk to you though, but I have to be there. I am only five minutes away, please let me help."

First point: Appeal to the subject.

"You can do that?" Jack was interested.

"Yes, but do you want me to help?

Second point: Get him to want you to help.

"Yes, Mary needs me."

"Good, so yes, I can help you, but I am going to have to come inside with you and George to talk to Mary. Can you trust me on that – I'll be unarmed."

Third point: Gain trust.

Jack wasn't so sure, but he knew he could pull the trigger at any moment. A bullet for Mary and a bullet for him. Death within seconds of each other, and escape beyond the reach of mankind. "You can come in, but I must warn you, Mary and I are only too happy to die, so no tricks."

"Believe me Jack, I just want to talk like you do. We both know that will help, and you know I can get Mary to talk to you, but I have to hear it from you first for it to work. Do you think I can help you?"

Fourth point: Get the subject to agree with you.

Jason had been using as calm and polite a voice as possible, whilst maintaining an air of gentle confidence. He was in negotiator mode.

Jack was surprised by his reaction. "Yes, I think you can."

Bingo, Jason had started a basic rapport.

With any luck, it might just save everyone's lives in that room, his own included.

∞-∞-∞-∞-∞-∞

As he peered over the window ledge, Pascal could see his governor on her mobile, and Glover cowering on the sofa beside her. He was tempted to try and find an open window somewhere to sneak in, either to hear what was going on, or charge into her, but he knew he couldn't take that risk.

Pascal also knew he could probably take a shot at her through the window, but the thought of shooting his boss seemed too difficult. He still couldn't believe it was her anyway. There had to be some other explanation.

As he was crouching there, a silver grey Jaguar turned up, with Ives and Carter in the back. Ives was also on his mobile as he stepped out of the car, leaving Pascal to hope that it was Bjorkman on the other side. His thighs were killing him as he crouched by the door, but he wanted to be able to take his chance and spring up when needed.

Jason motioned at him stay calm and wait for his signal.

∞-∞-∞-∞-∞-∞

Knock knock at the door. A short, gentle knock so as not to startle anyone.

Jack grabbed Glover by the scruff of the neck and dragged him to answer it with the gun clearly aimed at his head, just in case they were going to try anything clever. Glover gingerly answered the door, hoping some trigger happy sniper wasn't on a rooftop somewhere.

Standing alone at the doorway was Ives, with his hands in the air to show he was unarmed, as Jack motioned for him to come in as quickly as possible. Now Jack had Ives as well, an added bonus, another possible kill before he releases Mary and himself from their mortal cages set upon this foul Earth. Glover led them back to the sitting room with the noise of his dog barking from the kitchen.

Jack was impatient to start, pointing out where they could sit. "Mr Ives, I wish to converse with Mary Kelly as soon as possible, so I respectably suggest you begin. If you try anything clever, I will be wise to any tricks...

...so I firmly recommend that you avoid testing my resolve."

Chapter 64 – Mary and Jack

Glover was quite resistant, his nerves keeping him alert made it difficult to relax. But at last he fell into a full Awakening hypnotic trance, greatly helped by the fact that this was his second with Ives.

"Mary, I'd like to take you back to 1887 when you knew Joseph Ride... find a good time, a time when you were alone, but happy."

"All right dear, I can do that, but I'm not going to talk of any hanky panky, I told you that last time, you sauce pot."

Jason smiled. He was glad that he could draw upon a time when they were both reasonably happy, and she sounded like she was in good spirits on this occasion. "Of course, Mary, I just want you to be happy, and I have Joseph Ride here with me now. He wants to talk to you, is that okay?"

"What, my Joe's with you?"

Jack was looking on with a mixture of awe and impatience, so Jason waved him down a little to tell him to stay calm. Difficult under these conditions.

"Yes, he is here with me. I won't go away though, because I need to look after both of you. If you have any problems or get worried, just let me know. If you get frightened, then say the word 'Resolution'. Is that alright?"

"Of course, my dear."

"Good. First though, I need to pause a minute to have a rest. You will not be able to hear anything until I, and only I, have touched your left shoulder, do you understand?"

"Yes, dear."

Ives pulled Jack to one side, as far as he dared. "Listen

to me, I have taken her back to the year 1887, before you..." he looked at George, "spent that last night with her the following year and killed her. Do not talk of anything past that point, she might not understand and we might lose her. And if you scare her, she will retreat into George's mind. Do you understand?"

For a moment at least, Jason had Jack under his control. Jack tried looking in the old man's eyes once more, hoping that something might have changed. Only Mary's mannerisms when speaking had some semblance of what he recognised. Just enough to know he wasn't being tricked.

Jason saw Jack was ready, and tapped George on the shoulder.

Jack stumbled for a second, unsure of what to say after all this time. "Mary, it's me... Joe, can you hear me?" A good start, using his real name, from a time before the Ripper existed.

George looked directly at Sabina, both of them playing out their respective characters in their switched bodies. "Oh Joe, how nice to see you."

Tears were forming in Joe's eyes, the reconnection after so much time and pain. "I'm so sorry."

Ives tapped George on the shoulder again, pausing Mary's personal time.

"Joe, be careful, she cannot know about later."

Joe nodded as his humanity came flooding back, knowing that he should not put her through that pain again. Ives tapped George's shoulder once more.

"Sorry for what, Joe, not marrying me?" she said with a lilt in her voice.

A small ironic smile on 'Joe's' face as he remembered that time again. "Yes, that's right. I knew in Paris that I was making a mistake by making promises and by not being able to keep them."

"Oh I know that, my darlin', you're not the first man to ask me to marry him and then forget the next morning."

Joe stiffened on hearing this, upset and angered by the thought of other men. For a moment, Ives thought Jack was going to return in this difficult three person mix, but Joe managed to hang on, knowing he could not afford to get angry.

Mary grabbed his hand, seeing he was sad. "Oh, don't get upset. Let me tell you a secret, but don't tell madam. You are my special one, my favourite gentleman. No one treats me as well as you do, and we have an understanding, remember? Both of us have a bit of a temper, maybe it's my Irish blood, and maybe it's your father's doing, but we understand each other like that don't we?"

A smile returned. "Yes, yes, we do." Joe stopped for a second as a thought ran through his mind. "Are you happy, Mary?"

"I could be better, sweetheart, of that you can be certain, but I suppose I am in my own way."

Joe was struggling with something. He knew that her life was going to get a lot worse from this point. "I know, but are you happy in your new body?"

Ives shot him a look to say 'be careful', but Joe wasn't taking any notice.

"What do you mean, you silly sausage?"

"Mary, look at us both, we are freaks."

Jason tapped George again on the shoulder – Mary disappeared and went quiet. "Joe!"

"Get her back. Get her back this instant or I shall kill you." Jack was back in charge and pointing the gun at Jason's head.

"If you kill me you won't be able to ask Mary any more questions. Only I can bring her back, Joe."

Stalemate.

"Then I shall kill us all."

"And what will that achieve? You have come so far, Joe, and here you are at last, able to speak to Mary. Do you know how amazing that is? I need you to dig deep into your personalities, Joe. Right now you need all of your parts. You need your character as Jack to see how bad things can get, you need Joe to know the good person you had been, and you now need Sabina to show how good a person you can still be."

And with that Jason made a sign to Isambard standing on the other side of the window.

Chapter 65 – Twisted

Knock knock knock...

Jack raised the gun at Ives. "What are you doing?"

"Helping you, Joe, doing the best for you and Mary. My friend Isambard has found someone who can really help."

"I don't need anyone else's help."

"But you do, Joe, you know you do. Right now all we have is violence. Do not finish this life as you did before, with both of you dead. Do not murder her again."

"Murder her! I am freeing her. Look at her in that Negro's body. She is lost, it is a complete abomination."

Jason slowly walked over to the door. "Which is why I need to help you both. Murder is still murder, Joe, violence begets violence."

Jack started screaming at Jason. "Move away from that door!"

Too late, Jason pulled the catch and opened the door. Jack was furious, but even in his maddened state of mind, he could not bring himself to end the conversation just yet. He somehow needed to gain Mary's permission to die with him. Otherwise, this torture could all just happen again, and how deranged would that future world be?

Sebastian walked in, Sabina's twin brother. Jack just looked confused. He saw the spider's web tattooed across this otherwise handsome man's face and saw that his back was slightly crooked, giving him an unusual gait. Something in the back of his mind recognised this odd looking man and froze him on the spot.

Memories of Sabina as his body, and his mother's voice converged to reveal his current body's link. Flesh of his flesh. Peas in a pod, linked to each other's mind from sharing the same womb as only twins can.

Jack felt he was losing himself. "What trickery is this? Why have you brought him here?"

"Because you need to remember that you are not Jack, and you are not just Joe... you have been thousands of people before and you will be thousands of people in the future. Do not screw up your soul's choices by bringing more bad karma on yourself."

"Karma is a myth, it is a fool's idea of justice."

"Maybe, but are you willing to take that chance? I now know that your lifetimes between Joe and Sabina have all been blighted by tragedy, and so you have to consider the possibility that there has to be a link, a reason for your suffering."

Jack looked around him. George was sitting motionless on the sofa, sent into pause mode by Jason's tap on the shoulder. Jason a few strides from himself, and Sebastian at the doorway watching him with sorrow and regret. "What are you looking at, you tattooed degenerate?"

Sebastian raised his deep blue eyes to look directly into Jack's pain. He spoke softly, with a calm confidence. "You should listen to what Jason is saying, Joe, what you do now will affect your future in many ways. Now is the chance to change your destiny. Give in to Sabina's soft voice in your head, let her back in and we will do you right. We will help you more than you can ever imagine."

Jack rushed over to Sebastian and grabbed him by the neck, forcing him against the wall and pointing the gun at his head. Sebastian remained calm as he gazed upon his sister, even though he was in some discomfort.

"Let go of me son!" Sebastian barked.

That voice, that tone. No, it couldn't be, but Jack let go anyway, shocked by the command. "What are you doing?"

"Protecting you, Joe, as I have always done, as any mother should do, no matter what you may have been through."

Jack staggered back; his legs suddenly felt weak, as if they were going to buckle, so he sat down beside George Glover. "How can this be? How can you be in my head and in his body at the same time?"

Sebastian spoke softly to his captor. "My soul has been following you, Joe, to try and right the wrongs of our past. You for your crimes, and me for not protecting you against your father all those years ago. His cruelty mixed with your illness produced the madness that created Jack the Ripper. But your are not sick now, the pox was left behind with Joe's body. You can leave that hideous being behind and rediscover yourself as Joseph Ride. Then, with that peace in your heart, you can let Sabina back into her existence as it should be."

"How... how do you know all this? How could you follow me?"

"Because we are linked by being mother, brother, and daughter."

Jack could take no more, his mind was being assaulted from every angle. "Daughter?"

Sebastian knelt by Jack's side. "Yes, daughter. I have always heard voices in my head Joe, it is part of my personal madness, but over the last year I felt in touch with this Jack character. Incredibly, instead of making me fear him, I felt pity for him. Somehow I knew our link as twins had a purpose, and Adam Capello has explained everything to me."

Jack began curling up in a ball. He could feel Sabina taking advantage of his confusion and pushing back for dominance. "No... no!"

Sebastian continued to try and draw his sister back.

"Capello can see the links between bodies. He knows that my spirit followed you after your death as Joe, and I became your mother again when you were born as Jose Martinez in Spain. My soul wanted to set things right and make you a good person again, but you died as an infant. I didn't know my destiny in that body, of course, so I carried on living that life."

Then Sebastian pulled out a tatty piece of paper with notes and names scribbled on it from his brief phone conversation with Capello just a short while ago. A conversation that seemed to illuminate so many dark areas of his mind. Then he continued to explain what he had been told.

"Then you were born before me as Michael Kline in Germany, so I followed as your daughter years later. But again, I lost you, this time when you died in a bar fight when I was just an infant, our timelines becoming ever more divided. It meant that I could not be with you in your next life, and you just fell apart without me. It has been our tragedy borne from our karma, and right up until you were born as Sabina.

"We... Sabina and I, were born as twins for a reason Joe. At last we are as close as we can be. It is quite possible that we were also meant to be each other; you the boy, me the girl, but the mix has merged our minds even more."

Jack pointed the gun at his own head. Enough of this madness, he had to escape. His finger lingered on the trigger as he summoned the courage to leave this world once more. Now is the right time to die.

"**Joseph, no!**" Jason positively ordered the command, knowing that when we lose a grip on things, our mind searches for a direction to take, and so will take an instruction much more readily. It was time to appeal to

Sabina to draw her out. He motioned to Sebastian to help him. "**I understand your confusion Joe**, but, **everything will be clear soon**, just let Sabina breathe a little in your mind, **it will help you**." He was emphasising key words to calm Jack down.

Jack pulled the gun away from himself, then at Jason, and then back at himself again. His mind was in meltdown.

Sebastian was still there by his side, but now as his mother and brother, all rolled into one. "Sabina, you have looked after me my whole life. Without you I would be dead by now, I am sure of it. If you are going to shoot yourself, then you'll have to shoot me too."

Joe let go a little more, his memories flooding back, returning his humanity as if it were warming his blood. The time before the pox, even before he had met Mary, or travelled to London to study; a time when he was eighteen and the world was at his feet. He looked at Sebastian, but was still completely confused. "Mother?"

Sebastian took Joe's hand and shook his head. "I don't have her memories yet, but she is still very much part of me, I promise you. Now I am Sabina's brother, and I love her just as your mother loved you. Let Sabina back in and I give you my word that I'll take Awakening sessions to remember your mother properly. This is not an ending, Joe, it is a new beginning, this is the start of a better life."

Tears flooded down Joe's face as he let go of the gun, then he let go of himself.

Now it was tears flooding down Sabina's face.

She was back in the room; amongst her family, amongst her friends.

Chapter 66 – Secrets

A quietness filled the air for a few seconds after Sabina let the gun fall onto the floor. A period of readjustment as she took control back of her own body, pushed on by the presence of her brother. She looked around, trying to make sense of the scant memories she had of the last hour she had just spent, but remembered very little.

Later, Jason and Sebastian rode with Sabina in the police car, explaining what had happened, and giving her reassurances that she would be okay; but in truth, no one could really be certain. After all, how does one deal with such a strong past personality taking over your body and ruining your life? For the time being though, the Ripper is contained within Sabina. No more murders from this evil personality would be striking London tonight.

Within moments of setting off, a group message went out to everyone involved, stating that the events of the day were to be kept confidential, until an urgent meeting at Scotland Yard was attended. There was to be absolutely no communication regarding the matter until Commander Pashmali had given the go ahead. That was a strict order.

Thirty minutes later, Sabina was being sedated and looked after by a nurse whilst watched over by Carter. Everyone else was escorted to one of the main briefing rooms on the fourth floor. Ives and Pascal were joined by George Glover, who'd ridden over separately with Isambard, all wondering what the hell was going on. Pascal somehow doubted they were there to pick up a commendation.

Only two people were inside the oak panelled board room, Commander Pashmali and the Commissioner of the

Metropolitan police herself, both looking very grave. The commissioner shook hands with everyone as they came in, then took centre stage.

"I want to start by thanking all of you for your hard work over the last few months, and for bringing it to a safe conclusion this evening. Mr Glover, I also want to personally apologise for the position you have found yourself in since volunteering such personal information about yourself, and hope that we can still count on your support for the remainder of the investigation."

Glover looked uncomfortable with the sudden attention, so he just nodded. The commissioner continued.

"We have a problem. Several in fact, which is why I have asked for your confidentiality in this matter, and why I must remind my staff, and Mr Ives and Mr Smythe, that they have all signed the official secrets act as part of their working contract with us."

Ives was wondering what they had to be so secretive about. "What's happening here, ma'am?"

"Mr Ives, I'm sure you can appreciate how politically embarrassing it would be to the Metropolitan police, if news got round that our lead investigator turned out to be the very person we were looking for. Lives could most possibly have been saved, if we had appointed someone different from DCI Bjorkman. We all know hindsight is a wonderful thing, but it doesn't stop the media from attacking us for things we should have known."

"Are you saying we should keep all this quiet?" Ives was dumbfounded.

The commissioner looked uncomfortable. "Well... look at the advantages. If we went to trial with this, not only would all of your lives be paraded in the world news, but it would be almost certain that DCI Bjorkman would be prosecuted and spend a very long time in prison, maybe for several life times. I do not want that happening; it would not benefit anyone, especially in the light of what happened to her father. If we can contain this, we can use the time to give her the best medical and supportive assistance possible.

"Martin Kale called a little while ago, explaining that he had played a small part in this matter that he also wants kept confidential. He was looking for an update, and I mentioned our dilemma. He has made a personal promise that if DCI Bjorkman is held in a secure psychiatric hospital, he will do all he can to rid her mind of her Jack the Ripper persona, and if that means erasing the memory of Joseph Ride forever, well so be it.

"No!" Glover's voice boomed out into the room. "Bjorkman must answer for her crimes, Commissioner. She must pay the price."

"She will be punished for not coming forward, Mr Glover, of that you can be certain. In effect, this part of DCI Bjorkman's soul would need to be eradicated forever. Think of it as killing off that part of her, so that the Ripper would never be remembered, or exist in any of her future lives. It is a better scenario than going down the traditional route at the moment. And Sabina Bjorkman will probably spend the rest of her life in psychiatric care. I don't know about you, but I'd rather be in prison."

Glover thought back to his time as Mary, remembering the special relationship she and Joseph Ride had had. He knew it was the pox and madness that had turned Joe into the monster, and here was a chance to kill the monster from within. Although he hated the whole idea, it did make some kind of warped sense, and balanced out the scales of justice as best as they could in this unwinnable situation. He looked at the commissioner. "Okay, do what you need to do."

"Thank you, Mr Glover."

Jason was still not so sure. "And you honestly believe Scotland Yard can get away with this?"

The commissioner looked worried. "That unfortunately, will have to rest on my shoulders, Mr Ives. Our official justification and plan, is that this is an experimental sentence, that can only be carried out in complete secrecy, without having to answer to the media or governmental agencies."

Pascal didn't know what to think. "Sorry, ma'am, but surely we cannot just pretend that the Ripper was never caught. The media will be hounding the Met for years to come."

"Believe me, DS Pascal, I share your concerns, but the Met police is at an all time low when it comes to public and government confidence anyway. If this matter became public, it would honestly be the end of the Metropolitan police. The home secretary has already been talking of having to break up the Met and replace it with a privately run enterprise. To me, that would be the end of fair policing, as the budget and revenue schemes to run such a service, would compromise a balanced system of justice that has prevailed since its formation by Robert Peel in 1829. We don't want to end up like the Americans and their privatised crime service. It's like the bloody Wild West all over again."

Pascal had to admit that what she was saying rang true, so nodded in agreement.

The commissioner continued. "In short, it is more important to keep this quiet than to announce a short-lived victory. Unfortunately, as we all know, there will soon be more murders to report about, and more scandals to leak out... there always are."

The commissioner started wringing her hands together, as if trying to wash off some imaginary blood. Then looked up to confront the small group before her.

"Ultimately, though it greatly pains me to say this, Jack the Ripper will have to remain as much a mystery now, as he has always been."

Chapter 67 – Note to Self

Jason paid a quick visit to Sabina to make sure she was okay before setting off to the office in Charing Cross. The investigation might be over, but he still had a lot of paperwork to sort out. A few hours later, Pascal saw him in the busy corridor and motioned him over to the side for another one of their impromptu meetings.

"Hey Jason, well done today, good work. I was wondering though, how did you know about Sebastian?"

Jason thought back to that night in the office when Sabina had come on so strong to him. He'd flattered himself that it was just about sex at the time, but now he began to wonder if it was a lot more than that. He'd been surprised to find a note in his pocket when he'd arrived home, planted by Sabina when they were cuddling against her office door. It had been a curious note, but after their previous conversation about her personal life, he had thought that it was part of her opening up to him.

It had said, quite simply… 'If anything happens to me, please contact Sebastian', complete with his phone number and address. He'd also thought it was a bit of a cry for help, but hadn't realised just how much of a cry it had really been. She'd obviously used the sex to drive Jack out of her mind completely, then took the chance to pass on her message whilst Jack wasn't looking. So when Capello had told him about Bjorkman, he mentioned the note about Sebastian and they looked into it further to discover the past life links he'd had. Somehow, Sabina had guessed her brother and Jason could help. Female intuition maybe?

Jason didn't know quite how to explain the delicate details of this story to Pascal, so he made it very brief.

"Oh, Sabina had once told me about her brother doing well in rehab, so when this happened, I got Isambard to chase him up and bring him to Glover. I felt we could do with every little bit of help we could muster, to draw her back to us, and nothing beats family."

Pascal nodded, looking impressed. "Well, that's why you are the pro, I guess."

"Hmm, maybe, I've never quite worked it out myself," Jason replied modestly.

He patted Pascal on the shoulder and walked out the station exit.

Epilogue

The Dog and Duck public house was quite busy for such a cold winter's evening, but the fire was roaring on the hearth as Jason sat warming his legs. He'd arrived early to make sure of grabbing this sought after seat. After all, he wanted to make a good impression on this date, his first in almost half a year.

He sipped his glass of Rioja slowly, enjoying the aromas released by the warmth of the room, then smiled as he saw Samantha walking into the bar looking more beautiful than ever. Things had not exactly gone to plan in their short lived relationship, but now they both have a chance to see if there is still a spark.

His mobile is firmly switched off...

The End

Thank you for reading 'Killing Time'

I hope you enjoyed it.

Please leave a review on Amazon or Goodreads as every review helps get the book to new readers

M W Taylor

March 2017

For the origins of Awakening, or more about Adam Capello, take a look at my first book, 'The Many Lives of Adam Capello'. Available on Amazon.

Lightning Source UK Ltd.
Milton Keynes UK
UKOW03f0801090417
298672UK00001B/1/P